THE
PASSAGE
HOME TO
MEUSE

Noble
Press

THE PASSAGE HOME TO MEUSE

GAIL NOBLE-SANDERSON

Author of *The Lavender House in Meuse*

Noble
Press

Noble Press

Published by Noble Press LLC
Mt. Vernon, Washington
gnoble_sanderson@comcast.net

Editing by Spellbinder Edits
Cover Art by Kathleen Noble
Cover design and typesetting by Enterline Design Services
Author photo by Travis Christians

ISBN: 978-0-9991386-0-1
Library of Congress Control Number: pending

Printed in the United States of America

This book is dedicated in grateful memory to our Grand-Mére Extraordinaire, Edith Leoda Devore Kunsman. Our lives were enriched and encouraged because of your unconditional love and support.

TABLE OF CONTENTS

FROM THE AUTHOR

The book you are holding, *The Passage Home to Meuse*, continues the life of Marie Durant Chagall and is the second in a series, following *The Lavender House in Meuse*. The story follows Marie over a period of seven months—from December 1922 to July 1923.

As readers of the first book know, my writing of this story is based on memories I believe are from a past life I lived as Marie. This second book came to me in much the same way as the first, only I felt a milder sense of urgency to get the story down on paper. I am now becoming used to having the characters relate their tales and to knowing that what they have to say remains in my mind as I compose the story through prose.

What I did attempt in this second book was to more accurately describe the settings of events and capture the essence of the times and experiences of the characters. Both as a writer and a storyteller, my desire is to elevate the quality of the writing to convey in as much detail as possible the message of the people, the lessons of their lives, and to create a sense for you, the reader, that you are there in the moment, giving you your own individual experience.

Through constant reading and research of the history of the times and places of my stories, I endeavor to maintain historical accuracy, helping to ensure substance and perspective to the tales. Of course, there is a convergence of memory, history, and imagination throughout the telling. There are also times when the writer of historical fiction must use her creativity to move the story forward, fill in detail, and expand the personalities of the characters, using her craft to make a whole of the parts. In my case, I coalesce what is known from history to be true, my recollections of the people and events, and my imagination to unite each piece and bring the story to fruition.

As in the first book, my goal has been to remain true to the memories. The characters always surprise me by the decisions they make that shape their experiences and impact their lives. I have learned to trust this process and am grateful that I am able to recreate their stories. In the reading of their journeys, may we all contemplate our own and seek the greater good for others and ourselves.

CHAPTER 1

CHRISTMAS EVE 1922

The last light lingered, finding its way through the falling snow and into the frosted windows of the convent's refectory. A fire blazed in the hearth of the room, flames casting warm offerings of brightness onto the scarred wooden dining table. The time spent putting the finishing touches on the table settings had allowed me to lay aside all worries. My lingering concerns over a planned trip to see Papa and my sister, Solange, in New York City the coming April and anxiety about establishing my own nursing clinic had been weighing heavily on my mind of late, but not tonight. Tonight was to be made special for the Sisters, special for us all. And I had told the Sisters they were not to come into the room until my preparations were complete.

The new embroidered linen runner spanned the length of the table and was my Christmas gift to the Sisters. I had worked the simple design of holly and berries with threads of deep reds and dark greens, keeping my pattern of stitches evenly centered down the middle of the heavy cloth. The table was four meters long, with benches along each side, and the table runner extended each end by a generous half meter. Matching linen napkins, on which I had stitched a simple holly leaf and a single berry, were folded beside each plate, the china dishes brought from my house. The beautiful *bougeoirs* Henri had given to me when Solange visited I had placed intermittently along the runner, finding spaces between the clusters of leaves. The mismatched bronze candleholders, with their colorful cloisonné designs, looked like little floral arrangements among the embroidery. The small candles held inside these *bougeoirs* would be lit last, as they would burn more quickly than the larger candles.

The previous fall, the Sisters and I had experimented with new candle molds, taller and wider than our usual tapers, and these thick pillars of the palest yellow beeswax, the color reminding me of the wings of bees among my lavender fields, were now lined atop the high wooden shelf running along the wall opposite the door to the courtyard.

As I lit these tall candles, the refectory grew brighter with the glow of each flame, and light flickered and danced on the beamed vaulted ceiling. Although the white plaster walls were unadorned, save for the humble crucifix above the mantle, the wealth that filled this simple room reflected all that was in my heart. There was no place I would rather be; no place could be lovelier or more filled with love on this, my first celebrated holiday with those whom I had come to cherish. My relationship with this special group of women had grown close over the past year, as I slowly came out of my self-imposed isolation in my house in Meuse. Following years of recovery from battlefield injuries, both physical and emotional sustained while nursing at the frontlines of the battle of Verdun, the kind Sisters of this convent, along with Henri, our enterprising country peddler, walked beside me as dear friends as I began to find my way back to life.

The Sisters and I had spent these last several days baking and cooking for this evening. We had planned a feast, and after lighting the last of the candles on the table I paused and sat down at the end of one of the benches. I could smell the mouthwatering scents of roasted rabbit and herbs wafting through the kitchen door, and my stomach responded with a rumble of hunger. Looking over the table in anticipation of it being filled with steaming plates of delicious food, my contentment was interrupted by urgent knocking at the door.

I opened the door to a cold whirl of snow and wind and was surprised to see Henri a few steps away assisting a barrel of a man leading a large animal. All three were entirely covered in white, as though they had been outside for some time. The refectory's light illuminated more clearly their circumstance as they gathered near the doorway. It was Bernard with Henri, a familiar acquaintance, though not yet a friend.

Both wore expressions of worry. The animal leaning heavily against Bernard, its low bleating muted by the heavily falling snow, I now saw was a sheep. A large-bellied ewe, to be exact. She shed from her rear drops of warm red blood that shattered the snow's thin white crust.

"Henri, what's wrong here?" Even as I spoke those words, I realized the ewe was struggling and in pain. Bernard looked as though he was suffering as well.

"On my way to our dinner here, Marie, I met Bernard on the road. He assumed you were at the convent on this Christmas Eve and was bringing his ewe to you, so he accompanied me along the way. She has been attempting to birth her lamb since early morning with no success. He is hoping you might help bring forth a live lamb or one dead. But either way, he hopes you might assist the mother. His greatest fear is that she will die."

The wind suddenly swirled snow about the four of us, and the candles flickered in the fractured calm of what was to have been a quiet but grand meal on this most high of nights. I gave a great heaving sigh and let all expectations of celebration fall away.

"Come in, here inside the room," I said, taking Bernard's arm and leading both him and the sheep into the warmth of the refectory. Henri closed the door behind us as I fell to my knees beside the beleaguered animal.

"How old is this ewe, and has she previously delivered healthy lambs?" I asked, beginning to palpate the sheep's large girth.

When the animal's owner did not respond, I looked up at his face. Bernard was staring intently into the ewe's eyes, stroking her head.

Henri answered the question I had posed. "Yes, many times and many lambs. Now, though, she is not so young and possibly too old for such things. Bernard told me she is a good ewe, his eldest and most favorite. That he prizes her highly and wants only for her to be delivered from her pain."

"*Oui*, Mademoiselle, all Henri says is true. Please help us." This Bernard stated with such pleading that all my thoughts turned to the ewe, who by this time was lying prone upon the floor, bright red drops of blood beginning to pool on the rough-hewn tan and gray stone.

The space was close between the door and the table. With the help of the two men, we positioned her more toward the corner of the room, closer to the fireplace, so that I might conduct a thorough examination. I did not tell them that up until that moment I had never helped deliver any living thing from inside of its mother. But I had studied the anatomy and understood the rudimentary process of birthing. I hadn't thought it a complex process but streamlined and efficient, a wet passage down a narrow canal to another life. That is, of course, if the body of both the mother and the one about to be born were working together properly. And that is what I needed to determine here with this ewe. She was so weak that I knew I needed to quickly assess her and the state of the lamb she still held inside.

Bernard murmured softly to the ewe and continued stroking her head. Henri watched from the other end as I palpated my way round her middle, finally examining her birthing exit. The bloody drainage increased with each contraction, accompanied by weak bleats and sighs from the ewe. I was relieved to discover her uterus was still in the active stages of labor.

"Henri, go to the Sisters, explain what is happening, and bring back clean rags, lye soap, a bucket of clean water, and any sort of alcohol you might have in your wagon. Also, my basket is in the kitchen. Please have Sister Dominique boil the instruments and bring the rest to me." Henri knew what I needed to care for a patient, and regardless of beast or being, what was required was nearly the same, hence my basket with scalpel, shears, threads, and suture needles. "And an apron!" I called after him as he disappeared through the kitchen door.

Henri returned shortly, accompanied by Sister Dominique. She and I, along with the other Sisters, worked closely over the last years enjoying our business endeavors, producing honey from the hives of the bees in my lavender fields as well as creating beautiful beeswax candles. Dominique also showed a particular interest and keen knowledge of medicinal herbs and plants and was quickly becoming my very capable nursing assistant. She was both curious about and comfortable with the blood, smells, and sounds of pain and injury. I welcomed her calm presence as she hurried to my side carrying the items I requested. As I rolled up the sleeves of my dress she relayed a message from Sister Agnès that dinner would be kept warm, and I was to tend to what was pressing.

My hands and arms were tingling after washing with the harsh lye soap and rubbing Henri's dark liquor onto them. I then used a wet, soapy cloth followed by a rubbing of alcohol to clean the ewe's swollen genital area. After firm palpations, I slowly moved my right hand into her, evaluating each inner contour with probing fingers.

Although all the expected bumps and lumps were present, my hand found them higher up the birth canal and without detectable throbbing or movement to indicate a life about to emerge. After such a lengthy labor, the lamb should have descended lower into the canal. I probed a little higher until I felt small hooves, but certainly more than four, and two slimy heads, one significantly smaller than the other.

Two lambs were there! Each was vying for passage but suspended immovable as a cork in a bottle. The cords were not round their necks—relief there—but the tangle of limbs and heads made it difficult to assess which lamb to untangle and release first. If I could separate one set of four legs from the other along with the corresponding head, I could facilitate its release and allow free passage for the second as well.

Perspiration was dripping into my eyes, necessitating almost constant stinging blinks to clear my sight. Henri noticed and reached over with a dry rag, wiping my forehead and face and giving me a hesitant smile meant, I was sure, to instill confidence. He appeared almost as worried as Bernard. I felt very comfortable in my familiar role as nurse and returned his smile, hoping to instill confidence in him.

Assured as I could be that all cords and body parts not belonging to this first lamb were out of the way, I secured it round the neck in the valley of my thumb and index finger, closed my eyes to better see what I felt, and guided the head and legs toward its release. As the lamb's feet and nose emerged, I opened my eyes and saw the top of the animal's small narrow head, white and shiny as the new-fallen snow.

But then downward movement stopped, as though its twin were pulling it back to itself. I felt a sudden sense of alarm. Should I open the mother's belly or snip with my scalpel to make a larger passage for the head?

In the midst of these thoughts, the ewe shivered with a fierce contraction and a gasping bleat while I provided accompanying downward pressure to her abdomen, allowing the lamb to literally burst free from its dark confines. Sister Dominique gathered the wet newborn in a large thick cloth and held the still, small thing as I cut the umbilical cord. It had not yet taken its first breath.

"Rub it vigorously, Sister, and clear its nose and mouth of fluid as best you can. You should see it begin to breathe. Continue to rub and then wrap it warm," I directed.

I did not hear a reassuring sound from either Sister Dominique or the lamb, but knew I needed to quickly attend to the birth of the second; the mother was as listless as her firstborn. Surprisingly, she roused with one more fierce contraction, and again, applying firm downward pressure, the second creature came out squirming. This one was very small and very thin. Significantly smaller than the first. As I laid it upon a cloth, I was surprised to find its breathing regular, and it began to calm as I cut the cord. This littlest lamb's dark liquid eyes were open, and it seemed so peaceful, as though the last many hours literally suspended between life and death had been of no consequence.

While the ewe lay still from exhaustion, I reached up inside her once again to aid the removal of the twin-shared placenta. I sensed that she was perhaps in shock and surely dehydrated. She continued to lie on her side, her head heavy on the stone floor, her eyes closed. She was completely motionless, and I could barely see evidence of her breathing and found only a faint heartbeat.

I instructed Henri to soak a cloth and attempt to drip water into the ewe's mouth, for she was not interested nor capable of drinking from the bucket Bernard was continually placing next to her mouth, urging her to drink. I needed her to take even a small amount to know that she could reflexively swallow and to provide her with some immediate hydration. She could rest for a time, certainly, before she must suckle her newborns. They might, on the other hand, be too small to exert the needed pressure to the teats to expel the warm milk. But that was not of critical importance; we could feed them ourselves. That is, if they were still alive when needing to eat.

"She is swallowing, Marie. How much should I give her in this fashion?" Henri asked. The ewe had opened her eyes and did seem to be focusing on swallowing the dripping water.

"Until you see it running out the corners of her mouth. Then stop for a time and let her rest again."

I turned my attention to the new arrivals and was pleasantly surprised to see that the rest of the Sisters had glided silently into the room. They had wiped the lambs dry, swaddled them snuggly, hooves and all, into clean, soft cloths, and were now cradling them in their arms. The way the nuns were cooing over them you would have thought they held long-awaited newborn babes.

I checked each lamb's pulse and respiration, assuring myself they would most likely, with nourishment provided in the next couple of hours, live. Their eyes were open and both were breathing normally. Perhaps it was the attention of these loving women that allowed the lambs to hang onto their lives while their mother tenuously held onto her own. I hoped for Bernard's sake, as well as the lambs', that the mother would recover.

Bernard was still kneeling at the ewe's head, cooing under his breath to her as he had throughout the birthings. I walked over to him and placed my hand on his shoulder. He startled, as if surprised to find anyone else in the room besides himself and his precious sheep.

"She appears fine for now," I said. "Quite exhausted, of course, but if she lives through the night, she will most likely be on her legs tomorrow. She birthed two lambs, Monsieur, true twins, with one being much smaller. One may live, or both . . . or neither.

"We will leave the ewe here tonight, making a place for her and the little ones in this warm corner. Then we shall see what tomorrow brings."

Bernard did not look up at me but nodded over and over and, placing his hand over mine still lying gently on his shoulder, whispered a quiet, "*Merci, Mademoiselle, merci.*"

Henri gave the ewe more to drink and used the remaining water and rags to clean her, removing any excess fluid and blood and wiping from the floor all traces of the birthing. However, the pungent fragrance of earth and animal and the iron smell of blood continued to linger on the air.

Sister Dominique brought me a bucket of clean water, and I washed again, scrubbing hard my hands and up my arms with the bracing soap. She then wrapped my hands and arms in a large cloth and gently dried them as I watched her ministering to me. I removed my soiled apron and we looked at one another and smiled, gazing round the refectory still bathed in soft candlelight.

All but Bernard broke into subdued laughter, shaking our heads and marveling at how our well-planned evening in this room, with its elegant refinements of fine embroidery and pillared candles, had instead become a place of new life.

"To the kitchen! Our feast awaits us!" announced our ever-buoyant Sister Béatrice.

I glanced over to the two men. Henri had washed his own hands and now stood across from Bernard, who seemed oblivious to the rest of us in the room. "Henri?" I said quietly, an unspoken invitation to join us. He gave a slight wave of his hand, which I correctly interpreted to mean he would stay with Bernard.

The Sisters and I moved as one to the kitchen, talking over one another about all that occupied us these last two hours. They quickly piled high the more modest kitchen table with the foods kept warm, and we sat down to our Christmas Eve dinner. The roast rabbit with chestnut dressing, herbed browned *pommes*, succulent *haricots verts* with rosemary and shallots, and warm spiced olives were lifted from the heated platters to our plates. With heads nodding in shared acknowledgement, Sister Agnès offered up a prayer of gratitude before we commenced eating.

After several hurried mouthfuls to assuage my ravenous hunger, I discreetly slipped away from the table back to the refectory. Henri was now sitting on the cold floor beside Bernard, talking quietly to him of what I knew not. Approaching them, I asked if they were hungry.

"More than hungry, Marie," Henri immediately replied, standing up. I felt he now welcomed this interruption. He had, after all, been an invited guest to our dinner. Bernard, however, continued to sit still on the floor, his hand on his ewe's head. Her eyes were closed and her breathing was well measured. Henri had laid her lambs on nubby wool blankets he must have secured from his wagon. They were tucked in close against their mother's midsection, sleeping soundly.

"Well, seeing as how you two appear to be keeping watch over mother and babes, I will bring you plates of food with drink, and you can eat here at this finely decorated table."

"You bring two full plates, Marie, and I will take care of our drink!" Henri said with his usual good humor, the weary smile about his mouth telling me all was surely restored to rightness this night.

When I returned shortly with plates the Sisters had mounded with generous portions of each dish, Henri and Bernard had moved to the candle-lit table. Bernard sat facing the ewe and Henri faced the now half-melted candles. More wood had been added to the fire in the hearth and the room remained warm and inviting. Henri had long ago removed his hat, and the candlelight flickered across his pleasant face, catching the flecks of crimson gold in his dark brown eyes and illuminating the sun-bleached highlights in his thick brown hair. He looked satisfied and eager to eat. Bernard, on the other hand, still gazed upon the sleeping ewe. He no longer appeared as forlorn, and although his face was still lined with concern for the animal, he made motions to begin eating his meal. It seemed to me Bernard exhibited an exceptional amount of concern for a sheep. I made a note to remember to ask Henri later about his friend's intense regard for this animal.

I left them both there in the glow of the table and returned to my Sisters, the sounds of their knives and forks moving across the china plates creating a tinkling of holiday music. It wasn't the Christmas Eve I had eagerly anticipated, but it was the one I would always remember.

CHAPTER 2

FÉLIX –
EARLY JANUARY 1923

Donning my heavy leather boots over thick wool socks, my not-thick-enough long wool cape, and recently knitted hat and gloves, I tromped out the back door ready to complete my morning's chores. The air was ice-frigid in this early morning hour. The last snow had fallen in December, but it now seemed colder somehow without the white blanket insulating the landscape. An illusion, perhaps.

I felt frozen within a few short minutes, making it difficult to muck the stall and feed Horse and Chickens. I worried they would freeze and would have brought them into the house had I thought it reasonable. I had stacked sturdy bales of dry hay round the wire walls of the chickens' outside run, creating a hay house, hoping it would keep some of the warmth they generated among themselves confined within. Another illusion perhaps, but it helped ease my guilt.

And poor Horse, he had no other bodies to help warm his own, but I had purchased more winter blankets and kept him covered day and night. Hay was also piled high round the opening of the three-sided, three-meter-high wooden stall. This helped block the wind and hopefully preserved some warmth for him. Thank goodness all these animal homes were covered by solid roofs. I had to keep buckets of water in the house and lugged them out to their drinking cans each morning, where yesterday's water lay glassy and frozen, sometimes rotating them twice a day if the water froze quickly.

The chickens appeared to be sleeping as I approached. But their soft clucking sounds welcomed me as I entered their space and began tossing their feed to the ground. A few brave hens suffered the cold, hunger getting the better of them, and they strutted out of their cozy coop to eat. They were lovely, their rounded bodies covered in shiny feathers of russet-gold and orange-brown streaks with tinges of red in their long tail feathers. They seemed no worse for the cold weather, and as I ducked my head into the coop, the packed straw where they had lain was reassuringly warm.

Horse greeted me with more excitement. He was telling me he would appreciate a ride—some exercise to help warm his muscles. "We can do that when the sun rises and the day warms," I told him.

He nudged and rubbed my head and shoulder, and I took the time to give him a brushing interspersed with frequent hugs as we talked and discussed the cold weather and where we might ride later. Interesting, how I loved these animal friends as companions and how much we were mutual caregivers.

Carrying more wood from the diminishing stack laid by the back entrance to my home, I walked to the front room, boots and all, and deposited the heavy pile of fuel beside the stove. Embers still burned, but low, as I placed four pieces of wood onto the fire. I would not light the stove upstairs; I had been sleeping on the divan, moved close to this stove, to keep warm these cold nights. The kitchen stove I also kept aglow and now placed more wood into it as well. Flames burned bright by the time I sat at the kitchen bench and struggled to release myself from my boots and heavy outer garments.

After filling the kettle and placing it on the stovetop, I took out the skillet for two eggs with a slice of ham. This was my favorite breakfast—other than fresh fried trout from my river Meuse. I looked forward to fishing again come spring. Henri and I always managed enough fish each time we ventured to the river to amply fill our stomachs. My mouth was watering as I set the ham into the hot pan. Sparks of melted lard bounced out at me.

A rap sounded at my front door. Henri's rap. Sometimes tentative, sometimes bold, but always three knocks in measured succession. Today's rapping was rather strong. Wiping my hands on my apron, I thought I could add more eggs and ham to the pan, and we could share a good breakfast with hot tea. Perhaps he had a fresh baguette to share.

I opened the door and there he stood, his familiar floppy hat in his hands. But another pair of hands, small and blistered red, appeared from round his back and across the tops of his legs as third and fourth appendages. What was this?

"Henri, come in from this frozen morning. Are you hungry? I have just started breakfast and can make you some as well." Curious about those little hands, I waited to be introduced properly.

"Oui, we are more than cold, Marie. Might we stand by your stove?" he said, entering the house with short, jerky steps to accommodate two more feet, also small, which stumbled along behind his. Small hands and now small feet.

"You've sprouted extra limbs, my friend! And how did this come about?" I tried to peer round his back but the slight figure was having none of it and hid well into Henri.

"May I introduce you, Mademoiselle Marie, to my young nephew? Félix, come greet my friend," he said while attempting to dislodge the timid boy from behind him. Still the boy held fast to his protector.

"Félix and I are needing your medical advice. My nephew is suffering greatly from blisters and itching to his hands and feet. I am worried because it has become worse, and he is in pain. Would you take a look?"

The boy had not yet made an appearance, but I thought perhaps the bribe of breakfast might suffice to loosen his grip.

"I would be delighted to be of service, but at present I am famished and will need eggs, ham, and tea before I am to be of any good to you. Would you be hungry also?" I turned toward the kitchen to check the skillet and add more food. "And Henri, might you have a baguette in your wagon?"

"I do indeed, and we gratefully accept the offer of breakfast. Félix, let's take your coat off and you stand here by the fire while I fetch what is needed from the wagon."

And with that, he peeled the tight hands from his legs, removed the boy's coat, and quickly raced out the door before Félix could reattach himself. The child stood very still looking down at the floor.

"Please sit down by the stove, Félix. Henri will be right back and then we will eat. I am so pleased that you came with your uncle today and can share breakfast with me."

Félix slowly lowered his chilled body to the floor as I took measure of him. The smooth, pale skin of his face was in stark contrast to his wavy, unruly mop of ebony hair and matching dark eyes. Henri had removed from the boy a bulky, short wool jacket and a thick knitted hat that must have been his own. The boy's pants and shirt were threadbare, badly soiled, and too small for his thin frame. I gauged him to be perhaps five years old, maybe even younger. I took myself to the kitchen, humming a tune to let the shy youngster know I was close but preoccupied with breakfast. I would not venture too near this frightened little rabbit.

With Henri's return, after placing bread, cheese, and honey on the dining table, he set about laying forks, knives, and plates. We had eaten many such impromptu meals together over the last year, and it had become a familiar and pleasant comradery. Félix remained still and quiet, sitting close to the warm stove, his eyes following Henri's every move.

"That smells delicious, Marie. I will have three eggs if you have them. And at least two thick slices of the ham. Félix, do you want one egg or two?" I had come back to the table and watched as Félix lifted a red, swollen hand and attempted to bend three fingers and thumb down to hold up one finger. "One it shall be, then, with one slice of ham," declared Henri.

I filled the plates as Henri sliced the bread, cut into the small round of cheese, and poured the tea. By now some diffused sunlight was filtering through the dull winter sky, and the room brightened as we all sat down to eat.

I surreptitiously watched Félix attempting to pick up his fork, his fingers so swollen they barely moved. He stabbed the ham and brought the large piece to his mouth, fitting as much as possible between his teeth before tearing off a bite.

Without a word, Henri reached toward the boy, lowered the remaining ham-on-spear back to Félix's plate, and cut it into small pieces. Félix kept his eyes on the plate, looking impatient to continue eating.

"Eat the bites one at a time, boy. With your fork, please," Henri quietly instructed, as Félix began picking the pieces up with the stiff fingers of each hand, stuffing bites into his mouth. Henri was patient and kind. His fondness for this young child was evident, as was the worry and concern I saw on his face.

"Have you and Félix been long out in the cold, Henri?"

"Actually, we traveled here straight from home. I just returned this morning and found Félix in the small shed beside my house, and looking as though he had been there for quite some time. As I came upon him whimpering in the hay, he attached himself to me. When I realized the state he was in, we came directly to you."

Henri's fork made stabbing darts and dashes in the air as he spoke, as if sending me secret messages to help explain the situation. I could not interpret the fork's code.

"And the medical concerns, Henri? Can you tell me about those?" I asked, making my eyes wide in hopes he could interpret my implied questions. We were both sending signals neither could discern. It almost made me laugh. He had pulled me into his caution, and I was not sure what or how to ask about Henri's worry in front of the boy.

"His feet are in as bad a state as his hands, and I am worried that he might have frozen his fingers and toes." His fork continued its signaling as he spoke, again attempting to convey some unspoken concern I was left to deduce for myself.

Breakfast was consumed quickly between our words. The boy had made not a sound. I wondered if this silence was itself a concern. What else was going on here?

Félix began to fidget, and Henri told him to go out beside the house and relieve himself. While Félix did so, Henri spoke rapidly. "His *maman* passed away six months ago, and his papa has sunk into a deep despair. There are several relatives who have also tried to ease their pain and assist in caring for the boy but without success. The papa, my cousin, pines constantly for his departed wife. He doesn't seem to see the boy, doesn't take refuge in his son. It is as though he cannot bear to be near Félix. Perhaps the reminder is too difficult; Félix looks so similar to his dear maman. His papa has been gone now for over two weeks, but Félix is faithful and awaited his return with each new day. I was told that one day his papa loaded up some of his belongings, packed his personal effects, tied his second horse to the rear of his wagon, and without a backwards glance toward his son, he left. Although Félix, too, is my cousin, I have always called him my nephew. I am very fond of the boy and now have serious concerns for his well-being."

Félix came back into the house and sat once again on the floor, facing the stove. I thought this a good sign, that he was more comfortable now and not so wary. I poured Henri and myself another cup of tea and took one to Félix, setting it on the floor beside him on a plate with a buttered and honeyed slice of bread. Without a word, he picked up the bread and consumed it before I had returned to my chair. Other than his swollen red digits and frequent scratching of his arms through his shirt, he did not appear to be in great physical distress or otherwise ill.

"Henri, what do you and Félix have planned today? It seems too cold to be out and about on the roads, and Félix looks as though he could benefit from some daylong warmth by a hot fire. Might today be a respite for you both, allowing me to offer my home as such? Of course, I will put you to work, as you are not one to sit idle. Perhaps it is a fair trade?"

As I said this, Félix curled himself into a small ball on the woven rug in front of the fire and quickly fell asleep. I motioned to Henri to turn and look at the boy. He rose from his chair, picked Félix up in his arms, and gently laid him on the divan. I got a blanket to tuck round him and together we stood watching the sleeping child. He gave off a pungent odor made strong from the warming of his body that told me he needed a bath and perhaps had open sores. He needed food and warmth and, even more so, care for his young soul. I looked to Henri and he nodded as though my thoughts were his own. What was he to do with this poor orphan?

We cleared the table and washed the dishes, all the while commiserating regarding the boy. Henri was clearly distraught and unsure as to what to do next.

"Is he always this reticent and shy or is he just in both physical and emotional pain? To be left without either parent would be almost more than a young child could bear."

Placing the last of the dry plates on the shelf, Henri said, "I think I can assume his papa will not be returning. At least not soon. And I am happy to take Félix in. I have often thought about doing so, even before my cousin left. It has been difficult to watch and wonder when to intervene as his papa continued to disregard him. I thought that with some passing of time following his wife's death he would begin taking care of Félix. But the child has been abandoned by both death and rejection."

"When he wakes, we need to bathe him. During his bath I can examine him. Looking at the blisters to his hands, I would deduce he has chilblains. I saw similar symptoms with many of the soldiers during those frigid winter months at Verdun."

"He tells me it stings and itches. I know his toes are also swollen, and it is hard for him to walk. How did he get this, Marie?"

"Chilblains is caused from excessive moisture being trapped around the fingers and toes, and it worsens during the colder months. Sometimes it is an indication of poor circulation as well, especially when the hands are involved. Did his parents have similar concerns, that you know of?"

"Now come to think of it, his maman often had red, swollen fingers in the colder months that she said itched and stung much of the time."

Looking over at the sleeping boy, I thought it probable this was a condition he inherited from her.

The large pots of water I had placed on the stove had begun to steam. I pulled the bathing tub into the center of the kitchen, and we went to rouse Félix. He was so deep in sleep we were able to undress the exhausted boy without him waking. As Henri carried him to the kitchen I went ahead and poured the now-warm water into the tub. I knew the water would initially aggravate the pain, so we would bathe him quickly with soothing olive oil soap.

As I expected, Félix was none too happy about his bath. Henri bent the boy's legs to set him down in the tub, keeping his arms round the boy to calm and steady him as I quickly lathered the soap in my hands. I washed him gently but thoroughly from head to middle. I had Henri stand him up to soap the rest of him, then poured fresh warm water over his entire body. He was whimpering as Henri lifted him out of the tub. I wrapped the child in a large white towel, and Henri carried him back to my divan where I could thoroughly examine his small self.

Félix did have all the indications of chilblains to his feet, hands, and their appendages, as well as on his earlobes: swollen, general redness and many areas of raised sores between his digits. He must have been in terrible pain, one of the reasons he had difficulty eating and sleeping.

I applied olive oil infused with lavender to his entire little body and dressed him in one of my long-sleeved flannel shirts with a pair of my socks on his feet pulled up past his knees. All this time he sat wide-awake staring silently at me. Henri moved the divan in front of the fire, thinking Félix might again fall asleep. Before he did so, I explained to them both that keeping warm and dry, as well as assuring adequate sleep and nourishment, would go a long way in easing the pain and begin the healing process.

"Félix, might you want some warm milk with chocolate?" I asked, hoping he would answer and we might become better acquainted.

"Oui, Mademoiselle," he offered in a soft voice. "And I would like some more bread, please. I'm very hungry again."

"Of course, dear. You stay here with Oncle Henri, and I will come right back with your chocolate and bread," I said, smiling at him as he looked at me with his lovely dark eyes. He seemed a sweet child, and I felt myself wanting to take him in and see to his healing.

After Félix had more to drink and eat, and talking some with me as he did so, he then fell fast asleep. Henri had added more wood to the stove and piled a high stack beside it that would keep us sufficiently supplied throughout the day and night.

Sitting once again at the table, Henri asked, "What am I to do? I can certainly make my home available to him, but it isn't all a boy should have. How long do you think it will be before he is feeling better?"

"As I said, if he is fed and kept warm and free of moisture, and the oil is applied conscientiously, he should heal quickly. I would think, though, that this may be a condition he shares with his maman and will be something he must tend to throughout his life. I would like him to stay here with me for a couple of days so I can watch over him. It will be no problem to feed him as well. I would welcome such a fine fellow here to keep me some company, and I have no need to venture out for another few days. Do you think Félix would be comfortable here without your constant presence?"

"He has not had anyone to properly watch over him for some time. I am in and out and never home for long. I admit I feel guilty that I did not pay closer attention to the situation. Not wanting to interfere and hoping his papa would return, I checked on him occasionally as he stayed first with one relative and then the next but then went about my business. I do not know how he will feel about staying with you, but I would certainly appreciate him doing so until I can prepare a place for him at my own house. And I can stop by every day." I could see how very worried he was about the boy. Henri's gratitude and relief that I would help were evident by the smile that now returned to his face.

Over the next three days, Félix and I became great friends. I slept next to him at night on my mattress on the floor, laying it beside his bed on the divan, and during the day we played games. I brought out my paints and brushes, and he very much enjoyed making pictures. He drew one of his papa, maman, and himself that brought tears to my eyes as he described them in detail. He was such a sweet, lonely child. Between Henri and myself he would hopefully begin to feel safe and loved. And once again, as I had done here in this home after the war, I was nursing a boy.

CHAPTER 3

REFLECTIONS – MID-JANUARY 1923

When standing but a foot away, the clear reflection of myself from head to mid-calf nearly filled the surface of the looking glass. The small dark specks sprinkled close to the outside edges hinted at its age, and the heavy wooden frame of white with tooled gold filigree suggested its past grandeur.

It was a beautiful piece. A thoughtful gift. I preferred appreciating its beauty standing at an angle, off to the side, looking into its surface to catch the reflections of my home illuminated by the light from the windows or casting shadows as I lit the lamps at evening.

I had not seen myself in mirrored glass since I knew not when. There had been no need and certainly there had been no desire to do so. I took a hesitant step back in front of it again to take full measure of myself. To face the woman I knew to be me. As I stood there, I said, as I had each day since its arrival, "So this is what I look like." Still tall and thin, with dark gold hair pulled taut to the back of my neck, stray tendrils poking out about my face and curling round my neck. I loosened my hair and mussed it with my fingers. I had chopped it last spring when the weather turned warm, as it was too hot on my head, and now it had grown much longer. Tilting my head first to one side and then the other, I saw the hair was quite uneven, the left side hanging longer than the right. I would sharpen my cutting shears and even the locks tomorrow. Its crookedness would be all I would see—my world askew and needing to be set right upon my head.

My eyes were still their blue-green (had I thought they might be different with all that had changed?) and still flecked with gold around the color's edges—not unlike the specks at my mirror's edge. And I found this, for whatever reason, comforting. A bonding with my looking glass.

I turned to my right, my body now in profile, and my hand smoothed down the front of my dress, assuring me I had not turned to bumps and lumps round my middle and hips. My nose was Solange's nose, and I saw much of my sister in this profile, her younger self now an older me.

As my hands continued their contouring motions, I realized I looked from without not quite as I felt from within. I stood looking at a woman of almost twenty-seven years. One with smooth but reddened skin and thick hair, a firm and solid body, looking for all the world as a woman secure in her person and at peace with her world. The years of grief and strain and the occasional bouts of melancholy and fear somehow did not show on my person. When reflecting upon the nature within, I knew this woman to be tentative, self-protective, and often unsure of her abilities to live an adequate life in the present or the future. But, truly, the reflection in the glass did reassure me that perhaps I could become what I saw.

I knew also that these years in Meuse had done much to restore me and allowed me to move toward the woman I might eventually become. That piece of me that was strong, that could rise above and overcome adversity, had never left me. It simmered constantly within as it had throughout my life and would occasionally burst into flame with sparks of accompanying frustration bordering on anger when I could not order my world as I wanted. Especially when I thought others were intruding upon my will to conduct my own affairs. And with this thought came thoughts of Henri. Well intentioned was my constant friend and a never-ending source of advice and assistance—mostly unrequested but most often proving helpful.

Supposing myself without want or need of company, and surviving on inadequate provisions, my first weeks in this house of my mother's were spent in agonizing despair. And that is how Henri found me when he first pulled his well-stocked peddler's wagon up to the front of my home. Thus began our relationship of perpetual push and pull. He would push me to see possibility beyond my staid existence, and I would pull away in fear and protest. But this determined man persisted, and during those early months, Henri concocted plans and schemes to enhance the quality of my barren life. He eventually had the gall to suggest I should house and nurse three wounded soldiers that the convent did not have room for. Because he reassured me that he would find all goods and supplies needed for me to care for these young, injured men and because I could no longer sustain the will to oppose him, I succumbed and found my own renewal.

And now, after these years of mutual goodwill, what did Henri see reflected when his eyes saw my person in this glass? I think he saw the truth, saw beyond the hope his gift reflected. He came bearing the looking glass last weekend. A "belated holiday token" he had said.

A knock came mid-morning, my tea just poured, hot and steaming, my bread dripping honey over its edges. Snow had fallen overnight and was beginning again, fresh flakes falling from a gray sky. As I opened the door, Henri slapped his hat upon his thigh, throwing snow up between us. I saw through the flakes that his thick, dark eyebrows and lashes were covered in white, giving him the look of an old man.

"It is cold, Marie! May I come in to make a delivery?"

Stepping aside, my mouth full, and wiping lavender honey dripping from the corners of my lips, I nodded and motioned him to enter.

He took hold of a large piece of wood he had leaned up against the house and, awkwardly lifting it to fit through the door, carried it into my home.

"As soon as I saw it I realized there was only one perfect place to hang this jewel of a piece; the only wall it was intended to grace was one within your home," Henri said as he marched past me without even looking at me, gushing and talking too quickly. Attempting, I was sure, to brush past any reluctance on my part to join in his enthusiasm. He was hoping I would simply acquiesce to his intentions of bringing whatever it was he lugged into my home.

He had the back of the rectangular piece facing out toward me, and I could see only a solid piece of dark wood nearly as tall as the man who carried it. I thought it must be a painting. Some interesting artifact he must have found in his travels.

With some effort, he carried the heavy object to the wall separating the kitchen from the sitting and dining spaces and, turning it round, leaned it up against my china cabinet. And I realized it was a looking glass!

Henri threw his hands out wide and stated, "This is the wall on which it must be hung! It will reflect the light from all the windows. We will move this china cabinet to the wall by the dining table. I will assist you in removing all the pieces of china to the table top, and together we can move the cabinet and then hang the mirror," he continued without taking a breath.

Familiar now with Henri's forays of excitement into my otherwise sedate world, I sat down upon the divan. "It is a lovely piece, Henri. Where did you find it? How old do you think it is?" I was stalling for some time to settle myself and decide what was intended here.

"Certainly a great deal older than my forty-four years. Perhaps saved from a great house after the war. I was not told the history. The gentleman from whom I rescued it knew only that it was well made, the frame itself a work of art and much detailed." He ran his fingers over the contours of the frame. "The intricate scrollwork is hand-sculpted, and the delicate gold filigree took the fine hand of an artist to apply."

I got up, unable to resist the frame's loveliness. It beckoned to be touched.

"Alright, Henri, I concede it is a beautiful piece. Quite regal, actually. But don't you think it rather ornate for my home?" I asked, still admiring the workmanship.

"Your home becomes what you choose for adornment. Fine or otherwise. You have chosen thus far excellent pieces. All with a history and all cohabitating nicely into something you appear to find comfortable, and the whole of it is very appealing to the eye. This may add to your comfort as well." He now looked at me rather than the mirror. "When I saw it, I immediately thought of you."

My mouth turned with the hint of a smile. "Peering daily into such a large glass may not necessarily bring me comfort."

"Well, it is here, and it is my post-holiday gift to your home, *ma chère*. After it is hung and has graced your home for a little while, then you and your house can decide whether it will become a welcome addition. If not, I am happy to take it elsewhere. Truly, it is for you to decide."

I was drawn to the fine artistry of the frame's woodwork and the whole of the majestic looking glass and was filled with a sudden attachment and claim to it—as Henri surely knew would occur. In truth, it *would* fit nicely among the other fine old pieces in my home, all of them chosen by Solange and myself. Pieces long used by others in their homes and now adopted lovingly into mine. But accepting this as a gift from Henri was another matter altogether.

"Let me pour you some tea and cut more bread. We will need some sustenance if we are to make these changes to the rooms." And with those words that seemed to be uttered on their own, I resigned myself to the fact that I did indeed want this beautiful piece in my home and would deal with attempting to pay Henri for it once it was hung.

"And cheese, Marie! I must say I drove straight from Verdun, excited as I was to see the mirror hung in its new home, and therefore, I did not eat and am now exceedingly famished."

We stood for a moment, side by side, looking into the glass at our shared reflection. I remembered I had not asked him about Bernard when Félix was here.

"Henri, how is Bernard? And have his ewe and her lambs continued to do well?"

"The sheep and her young are doing better than Bernard. He has been in an agitated state of melancholy and not a pleasant person to be around these days," Henri answered as we addressed each other's reflections in the mirror.

"I am curious as to why on Christmas Eve he seemed excessively concerned about his sheep. To the point that I was worried for his mental state."

"The flock of sheep and the birthing and tending to the lambs was his wife's occupation. She loved those animals and especially the ewe you attended to that night. Bernard lost his beloved wife four years ago and has continued to mourn his loss every day since. He has never been a very agreeable sort, but since her passing he has become even less so. People tend to keep their distance from him, making him even more unsocial. I believe this favorite ewe of his wife has become his only source of comfort. He cares for her as he did his spouse. Four years seems a very long time to live such a solitary existence," Henri said.

"Well, if he means to keep that sheep, I would suggest she not bear any more lambs. Can you mention that to him when you see him next?"

"I make it a point to stop in on him each week or so and almost force a conversation. Your advice will give me something to discuss with him. Although he has not said so, Marie, I know he is much appreciative of your care that night. It is difficult for him to express his feelings."

Henri turned from the mirror to face me. I faced him as well, letting many seconds fall between us before he broke the moment.

He turned back to the mirror and chuckled. "Do we not look like a pair of very hungry miscreants?"

Yes, indeed we did, I thought as we beheld once again our reflections in the looking glass. We seemed to always be in cahoots as we moved about in each other's lives.

CHAPTER 4

BESOTTED PEDDLER – FEBRUARY 1923

What did I do before I cared for so many? I've spent less and less time on the road these last months when I should have been out selling and buying from customers. Why don't I feel put upon—frustrated and worried that I am neglecting my own affairs? It isn't my business to entangle myself in the concerns of others.

True, it is winter and my clientele are settled in during these cold months and holidays. Truer still that I was never before daunted by inclement weather or my customers' hesitancy to purchase once the holidays had passed. I was always busy stocking and storing goods and acquiring furniture and wares for the next season. But here I am, myself settled to traveling back and forth a stretch of road so short that I could almost walk between the lengths of my intentions.

Besotted. I am besotted, and my foolishness for being so awakes with me every day that dawns. True, that more of my time and attentions have turned toward Félix. But he is a companionable child, curious and eager to travel beside me on the wagon, to take his lessons at the convent or spend days with Marie when I am off on business. It bothers me that I am spending more days than not with him and Marie, neglecting business.

And there lay the thorn that catches at me. The thorn that pricks me so often unawares and has begun to embed itself with particular pain around the edges of my heart. Besotted. Quite an ungainly word. Sounds like something one would do with a plant. Perhaps that is more what is occurring. Those you come to know and care about do plant themselves in your heart, I suppose. Certainly family, at least some of them, you gladly watch over as I do Félix; certainly, friends and, of course, the Sisters.

But my concern for them does not keep me awake at night. Does not befuddle my mind. Does not cause me to conjure pitiable reasons to seek out their presence, or cause me to question my sanity. I am not besotted with them.

Mon Dieu! I tell myself it has something to do with her mother. That I am getting old and attempting to draw the years back again through her to that earlier time of youth. During those few summers when, as a boy, her mother caught my attentions. And yet, now I cannot see clearly as I once did that young girl's countenance. She is a vague memory, a long-ago story from a young boy's carefree summers that has faded as all youthful memories do when the present is so vivid before us.

Throughout these three years of becoming acquainted, at first watching Marie struggle to heal herself as she nursed the young soldiers, I tried to help right her world after the war. Then finding myself drawn back again and again into the presence of this compassionate and strong woman, I desired to assist her in any way she might find comforting. How pleased I was when later she allowed the Sisters' beehives residence in her vast lavender fields, providing yet another opportunity to spend time together. Her friendships with the Sisters as they worked together making and selling their honey, candles, and lotions further helped Marie become whole again, ready to seek her greater destiny. And now, I find opportunity again to come alongside, to befriend and support, by providing her the clinic space.

I try convincing myself that my ministrations are only acts of friendship and appreciation for her skills as a nurse, her kindnesses to the Sisters, and her loving care for Félix. And I know this to be a rightful assessment. Friendship and comradery, a sense of mutual respect and admiration—all of that true. True also that these aspects of our relationship have never been spoken aloud.

Not a comment or affirmation is needed. That is true of most friends. A sincere "merci" is all that is expected.

But being besotted is a different matter altogether. It begs confirmation beyond a merci. It seeks mutual acknowledgement. It demands the thorn to either flower or be plucked permanently from its painful residence.

And my recourse for this befuddlement of mine? That I offer up myself and watch for any sign from Marie that she could return the same feelings. And if she does not? How long do I continue to wait before I castrate my longings and never again speak of my loving regard? It is hard to admit that I love her, for I do not want the pain of not having it returned. There lies the hope I hold to so tightly, that she might see the possibilities—the fruit, both practical and pleasurable, that our union might bear. I tell myself it is better to wait expectantly, allowing this hope to remain vigilant. Our world is changing quickly. I sense the urgency all around us to grasp what we desire, knowing firsthand it can so quickly be taken from our hearts.

CHAPTER 5

THE PROPOSALS – FEBRUARY 1923

I woke to sunlight coming through my window. It was much later than usual for me to not be up and about my morning chores. But I felt no guilt for sleeping in, for I had the entire day before me to do as I pleased.

As usual, I hastened to bring wood in for the stoves from my woodpile just outside the kitchen. As I opened the door to gather as many pieces as my arms could manage, I was stopped short by the sounds of Henri's singing. Singing in a loud voice accompanied by what sounded like a saw cutting wood.

What in the world was he doing? I walked to the corner of my house to peer across the road to the riverbank from where the sawing and singing were coming. There he was, in his familiar worn red corduroy jacket with the faded green wool scarf tied round his neck. But wearing no hat and no gloves.

A thought that had been lingering long and restless in the back of my mind suddenly seized the moment to present itself as urgent, and I was struck with stubborn resolve bordering on a feeling of injustice. This man, my friend of almost three years now, knew all and everything about me. I knew almost nothing of him. Yes, I knew he was a kind man, a helpful friend to many, a man of integrity who worked what seemed endless hours. Today was the day he would share with me where he lived and with whom besides Félix. I knew he had to have a house and probably buildings large enough to store all he brought back and forth to sell and trade. But how did he come to live here and for how long?

I wanted to know his history as he knew mine. I had many questions he needed to answer to put us on an equal footing regarding our friendship.

I hurried back to the kitchen door, grabbed up the wood, threw it into the stoves, and ran upstairs to change into warm clothes before embarking across the road on this mission of disclosure. He would not dissuade or distract me by answering my questions with questions of his own as he had done so many times before. Today was a day of reckoning.

Wool trousers and heavy flannel shirt on, I hopped in place trying to fill my heavy boots with my stockinged feet. Assuming I would be spending some time in the cold visiting with Henri, I donned my long heavy wool coat, hat, and gloves, and grabbed a wool blanket on the way out the front door. It was quiet as I ran across the road to the river's bank, and I feared he might have left even before I began my interrogation. But no, he was there, standing behind a poplar tree smoothing its bark.

"Bonjour, my industrious friend! And why are you sawing branches off these poor frozen trees?" I asked, taking note of the large pile of orphaned branches.

"It greatly increases one's comfort to lean against the trunk of a tree if the low limbs are not poking you in the back," he said without looking my way.

"Let's stop for a while and see if your theory proves itself to be true." I hastily shook out the blanket so it lay close to the trunk of a freshly limbed tree.

Henri took out a handkerchief and wiped his brow. "There are only four more trees to limb and then a respite. You sit and watch."

"I count five trees already limbed. That is more than enough for comfortable reclining." I sat down on the blanket and patted a place beside me. "Sit down, Henri. We need to talk."

Henri dropped his saw and hurried toward me. "What has happened? Are you not well? Bad news from your family?" he asked as he sat down on the blanket.

"There is something disturbing me. It is you, Henri. You and what I feel are secrets kept and truths evaded each time I venture anywhere near wanting you to share more about your life, apart from the little I know. You know everything about me and I know practically nothing about you!"

Splaying his hands in front of him, he replied sincerely, "Secrets? Evasion? Whatever are you talking about?"

"Am I your friend, Henri?"

"Yes, of course," he stated with a terrible look of consternation on his face.

"Are you my friend?"

"Why these questions we both know the answer to? Yes! Yes! You are my dear friend and I am your friend. I must say I am prone to think you are either sleepwalking or running a wild fever."

"You would almost certainly know if I were running a fever, and if so, you would then promptly pull from your wagon some elixir as a remedy. I, on the other hand, would never know if you were ill or in need in any way. You would just keep to yourself in whatever place you keep yourself. How would I, your friend, ever be able to bring you something you might need in a time of illness or trouble? For I have no idea whatsoever of where you reside, where you make your home. And Félix, where does that boy stay when he is not with me? Fair is fair, Henri, and this friendship is not."

Henri sat stone-still saying not a word. No quick retort, no question asked, no rebuttal—not one word or gesture. And thus, we sat staring at each other for what seemed endless minutes. I was not going to be the one to look away, and just to be sure he knew that, I crossed my arms in front of me for good measure. I could sit there and wait forever.

After what seemed such a long time that I was beginning to shiver from the cold, I saw his shoulders drop, and he released a long sigh. He had come to a decision.

Henri looked at me, his face set with determination. "You are right, Marie, but truly, I bear no secrets, not from you or anyone. There is simply nothing to impart. But I understand that you would not know that. I acknowledge your perspective, and we will right this inequity today, immediately after I limb these last four trees. We will then take a ride to visit my home." He got to his feet, picked up his saw, and walked to the cluster of trees.

"Thank you, Henri. I will go pack us a lunch," I said, rising. I shook out the blanket and walked back to my own home, feeling that perhaps I had not won the victory I so strongly fought for. Something in Henri's manner stirred caution in me, and I was not sure of what I had just accomplished, if anything. I felt not satisfaction but a mild sense of foreboding.

By the time I had a simple lunch of baguette, cheese, two apples, and a small jug of water ready for our ride, Henri was stowing his saw in the back of his wagon. He climbed onto the seat, picked up Donkey's reins, and offered a hand as I approached. I settled in beside him, our lunch stored on the floor in a basket between my feet. With only a word and a slight slap of the reins, Donkey turned the wagon round, and we headed north, toward Verdun.

"I thought you lived south of here!"

"See? You did know something about where I live. Yes, I did live to the south, but now I live north, actually very close to the convent."

I did not want to ask any more questions. He was in an answering mood, but each time he answered I was more confused. Where in the world were we headed?

The morning remained cold to the bone, and I was shivering by the time Henri pulled Donkey up to the front of a house. From where we sat atop the wagon, I could just make out the shape of the convent's tall chimneys farther up ahead on the other side of the road.

"Is this not the house belonging to the doctor?" I asked.

"No, Marie, it is actually the house belonging to me," he said solemnly.

I knew the house had been closed up since the young doctor, whom I had never met, left for the army as a field physician. He never returned, and no one had heard from him in all these years following the war. The house had remained empty and idle.

Jumping down from the wagon, Henri extended a hand to me, and I jumped down as well, holding our lunch in my other hand. I felt no appetite, though, but rather a dull nausea. Why was I so scared? Yes, that is what I was! But what brought this sense of fear?

"You see, the home I lived in previously was one I occupied for more than twenty years. It was ramshackle and small. Too small for more than just myself. And I want to provide Félix with a home that is closer to town. After many months of searching, I only recently tracked down the physician's family. The doctor was killed in the war, and his family had not the heart to pursue selling his home. I told them I wanted to purchase the house from them, and we quickly came to an agreed price. I have only just taken possession this last week and have begun moving in. It needed some minor repairs and updates, including painting the whole of the interior and the clinic space. The foliage around the house has grown high, too, and still needs taming before it resembles a proper home."

The house was a long edifice of stucco washed an apricot gold. The red-tiled roof offset the blue-gray wooden doors and shutters at the front entrance to the actual house and what appeared to be the clinic's entrance, where I knew the doctor had seen his patients. There was evidence of lavender dried and gone to seed, and a brown vine meandered up the wall beside the clinic's somewhat weathered door. Indeed, the lavender had overgrown its intended bounds beside the three shallow steps leading up to the door and would need trimming before spring.

"Yes, I do remember the Sisters saying that the doctor had barely finished his house and opened the clinic before he had to leave." I was more than eager to see this space where he had practiced.

Walking up the steps, Henri said over his shoulder, "We'll go in here. I anticipated you would want to see it first. This enters directly into *la clinique*, which is separate from the rest of the house."

Ah, how well he knew me.

As we walked into the room I was surprised by how large it was, at least five meters wide and over seven meters long. The wood plank floor was painted white to match the walls. Two wide cupboards with glass-fronted doors hung on the wall directly across from the entrance, and each cabinet had five shelves filled with evenly spaced medicinal apothecary jars of blue and white porcelain. The jars were labeled with familiar names of ointments and tinctures, dried herbs, and oils, including arnica, St. John's wort, witch hazel, and oils of clove, eucalyptus, lavender, and peppermint, among others. Under the cupboards ran a long, wide countertop with a sink at its center and a row of drawers directly below. Beneath the drawers was a long empty shelf where the doctor must have placed larger instruments and implements.

In front of the wall of cupboards stood a wooden plinth table with a shelf below. This examination table was at least one and a half meters wide and two and a half meters long. Other than the table and cupboards of jars, the room was empty and spotlessly clean. It was an ideal space for a medical office.

"I think the room looks ready for patients. Do you not agree?" Henri was looking not at me but round the room as though he had never seen it before. I tingled with cautious curiosity at what he might be leading up to.

"The other door," he said as he motioned toward it, "leads into the house. But I wanted to show you the clinic first, Marie, as I have a proposal to make to you. Actually, two proposals." He walked to the plinth table and placed his hat on it. I walked between the table and the cupboards with the sudden compulsion to hold on to something.

"I have spent my life appraising the value, the worth of things loved by others. These I must judge to be of this or that value as they pass from the lives of one person and I place them into the hands of another. I am not an educated man. Not in the formal sense of the word. But I have come to have great knowledge as to what is worthy and to be prized in this life. Some prizes are found quite by accident and prove to be great treasures. Only a few of these have I kept for myself over the years as they became precious to me."

Stepping closer, the plinth table now between us, Henri looked at me beseechingly and said, "Do you remember the unripe pomegranate I brought you almost two years ago, assuring you that with good tending it would grow into a luscious, ripe fruit? Did you know at the time I was speaking of you? That you are a treasure? That you are a gifted nurse tending to the needs of us all in ways you do not even realize?" His brows creased as he spoke.

He paused and took several breaths. I was now holding the sides of the plinth table so tightly my fingers were becoming numb. My heart was racing and my breathing so fast I feared I would faint.

"Marie, I want to propose that this room, this clinic, become yours. Here you can see patients from all over the area and even ones that might come from Verdun. Here you can do your tending in a fine space worthy of a fine nurse."

Again he stopped, and I thought he was as close to falling down as I was. He took more deep breaths and continued, "And I have a second proposal. One that stems from my own need. Today we talked of being friends and we are surely that. But, Marie . . . I want you to consider becoming more than my friend. I propose that we marry. In my experience and observation of many husbands and wives over the years, the best of couples are above all else the best of friends. I believe we could be both as well."

We stood there in pregnant silence. I knew it was my turn to speak, but I barely had breath, let alone words.

"Henri, while you talk of your experience, I have none. Both of your proposals find me stunned. To the first I want to say yes immediately, and to the second I need to say I must have time."

"It must seem to you a bribe. The offer of this clinic with the offer of marriage. And I want you to understand clearly that they are not one and the same. You may say yes or no to either or both. I will understand, or try my best to be bravehearted."

He began walking round the sparse room, moving slowly from corner to corner. Coming back to the table, he looked me straight in the eye. "I have watched you fill your house with items scarred and worn. And you rub and polish the old, making it shine. The marks of time and wear become the patina of what you now cherish. You know how to choose what you can love and tend, what brings harmony and beauty to your life.

"As you think on what has been offered here today, please trust yourself, Marie. Trust that your heart will know what will make you most happy."

With that said, he broke our locked eyes and moved toward the door leading into his new home.

"Today is Sunday. Linger here in this space as long as you desire. Examine every nook and cranny to see if it meets your needs. And then look into your heart to see if I might meet your needs as well. I ask that you let me know tomorrow of your decision."

I felt my throat closing on itself as I choked out, "But, Henri—must I decide so soon?"

With his hand on the doorknob, he stopped and glanced back over his shoulder, saying with impatience bordering on agitation in his tone, "It is time, Mademoiselle. Time we make some decisions." Turning the knob and opening the door, he stepped with great resolve across the threshold and silently closed the clinic door behind him.

And I was left unpeeling my frozen fingers from the table as I attempted to slow my breath. From the light outside the window, I guessed it must now be early afternoon. The Sisters would be in the gardens or reading in their rooms. I desperately needed to find Sister Agnès. My soul needed counsel and my heart needed solace. It would be my decision alone, but I did not want to be alone as I sorted out my feelings. Sister would listen and, I hoped, give wise advice.

I did walk around the room several times. Not to examine it, as Henri suggested I should, but in an attempt to calm myself. I finally opened each drawer under the counter, finding evidence of mice and half-eaten lengths of bandages. I tried to imagine myself in this large space with my own instruments and supplies, but my mind could make no determining beyond the fact that the room was ideal and, more than anything, I wanted to nurse here.

Having opened and thoroughly taken account of what detritus was contained in every drawer and cupboard, I could not help but walk to the door to Henri's home and lean my ear up against it. There was no sound on the other side. What was he doing in there? Pacing and worrying as I was?

After taking a last look around, I left and walked the five minutes north to the converted farmhouse that was the convent. My pace quickened the closer I got. My dear friends would take me in and perhaps right my teetering world as I attempted to navigate such foreign matters. And then I smiled. I was going to seek advice on matters of the heart from Catholic nuns. But then, who better to discuss such matters with than those devoted to loving?

Félix's short stature appeared at the front window as I drew near, and he opened the door for me moments later, propelling himself directly into me and wrapping his arms round my middle. My heart jumped as usual at the very welcome sight of this dear child. I ruffled his black curls and felt my soul settle. It was so easy to love this boy. So easy to trust that his own devotion to Henri and myself was pure and true and real. Could Henri and I do the same with each other? Could this child be the bridge between us that I would need to make that happen?

"My hands are much better, Marie. Do you want to see?" he asked, his voice muffled against my body.

"Let's go inside and have some tea, and I will take a look at those wonderful hands of yours."

Hand in hand, we entered the convent and made our way to the kitchen. The kettle, as always, sat simmering on the stovetop. Sister Jeanne and I greeted one another warmly before she settled Félix and myself at the table and poured us our tea.

Of course Félix would be here. I suddenly realized that Henri had planned all along that today would unfold exactly as it did. Had I not gone over to the river and demanded he answer my questions, he would have come to the house asking if I wanted to see where he lived. But he counted on my curiosity and coming to find out what he was up to with his loud singing and sawing. I was almost overcome with emotion and felt myself close to tears. Of course I loved him. He was my dear friend.

Félix held his small hands out to me from across the table, laying them flat, palm-side up. I took them gently, kissing each palm, and assured him that, indeed, his hands were healing, and the rough redness, if he continued to take care, would soon be replaced by new, smooth skin.

"Remember, Félix, every day before bed you must continue to apply the salve I gave you to both your feet and your hands and to any other red areas on your body. If you can keep them mended through winter, you may not need to use the salve in summer."

"Oui, Mademoiselle, I rub it on every night and wear socks to bed—even socks on my hands!"

I continued to hold his hands in mine as we smiled across the table at one another. Again, my heart stirred at the knowledge that if I accepted Henri's second proposal I would in essence become mother to Félix. That to me was the most appealing aspect of Henri's proposition but surely not a logical reason to accept an offer of marriage.

Sister poured Félix and me more tea, and as they engaged one another, I left with my teacup in hand in search of Sister Agnès. I was relieved that I had calmed sufficiently before now going to speak with her. Agitation is never a state in which to sort through feelings and emotions.

As though expecting me, Sister met me in the nave as I rounded the corner.

"*Bonne après-midi*, Marie! What a nice surprise, as it is always a pleasure to see you, *ma chère*. It has been a little while since you and I had a visit," she said, placing her arm through the crook of mine and leading me off to her room. Her actions had me wondering if Henri had shared his plans and she had been expecting me.

"How are you feeling, Sister? Any continued dizziness, fatigue, or pain?" I asked. Some time ago, Sister Agnès had taken a very bad fall onto a hatchet in the garden shed and sustained a significant wound to her head. Although she appeared to have healed completely, I remained unconvinced that there were no lingering issues to be resolved. I had noticed on the last few occasions we spoke that she would frequently take the first two fingers of her right hand and run them several times in quick succession under the band of her headpiece. The band fell directly across the suture line where I had stitched her deep head gash. I thought it possible that the constant pressure from the tight cloth to the wounded area kept the skin irritated and prevented it from healing completely. It would certainly help if the headband were loose, but when I had mentioned this to her on several past occasions, she assured me the hours in her bed at night with no wearing of her habit provided the scar plenty of time to heal. There was also the possibility that running her fingers under the band was now a nervous tendency indicating some level of anxiety.

"What brings you here for tea, Marie? I heard no sound of your wagon and Horse pulling up outside, and surely you didn't walk." Her face held a wry smile as she sat and indicated the other chair for me.

"I came with Henri. I insisted early today that he show me where he lived. That friends knew that about one another. You can imagine my surprise when he acquiesced and headed the wagon north instead of south." I couldn't meet her eyes but kept my gaze on the teacup as I swirled its contents round and round, much as my own thoughts were doing.

We sat silently then, she sipping from her own cup and me avoiding her knowing looks.

"And what did you think of Henri's proposal?" she asked, as though it were an issue of inconsequence. So she was indeed aware of Henri's offers. He may even have sought her counsel as I was now.

"Which proposal are you referring to, Sister?" I said, hoping to match her same light tone of voice.

"Ah, I see. He told me of the one: offering to you the room that might serve as your clinic. I heard the unspoken second proposal as well and wondered if he would find the courage to speak of it."

As I looked up at her, I hoped beyond hope that I might see reflected in her wise face the direction I needed to take. That she would share with me what she believed to be my future. I did not find that in Sister Agnès's kind eyes or in her words.

"I assume that you have come today to talk, and I will gladly listen, dear, should you be inclined to share your feelings and thoughts. But I will offer no opinion, as this is your journey, your life, and you must make the choices."

"As he told you, Henri's first proposal was to offer me the use of the clinic room. The second proposal was an offer of marriage. I do not know, although he assured me it was not the case, if the first offer is in reality contingent upon the second. The clinic room I very much want. I could not ask for a more perfect place in which to see patients. However, I am very sure that I do not want to accept Henri's second proposal. But if I do not, would he truly agree to my using the clinic room or might he feel I was taking advantage of his generosity accepting only what is beneficial to me and denying him what he desires?"

She set her teacup on the table. "Did he say that, Marie? That if you did not marry him you could not use the clinic room?"

"No, he did not say that. But he did say that I had to decide by tomorrow morning and let him know. That seems a brief time to decide such an important issue." I stood up and began pacing Sister's small room, my hands nervously running up and down the front of me.

"Perhaps since you know you would like to accept his offer of the clinic, you begin there and take time to contemplate the other."

"I do not think his deadline of tomorrow was really about the clinic room. He was indeed talking about our relationship."

Did I love Henri? Of course I did, but did I love him beyond the bounds of friendship? Could I see beyond into a future where we were husband and wife? He was obviously already at that place and, if I was honest with myself, over the years I had seen his care for me extending to desire and want. Pretending it was only my imagination allowed me to believe it wasn't true. And now to even entertain his offer filled me with fear—and possibly dread. Not the way a woman should feel, I suspected, if she were truly in love. But again, I had no experience, so what did I really know?

"I realize Henri loves me in a way that I find quite frightening. How can one ever know if someone's love is real or sustainable? It provokes great confusion in me, to say the least," I said, continuing to pace.

"Marie, sit down. Why would you think there would be no fear when you love? It is always a risky endeavor—promising into forever to love another person when it is so hard to even love ourselves from day to day." Sister Agnès calmly dabbed her mouth with a napkin as though we were having an ordinary chat over tea. "And that is a risk only you can determine is worth taking or not. And I don't think it reasonable that one thinks that all they have to give another person is what they have to give on this day. We all change, and hopefully when we profess love and commitment we change together and become what is mutually agreeable and comfortable as a couple. The miracle of love is that it allows us to grow beyond ourselves, our capacity to love the other increased by the love we receive. The other becomes our beloved because we are secure in their love for us."

I wasn't really listening anymore to Sister's words. She sounded as if she thought I should just run back to Henri, say yes, and have it over and done with. I wanted to run, but not to Henri. Just yesterday I was dreading leaving all I have here and traveling to New York City for a visit with my family, and now all I wanted to do was escape to anywhere but where I was at this moment.

"I wish I were dreaming and would wake up and find all was back to normal," I said in almost a whisper but loud enough that Sister caught my words.

"Stay here tonight, Marie. Spend this evening in contemplation and prayer. You must above all else be honest with yourself and then be so with Henri." Sister Agnès took my hands into her own and looked deep into my eyes. "There is nothing more damaging to oneself and to others than making a commitment one has no desire to fulfill. That will always end badly. Henri is right: you need to make a decision or two."

CHAPTER 6

THE DECISIONS – FEBRUARY 1923

I did spend the night at the convent. There had been no need for serious contemplation or prayer, for when Sister Agnès said to be honest with myself and then with Henri, there was only one decision to be made this morning. I slept badly, waiting for the dawn that I might appear at Henri's door and honestly respond to his proposals.

As I made my way to his house at first light, I found my feet heading for the clinic door. How I wanted to be in there planning the arrangement of my medicines and equipment. But since that may not become my reality, and allowing my good sense to rein me in, I turned to Henri's front door and gave it a solid knock.

He answered so quickly it was obvious he was expecting me—as I knew he would be.

"Bonjour, Marie. The kettle is ready to boil over. Come in, please, and we will have tea." He abruptly turned and departed, leaving me standing in his doorway, the decision to enter or not mine alone to make.

He was nowhere in sight as I stepped across the threshold and into the passageway of his home. I was curious, of course, to see this house of his, and looking about for a few minutes would hopefully calm my nerves. Perhaps he was giving me time to explore the house on my own; perhaps he, too, needed time to settle himself.

As I walked into the house, a wide sitting area opened to the right, with tall, mullioned windows that light had not yet illuminated, as the early sun had not reached high enough. But Henri had lit candles, many candles, our own beeswax candles from the convent, placing them all about the room in duets and trios. The glow of the flames cast gentle wavering shadows that enticed one into this space, and the effect was indeed very calming. I moved my hand across the walls and found they were textured, like sand beneath the paint, which was the color of hay before the harvest. However, this room was given definition not by its walls but by the carefully considered placement of furniture, so clean of design and sparse in detail I felt I had entered another world altogether. I had never seen such a room.

Sitting upon the inviting divan, upholstered in a fabric two shades darker than the walls, I allowed myself to take in the whole of the space, made beautiful by each piece of furniture situated seemingly at random. But I knew Henri considered the placement of each chair and table carefully to create such an inviting ambience.

A low coffee table was placed in front of the divan, and two side tables, small and square, were set next to the room's chairs. The tables were similar in that they were made of the same two woods, one blond in color and the other dark brown. Marquetry, geometric patterns of dark wood inlaid within the surface of the lighter, decorated the center of each table, and dark wood matching the inlays bordered the edges. Legs of blond wood tapered from wide at the top to very narrow at the bottom. Straight edges with complete symmetry of form.

The three chairs in the room were armless and covered in the same nubby fabric as the divan, the colors a variation of a theme. Two chairs were a light sage and the third just a shade or two darker. Again, simple in design and exquisite in form.

All the pieces blended and flowed in the light of the flickering candles. Calm, peaceful, simple, and splendid. One felt at ease in such a room, and I found my heart was beating more slowly once again. So much so that I did not feel fear or apprehension about the conversation that was shortly to take place.

Henri carried in a tea tray complete with croissants and set it atop the table in front of me. Taking a chair to the side, he poured our tea and said, "You'll be better able to see the room when the sun rises higher."

"This is lovely, Henri. I feel as though I've entered a dream in which I would be happy to remain," I said before I could stop myself. Whatever would he think?

Smiling and nodding his head, he handed me my cup and took up his. We stirred and sipped and looked about the room for several minutes, and I knew, once again, he was giving me all the time I needed before speaking.

Taking a deep breath, I started my practiced delivery with, "After speaking with Sister Agnès and spending the night in the convent thinking on what you put forth, I would like to propose what I hope might be acceptable to you. I would like to rent the clinic space from you four days a week beginning as soon as possible. Once you and I have spent time in such close proximity and over a period of, say, six months from the time I return from America, then I would be prepared to make a decision regarding your other proposal." I said this as straightforwardly as possible, looking directly at Henri the entire time.

He remained calm, sitting very still, as though he were afraid of spooking me, as if I were a young mare he was trying to gentle into a bridle. Perhaps a very apt comparison.

Henri set his cup on the table and squared his shoulders. "The clinic room is available, and you can move in your supplies and equipment as soon as you secure what you need. Are you planning to advertise your services in order to build your practice? Most likely it will grow slowly at first but steadily; you already have a reputation as an experienced and accomplished healer.

"I would like to propose that rather than a monthly fee for renting the space you would be amenable to allowing me to share in your profits—say, twenty percent each month? That way, as your practice grows, so does your income, and I continue to take twenty percent." He countered as though the only proposal under consideration was the renting of the clinic.

I found I was enjoying this banter; it was impersonal—solely a business proposition. Gone was Henri's tone of voice from last afternoon when it had gone from softly pleading to strident and almost angry. This was the Henri I knew and, certainly, a safe place from which we could speak.

"Yes, that sounds quite reasonable and fair," I said, reaching for the teapot to pour us both another cup.

He leaned forward, extending his saucer, and we smiled at one another. We were both glad to be on familiar ground once again and seemed to have silently agreed not to speak anymore of the second proposal. He did not attempt to counter my six months of watching and waiting, and my relief almost made me laugh aloud. I had my beautiful clinic space without the caveat of having to become a reluctant wife.

Bringing me out of my reverie, Henri said, "You can have leaflets made to distribute in Verdun and the surrounding area announcing your clinic's opening and hours of operation. When are you thinking of opening your door to patients?" he asked very matter-of-factly.

"The leaflets are certainly a good idea. I will see the printer and discuss the design and what information to include, but I won't have them printed until I return. As to when I might open, I have very little to bring into the clinic. I was certainly not expecting such a wonderful opportunity.

"I am writing a letter to La Pitié-Salpêtrière hospital, in Paris, where I originally trained and worked for three years following the war before returning home to Marseille. I am hoping they will allow me to do a six-week course of study to upgrade my skills and sit for the certificate of nursing exams when I return from New York.

"Now that I have a clinic space, I plan to consult with Papa about purchasing instruments and necessary items such as basins, basic supplies, and perhaps a microscope. I could see patients in the clinic now, but I won't be able to do much other than basic care," I said, thinking ahead as to what I could bring from my house. Those I had been providing care to I had been seeing at the convent.

"Regarding the clinic room, I will definitely need a barrier placed between waiting patients and the one I am treating. Framed screens, perhaps, with hinges, that can be folded forward or back to fit the space and placed on the other side of the plinth table. Ideally, four hinged screens each approximately one meter wide and two and a half meters high. Have you ever seen such screens in your travels?" I didn't want to take advantage of Henri's good nature and willingness to help. Nor did I want to become dependent upon him any more than I was. I was very happy that he would be paid a part of the clinic's earnings. It would ease my continual sense of obligation toward him.

"Oui, Marie. I am sure such a barrier can be either found or built. I will take care of that. For a fee, of course," he added with a sly smile.

I felt a compelling need to make a list of all that I might accomplish before I left for America. First, I must meet again with the physician in Verdun, coaxing him and pleading, if necessary, in hopes that he serve as the clinic's physician supervisor. I had already made initial contact with him, a late-middle-aged gentleman, and although he was supportive of my "nursing aspirations" to those who could not travel into Verdun or did not need a higher level of care, he would not agree outright to provide the oversight I would need.

He informed me he was giving serious consideration to closing his practice of thirty-five years and retiring to the warmer climes of Nice. His wife, in fact, told him she was leaving with or without him come June. He appeared much inclined to pack up and move with her but, he said, he was too exhausted to even contemplate the effort it would take to dismantle his practice. He also confided that the thought of spending all his time with his wife, although he assured me she was "a gem, just a gem," was cause for taking things slowly. But his practice was overwhelmingly busy, and he contemplated retirement every day he continued. I left with his good wishes and a promise that when I returned I might again approach him, should he change his mind, pointing out that the outlying clinic would lessen the demands on his practice in town, thereby providing him more leisure time. He made no comment, and closing his office door, I realized this was not a man who wanted me to open the discussion again.

I did not know of another situation in our immediate vicinity such as the one I was proposing, where a nurse in a formal medical setting acted as the first point of contact for care. I knew a physician would need to work in the clinic every so often to meet the requirements for a rural facility staffed by a nurse, but I did not know the frequency or the particulars of physician oversight. This was one of the many questions I planned on finding answers to when I, hopefully, spent time training in the hospital in Paris.

"Henri, would you have paper and pen available? I would like to make some notes. And might I please go into the clinic room again—now?"

"Yes, of course, and I will get paper for you as soon as I give you something else you need." He stood and took from his pocket a key that I immediately knew was to the door of the clinic. "I took the liberty of attaching it to something larger, making it easier to keep account of."

And with that, he extended to me my clinic's key, which I gratefully accepted. Attached through an opening in the top of the heavy bronze key was a bright gold chain, and on the end was a gold medallion stamped with the imprint of a bee. The image of the bees in my lavender. The medallion was fifty millimeters in diameter and fit perfectly into the palm of my hand. Closing my fingers round the gold, I stepped across the space to Henri and kissed him on each cheek, adding a thoroughly adequate hug. Yes, Henri was my dear friend. I hoped we could remain as today, even after the many days of tomorrows when I would tell him once again I was not meant to be anyone's wife.

CHAPTER 7

LETTER TO THE HOSPITAL
– FEBRUARY 1923

15 February 1923
Hôpital universitaire Pitié-Salpêtrière
13 ᵉᵐᵉ Arrondissement
Paris, France

Dear Madame Registrar,

I am writing to submit a request to advance my nursing skills and sit for the Certificate of Nursing exams.

I completed my extended Red Cross nurse's training at l'Hôpital de la Pitié-Salpêtrière in April 1916, receiving my Initial Diploma of Nursing, and was then part of a field surgical team serving on the northern outskirts of the Battle of Verdun. After being injured in a shell attack in December 1916, I was transported to la Pitié-Salpêtrière, where I recovered and worked as a surgical and floor nurse until April 1920. Before returning to my home in Marseille, I received the Diploma of War certificate and the State Diploma of Nursing.

My home is now south of Verdun, along the River Meuse, and after the war I opened my home as an extension of a nearby convent for the convalescence of men wounded both physically and emotionally. At this time, I would like to update and advance my nursing skills, as I once again want to begin actively nursing in a clinic close to Verdun.

I will be traveling to New York City to visit my family, departing 1 April and returning to France on 26 April. Would it be possible on my return to attend classes and lectures for a proposed period of six weeks, beginning in May? My particular interests are medical-surgical, obstetrics, and pediatrics. I would also greatly appreciate the opportunity to observe lectures by professor physicians discussing the latest developments in medicine as it relates to nursing. I trust the files from my time training, in recovery, and my three years of nursing at la Pitié-Salpêtrière remain in your records for your review. I would hope to sit for the Certificate of Nursing exams before my departure.

The name on my files would be Marie Durant Chagall. If you dispatch your reply to reach me before I leave for America in early April, please direct it to my Verdun address. If you dispatch your reply after 1 April, please direct it to the New York, USA address. I have enclosed both addresses on a separate sheet. Thank you for your consideration in this matter. I look forward to your reply.

Respectfully,
Marie Durant

CHAPTER 8

THE TRUNK – MARCH 1923

I had asked Bernard if he might pick up the trunk that had arrived from New York and bring it to my home. Solange indicated it was a very large steamer trunk and full to overflowing. Bernard was twice my size, and I knew he could maneuver it from his truck to the inside of my home without trouble. And he relished doing favors for the nurse who saved his favorite sheep. The trunk now sat on the floor in the space between my dining and sitting rooms.

Solange loved surprising me, as she did when bringing my replenished sewing box during her visit almost two years ago. Thus, I knew within this deep dark wooden trunk she would have placed a wide variety of items. Some would be essentials and some tokens of her sisterly regard for me. The trunk certainly wasn't new. Its wood was cracked in places and the steel bands around the outside and across the top were dull and burnished with age. I could envision her face, a look of satisfaction in her smile upon finding this perfect trunk to house all I needed for my New York visit and voyage on the *SS Paris*.

Unlike my reticence in opening my sewing box, knowing I'd be overcome with scents and visions of my home in Marseille, I was more than eager to unlock this trunk. Solange had mailed the key to me earlier along with my ticket and funds for my journey, and now, as I attempted to turn the lock, it stuck, the key not budging. I sat upon the top, thinking it might help align key to keyhole and, voilà, it worked! As I jumped off the trunk, the top lifted immediately, pushed up by mounds of material.

Solange had informed me that she was sending what was "fashionable and appropriate clothing" for a woman my age traveling first class and that I might initially find her selections questionable but to trust her judgement (when had I not?) and to try on each garment keeping an open mind. She wrote she was also sending me newspaper clippings and fashion magazines to aid my understanding of why she had sent these particular garments and how they should look when worn. On my! Did she think I was so out of touch and isolated that I could not remember how to put on and wear a piece of clothing?

I pulled the heavy trunk over next to the divan, across from the large looking glass. Lifting out each garment one by one, I held them against me for an initial inspection in front of the mirror, after which I carefully laid them out over the back of the sofa.

Each gown was wrapped in thin white muslin, which I assumed meant I needed to do the same when repacking for my trip. Peeling away the cloth, I first found a formal dress, one that would most likely be worn during the evening to dinner. It was exquisite in design and beautiful in its details. A soft dove gray of luminous flowing silk charmeuse. Sleeveless and loosely structured with a drop waist and a hem ending mid-calf, it was a style I had not seen before! The fact that it was flowing and loose certainly met my definition of something comfortable to wear. However, I didn't know what to make of the dress not having sleeves, especially for evening wear. Suspending judgment, I draped the beautiful dress across the cushions.

There were two more dresses. One was a pale sage green *crêpe de Chine*, again sleeveless but with a delightful matching short cape. The other was more formfitting and appeared to fall almost to my ankles. It did have sleeves, long slender sleeves, and ruching across the hips. The material exhibited a stretch-like quality and was cut on the bias, allowing the fabric to hang gracefully across one's body. The color was a deep shimmering blue—almost black. The tag inside the dress indicated it was designed by "Chanel."

Three beautiful dresses now graced my divan. I was overcome with both excitement and trepidation, knowing soon I would be wearing the elegant gowns. Perhaps Solange was right in sending those magazines. So long had I lived in my well-worn trousers and flannels as I trooped about completing my daily chores and activities that my hope was I could remember how to carry myself with the deportment worthy of them.

Taking a deep breath, I once again peered into the trunk, hoping there were also items of a more casual nature. I found three light wool skirts and very loose-fitting matching blouses. And belts I assumed were to be worn with the skirts. I really was not sure how to wear those ensembles. I uncovered two more blouses, one a sky blue and the other one white. All but one blouse had sleeves.

The next parcels in muslin turned out to be a most welcome surprise. Trousers! Two pairs of loose, long, wide-legged pants, one gray and the other light tan. The fabric appeared to be a lightweight wool, thin and soft to the touch. Those I would surely get the most use out of, and I could alternate between the various blouses. Next, I found two cardigans, one a soft beige and the other black, woven sparingly with silver threads creating a simple but elegant gossamer effect. Wrapped with these were two pairs of satin silk pajamas, one in pale blush pink with a delicate hemstitched trim and the other cream, both with long-sleeved, boxy jacket tops and matching loose long pants.

Dropping to my knees to more easily see what was left, I found three pairs of silk hosiery, two garter belts, lovely silk panties, two brassieres by "Maidenform," and three pairs of thin wool socks. I was more than grateful not to find tight restricting corsets or girdles anywhere in the trunk. The non-binding lingerie and flowing garments in beautiful fabrics were ones in which I thought I could feel comfortable.

Next, the trunk presented a light beige wool coat with two hats, one matching the coat and the other in navy blue. The hats looked like helmets made of felt, and when I placed one on my head it was somewhat snug. It looked rather odd with my long hair hanging down from below the hat's rounded brim. The beige coat fit very well and would be quite suitable for the spring weather. The vision of me from the neck down was pleasant; however, the vision from the neck up was rather discouraging. What did one do with all one's hair and these hats? I took off the coat and laid it over the trunk's open lid and tossed the hats to the divan.

Solange had placed five pairs of shoes all along the bottom of the trunk. Two were in basic colors of black and brown with curved, slightly thick heels and a top strap adorned by a silver buckle. Two other pairs were more delicate and formal and covered in silk, one matching the dove gray of the first dress, the other a cream-colored silk. The last pair I lifted out resembled a pair of men's lace-ups, which I was sure were meant to be worn with the trousers.

And lastly, there was a small tapestried box filled with jewelry. As I moved the clasp to the side and lifted the lid, I found three long necklace strands of small brilliant gemstones in many colors and two even longer strands of luminescent white pearls. There were also earrings, one pair a small cluster of diamonds and the other composed of a single pearl slightly larger than the ones on the matching necklace. The last lovely items in the box were rhinestone hair clips and a small watch encased in a very thin band of gold.

I felt like a pirate who found the long lost treasure. Unlike a pirate, however, I could not believe this booty really belonged to me. My sister had outdone herself sending me all the clothing and accessories I would need for my journey. I also knew I could wear the trousers, skirts, and blouses in the clinic under my nursing apron when I returned home. I certainly wanted to look professional and worthy of tending to my trusting patients!

Solange had also placed a very large envelope in the trunk with instructions printed on the top stating: "*For your reading enjoyment.*" The parcel contained three magazines: *Vanity Fair*, *Cosmopolitan*, and a new publication called *Time*, along with several newspaper clippings of women wearing the latest fashions, including hats, the styles all similar to what she had sent. Since Solange's visit, and because she was now living in America and wanted to improve her English reading and writing skills, we wrote our letters in English rather than French. On a note clipped to the first magazine, Solange had written in English, "*Enjoy these as they are an education in fashion and how to dress for your upcoming adventures on sea and in a new land, and Time magazine will update you on what is happening here. We eagerly await your arrival?*

Sitting down upon the floor and leafing through the two fashion magazines, I was able to understand how to wear the skirts (low on the hips with belts) and the blouses. I could also wear the cardigans over the blouses and then a belt round the waist of the sweater, and the hats worn in all the pictures, cloche hats, were atop the heads of women all with very short hair.

With those mysteries solved and too weary from the unpacking to actually try on the garments I instead went outside for a brisk walk along my river.

It was difficult to imagine living shipboard with hundreds of strangers. I knew I could retreat to my cabin at any time, however, I hoped I could become that person that mingled with others on a large ship for several days. That I could be that person who welcomed lighthearted or more serious conversations with my fellows onboard. That I might even feel lovely and admired as I walked in to dinner wearing the beautiful gowns sent by my thoughtful sister. For I had been in virtual seclusion for this long time now but indeed felt almost ready to move again among the living and the vital. I wanted to feel healed of my injuries from the war, no longer fearing that at any moment I might find myself falling apart by a sight or a word that sent me back to Verdun and the horrors of that time. That my wounds were now but scars. The scars reminders that I had survived intact and was ready to move forward. I was changed, surely, a different person now, someone stronger because of those experiences. I hoped the time aboard ship engaging in the social graces necessary when living among others would prepare me well to share precious time with my beloved family.

The afternoon was fading into evening by the time I tended to my chickens and Horse and brought wood in again for the fires. The nights were still chilly enough that the stoves, with a lighter load of tinder, were needed to keep the house warm and snug. Ah, just like the hats Solange sent.

I knew it would be most prudent to try on all the garments this evening and note any alterations that I might need to make before placing them back into their muslin cocoons. After washing my hands thoroughly, I made a tight, neat chignon to the back of my neck and lit my lamps. I then ventured into the trunk's presence and, one by one, slid each garment over my body. The silky material of the gowns was cool as it slipped down across my skin and lay over my form with ease. Looking into the mirror, I turned first to the left and then to the right side. I knew from the magazine pictures that the silhouette was intended to be flat and straight. The articles informed the fashion-conscious woman that if her bosom extended too far forward, "wearing a tight-fitting, binding garment would secure a flatter chest." And if the buttocks extended too much the other direction, there was always a girdle to remedy that problem. I was fairly straight of form by nature, and the clothes created the desired effect without needing restrictive bindings, which I considered torture. I pitied the poor woman who felt she had to cajole her figure into submission just to wear such clothing as fashion dictated. It was fortunate for Solange that I was not an overly endowed woman, for I would not have taken kindly to wearing anything that restricted the natural form of my body. Certainly not after years of freedom from all of that.

Finding the pages showing how to wear the skirts and blouses, I secured the belt on the skirt and pulled the tucked-in blouse out around the waistband to what I thought was the correct amount to create a similar image as the ones shown in the pictures. I did not try on the silk stockings, but slipping my bare feet into the shoes, I walked round the house and up and down the stairs. The shoes fit well; however, the skirts felt as though they might slide down to my knees. I tightened the belt another notch or two but continued to worry they could slip past my narrow hips. How disastrous would it be to find one's skirt around one's ankles while taking a stroll around the ship! I laughed out loud at the thought of such a *coup de grâce* occurring on my maiden voyage and adjusted the belt tighter still.

CHAPTER 9

SS PARIS – APRIL 1923

Bernard kindly drove me to the station in Verdun to catch the morning train to Paris. I would spend the night there, traveling the next morning to Le Havre, where I would board the ocean liner *SS Paris* late in the afternoon. I could hear my trunk literally bouncing up and down in the back of Bernard's old truck, and I was sure my valise, which had been Papa's, was no longer upright. Bernard, always a quiet one, spoke even less than usual on the ride, with only a "humph" in response to any questions I asked. Finally, I inquired as to his health. Was he not feeling well? Were his sheep a concern to him?

"Both the sheep and myself are very fit, thank you. And we are very fine to stay here at home as well. We could not think of any reason for leaving and traveling to some place as far away as New York City and leaving our friends and animals," he said adamantly as he drove even faster down the dusty road.

"I will be gone only a short time, Bernard, and I expect I will be homesick the entire time I am away. While you may be in fine health, my papa is not, and it is most important that I visit him and my sister. Henri and Félix will be tending my animals during my absence, but I would certainly appreciate you checking on them from time to time."

"Humph."

The Sisters also regretted my leaving, and more than one expressed concern that I might decide to stay in New York. I could not imagine anything further from my desires. While in New York for just two weeks, I hoped to receive confirmation that my request to spend six weeks at the hospital in Paris had been granted. And while the Sisters and Henri did know of my intention to layover in Paris on my return, there was no reason to share that with Bernard and risk increasing his grumpiness.

We arrived at the station with thirty minutes to spare. Not one for goodbyes, Bernard pulled up to the station's entrance, leaving the truck's engine running as he hastily lifted out of the back the heavy trunk and then the valise. He set them down rather abruptly beside me as I stood next to the door. Without making eye contact, his mouth set in a fierce grimace, he tipped his old hat as he bowed slightly before me and quickly hopped back inside the truck and drove off. It was my turn to say humph. And next, to find a porter to help with the trunk.

I did not have to wait but a few minutes in the small station for a porter to find me. I showed him my tickets, and he said he was working the same train to Le Havre the following morning.

"Do you require assistance in Paris, Mademoiselle?"

"I do indeed. Would you be available to help in securing my trunk once we arrive and in finding a taxi to take me to my hotel?" Depositing a persuasive number of coins in his outstretched palm as I made these requests, he assured me this would be done.

By now, I was hungry and sat on one of the long wooden benches in the station, pulling from my valise a baguette with cheese. I loved toting the bag Papa had carried all those years on his sea adventures. How many ports of call had this bag seen, accompanying him from country to country and city to city as he traveled on his merchant ships with his crews, delivering and picking up goods? And during the war I knew he had worked with the government, trading in arms and supplies to support the troops. It had been so kind of Solange to bring it when she visited. Papa would take great satisfaction knowing that on my first ocean voyage I too carried the same leather portmanteau that had served him on countless excursions.

True to his paid word, the porter appeared at the station in Paris and, having already secured my trunk, escorted me to the line of taxicabs awaiting passengers at the front exit of the station. The ride to the hotel took barely five minutes, but

I felt the cost reflected a journey of a much greater length. Ah well, I was already enjoying these experiences, and certainly Papa gave me enough money to cover any contingency I might or might not plan for.

Since I had placed my nightclothes and personal sundries into the valise, the trunk stayed closed and locked. I would wear the same clothing again tomorrow, a dark gray skirt with matching jacket, a pale cream blouse, and quite sensible shoes with only the thought of a heel. There would be no reason to open the trunk till it and myself were deposited into our cabin onboard the ship. An unbidden thrill of excitement passed through me for a brief moment as I envisioned myself in that cabin. Tomorrow I would step into a new world.

My sleep was restless and disturbed by vivid dreams about any number of unknown people encountering harrowing events. At eight the next morning, I used the unfamiliar telephone in my room. As the bellman had instructed me on my arrival, I called the front desk to let them know I was ready to depart the hotel and that I required a ride to the station to catch train to Le Havre. Having become quite self-sufficient and independent, I found it unsettling to have to ask so many strangers for help.

The journey to Le Havre was uneventful, and as we pulled into the station, I felt myself becoming excited and slightly anxious. This would indeed be a novel adventure, and as much as I looked forward to the voyage and to seeing my family, I also realized I had never been with so large a number of people nor so great a distance from my home. My dear friends in Meuse were truly few, and there were many days each week that I was happy in my solitude with my animals the only company I sought. I told myself I could always retreat to my stateroom and mingle or socialize as much or as little as was comfortable for me.

Up to this point, I felt well and cautiously optimistic that my anxieties brought on by the war had abated significantly. The terrible memories had lost the sharp edges that would rise up and wound unexpectedly. But I knew when I became overly nervous or worried that they were there, lurking just behind the thin curtain between panic and calm. I would remain ever vigilant, careful each day of this adventure to take measure of my level of concern. Should it become necessary at any time I planned to physically remove myself from a situation or circumstance that might escalate into panic. If I began to perspire and feel claustrophobic, I would know it was time to seek solitude.

Often when I could not fall asleep I still practiced the breathing methods taught to me by the kind physician counselor Dr. Renard. I met with him weekly for several months during my recovery in the hospital in Paris. When memories began to crowd round me and threaten to take me under, he instructed me to take long, slow, measured breaths in and out as I pictured the most calming scene I could imagine. While at the hospital, both in my sessions with the doctor or when working with my patients, if I felt the need to quiet my mind, I would picture the loving faces of Solange and Papa as we sat round our dinner table in our home in Marseille. Now when unable to sleep or feeling uneasy, I would breathe slowly, picturing myself in my peaceful fields of flowing lavender, the tall stalks of blue swaying in the fragrant breeze. This technique helped calm me in situations in which I could not immediately remove myself, such as in the clinic room when Henri made his surprise proposals. If the methods worked during that tense and unexpected conversation, I felt prepared to meet any challenges on what I hoped would be a fascinating and pleasurable passage to America.

As the vehicle drove onto the area in close proximity to the ocean liners, two observations were paramount in my mind, and both caused me to swallow hard and take a deep breath. One, this ship was massive; and two, people were already boarding—hordes of people.

My driver had evidently assisted many passengers who traveled the seas. After opening the car door for me, he immediately carried my trunk to the designated area and placed it beside others positioned for loading. I got out of the car with my heavy valise and followed him. A uniformed porter was placing tags on each traveler's luggage, and the driver indicated I needed to show the porter my ticket, which I produced. The porter wrote out my name and stateroom number onto a luggage tag and knotted it to the handle of my trunk, assuring me it would be waiting for me in my cabin. After I paid the driver, thanking him several times for his help, he wished me bon voyage and was on his way. The porter then directed me to the first class gangway where other passengers were signing in and boarding the ship. The line moved quickly, and soon my ticket was marked and I was directed to follow others up the long narrow ramp.

Stepping onto the ship, a young man in a different uniform asked for my ticket and said he would escort me to my cabin. "I am Maurice, Mademoiselle Durant, your valet for this voyage," he told me.

As we moved into the interior of the ship, I was immediately taken in by the beauty of the ship's design and decor. Each time we turned a corner or entered a new area en route to my room, I nearly gasped. When we came to the grand staircase, I had to stand and just gaze at the design and patterns of the floors and the pillared arches rising high on each side of the wide stairs. Eleven steps up took us to the landing where a large circle of patterned carpet was centered in front of a purple velvet divan. The divan itself was set into a soaring niche with tall inlaid lights on either side as the stairs branched up to the left and right. Vibrant colored tiles and glass in intricate geometric patterns were everywhere, and high above the landing the expansive domed glass ceiling allowed the sun's rays to illuminate this magnificent interior. It was like nothing I had seen before. As my escort motioned me up the staircase, I had to stop again at the top and turn to take in the grandeur of the light and colors and interesting use of textures and patterns.

Solange had mentioned in a letter that my first class stateroom was to be one decorated in the new Art Deco school of design. Upon reading that, I had no idea what to expect. As Maurice opened my cabin door, I realized my stateroom's decor reflected the style of the grand staircase: sleek and modern, with a simplicity that drew the eye to the asymmetrical use of tile, glass, metal, and wood. I immediately identified with the spirit inherent in the design and materials used to create these spaces. I also realized that what Henri had created in his home reflected a similar style.

My cabin was larger than I expected, with square rather than round portholes looking directly out to the sea. I found again the recurring use of geometric motifs in the cabin's furnishings and fixtures and the now familiar colors and fabrics used throughout the ship.

Though my bed was narrow, it was certainly ample enough, even for a person of my height. The headboard was placed against the wall to the left as you entered the room, and directly across, the unique square portholes framed a brilliant blue sky. In addition to the bed and small side table, angled off the wall to the right of the door sat a small, low-backed plush chair upholstered in a tapestried fabric of turquoise and mushroom brown. In front of the chair stood a small ottoman covered in a complementary brown fabric. Another small table of metal and wood, almost identical to the one beside my bed, was placed next to the chair, and on this sat a small lamp with a chrome base. The shade was comprised of little pieces of tile in random shapes and colors, reminding me of a stained glass window in a chapel. Behind the chair, against the wall, stood a tall mirrored armoire. A compact bathroom completed the space, and all felt very much like a cozy, comfortable home at sea. I looked forward to exploring this vast ship but knew I would enjoy most my time spent here in this lovely space.

"My room is conveniently located close to yours, should you need assistance in any way," Maurice said. "Should you have questions or need help, you may contact me directly using the telephone," he added, pointing to the black telephone on the small bedside table. My experience with using a telephone was limited to this morning's in Paris. I had, however, no intentions of bothering Maurice with any requests. "And may I now assist you with unpacking your belongings?"

"Merci, Maurice, but that will not be necessary. I am looking forward to a relatively quiet voyage, and I doubt you will hear much from me." I extended to him a large gratuity.

"*Merci beaucoup*, Mademoiselle Durant. I will be checking in with you from time to time to assure you have everything you need to make your journey a pleasant one."

We said our adieus, and I closed the door as Maurice departed with measured haste, I assumed to assist other passengers.

I walked to the square window framed in bronze metal marked with deep lines in a crosshatch pattern. Turning the latch on this porthole and opening it wide, the scent of salty air, smoke from the ship's stacks, and the cawing of seagulls as they flew close over the vessel filled my room and my senses. We would not depart for another hour, so I had time to unpack and take a short rest before we set sail. Before stretching out across my bed, I did hang up one of the lovely dresses; the one I would wear tonight at dinner.

The bed was firm and the coverings luxurious and plump, lulling me into sleep. I was jarred awake sometime later to an unfamiliar sound. It took a few moments to realize it was the ringing of the telephone. I stretched to reach the side table, picked up the receiver, and placed it to my ear. It was Maurice, reminding me I had a first call to dinner in one hour and did I need him to escort me to the dining room. I declined but did ask where the dining room was located. He said there were several but the *salle à manger* in which I was to have evening meals was located on the same third level as my cabin. He gave me more specifics, and then in closing said, "Do you need your formal wear pressed or freshened before you dress for dinner?"

"I think not. However, should that change, I shall let you know," I replied.

Having fallen asleep, I had missed our grand departure but felt no pangs of regret. I might have had second thoughts as we pulled away from the familiar and set sail for what to me was the unknown.

Feeling a bout of nerves knowing I must present myself for dinner in an hour, I briefly wondered if dinner in my room was an option. But no, I promised myself I would experience all I could on this trip Papa had paid for at what, I assumed, was an exorbitant price. And the clothes were so beautiful and enticing. I couldn't wait to put them on and, I hoped, blend suitably into the crowd.

I had chosen the dove-gray drop-waist silk to wear that first evening. I did my hair in a chignon, securing it with the lovely pins and one mother-of-pearl comb. Cream silk stockings and the soft leather pale beige shoes complimented the hues of the dress. Picking up the shawl woven of silver thread, I turned to leave the room and caught my reflection in the full-length mirror of the armoire door. I looked quite nice. I realized, though, that my face was pale and my hair looked not quite right for the beautiful clothes flowing so gracefully over my slender frame. When I had thumbed through the fashion magazines, I saw women wearing their hair not in chignons but in a style they referred to as "bobbed," which was short, about chin length, and I did like the simplicity of it.

With that thought, I left the cabin and proceeded to the dining room. Were my hands shaking because I was terribly hungry or because I was terribly concerned that I was going to be with strangers and knew not how this body and mind would respond? I could hear Papa telling me as he always did to "have courage." I knew by now that every act of courage required an equal act of faith.

The first class dining room was almost as impressive as the grand staircase. The ceiling was three stories high, with a second level of seating around the perimeter that overlooked the main floor full of rectangular tables. Everywhere one turned there were stewards directing passengers to tables accommodating groups of four or six. I was escorted to a table for six near the center of the long narrow room. The farther we went into the close, crowded dining room, the more my anxiety increased. Finally arriving at my table, the steward pulled out my chair, into which I thankfully sat, and with one swift motion he picked up the starched linen napkin from atop the table and laid it across my lap. Looking up at him and then beyond, I was very relieved to find that my chair faced the entrance of the room, allowing me a clear path out should I need one.

"Enjoy your meal, mademoiselle."

"Merci," I mumbled before he quickly departed to seat others.

I slowly scanned the room, taking in the beautiful decor and multitude of tables full of well-dressed diners, before I found the courage to greet the others at my own table. When I did look at their faces, they were all engaged in speaking with the person beside them or to others across the table. The noise was becoming a loud cacophony of conversation, making it convenient to just smile and nod at those with whom I made eye contact without having to say a word. I reminded myself that the volume of excited voices was to be expected and nothing that I should find alarming. As soon as the last of the diners was seated and the steward delivered our first course, voices had settled down to a modicum of low rumbling, allowing the passengers at each table to converse with one another comfortably.

As *l'aperitif* arrived, a fragrant deep red liquor, my tablemates introduced themselves, and I did in turn. We sipped our drinks quietly until the next course was served, *l'entrée* of salmon mousse with capers, and people began side conversations with one another. The discussions at my table all seemed to be taking place in English. Although I found my written English to be quite passable, my spoken English was more of a challenge. I hastily attempted to recall appropriate phrases to greet my fellow diners. But I could, of course, use my lack of conversational English to continue to merely listen and nod, which I did after explaining that my English was inadequate to keep up with the conversation and for them not to mind if I did not join in. This suited me quite well and allowed me to concentrate on course after course of beautifully presented food as well as maintain a calm demeanor.

The composition of each delectable dish was exquisite, and *le plat principal* that arrived next was no exception: tender tips of beef with a dark, rich mushroom gravy, asparagus perfectly *al dente* with a light lemon sauce, and a small browned mound of puffed potatoes au gratin. And, of course, the wines that flowed glass to glass were excellent, paired perfectly to each course. I feared I might, at some point, need to place my hand over my glass. I was beginning to feel slightly woozy and did not think the ship's motion was in any way responsible for the slight swaying of my body, my extreme satiation, and the sense that all was very well with my world.

Many of the rich dishes reminded me of foods from my childhood. Our cook, Elise, would prepare such lavish meals, serving them to Papa's many business partners at monthly dinner parties planned and orchestrated with great finesse by Solange. But now, living very simply at home in Meuse, my menu was severely limited by my own disinterest in cooking and consisted mainly of bread, cheese, eggs, oats, and seasonal vegetables and fruit. I occasionally enjoyed fresh fish from the river and meat prepared in the simplest way possible. My tongue exploded with pleasure at the flavors of these succulent courses. Would we be eating such quality and in such quantity every day of the voyage? I certainly hoped so and was happy to remind myself that the clothes Solange sent would certainly allow for a few pounds to be added to my waistline.

To my left was, I discerned from their conversation with the others at our table, a young couple newly married and on their way home from their honeymoon in Paris. The bride sat directly to my left and turned my way, asking in perfect French if was I enjoying the food.

"Oui. It has been quite some time since I have eaten food this delicious and so beautifully prepared," I replied in French.

"I take it from your lovely speech that you are from France and perhaps going to visit the Americas?" she asked.

"Oui. My home is close to Verdun, in northeastern France. I am going to New York City for a visit with my papa and sister. Though my understanding of English is somewhat limited, am I to understand that you are returning from your honeymoon? Where in the United States do you live?" I asked, very appreciative that we were conversing in my language.

"We will be traveling to Boston, by train, once we get to New York. My husband is to be a lawyer there. We combined the trip to Paris to celebrate both his passing his legal exams and our marriage. He will set up practice with his father. My family are all in the Boston area as well." She paused, her face becoming thoughtful. "Do you miss your family, living so far from them?"

"Yes. I miss them every day, but every day I am thankful that I continue to live in France," I said, hoping no more questions would be forthcoming as I watched the steward place two long boards on the table. *Le fromage* consisted of a great array of different cheeses, nuts, slices of pear, and, of course, baguettes. How could I possibly manage to eat another bite? Perhaps just two slices of pear with some of that lovely soft Camembert. Another wine appeared in yet another glass and, of course, it had to be sampled with the cheese and fruit.

As we nibbled and tasted, the woman asked my name and I asked for hers as well.

"We are Mr. and Mrs. Paul Levinson. My name is Kathryn, but I much prefer being called Katy. Now that I'm a married woman I hope I can continue being Katy and not stuffy Kathryn. Katy has much more fun!"

"I shall definitely call you Katy, however, I am sure others enjoy your company regardless of your name."

I realized I wasn't making too much sense when both Katy and I gave in to a bout of giggles as she raised her glass to mine and said, "Long live Katy and Marie!"

Katy's husband inquired as to the source of our mirth, and I left it to her to try and explain. I once again looked round the table and beyond to include the other diners in the large, opulent room. I was intrigued by the elements of Art Deco present in the light fixtures above our heads, the interesting shape of the metal dividers of the dining sections, the asymmetrical tiles adorning the floor, and the unique design of our chairs.

After two enjoyable hours, our bountiful repast was coming to an end. *Le dessert* accompanied by *café* was presented with some fanfare and laid elegantly before each diner. I was barely able to consume two bites of the chocolate profiterole, which I downed with half a cup of coffee, before taking my leave. I sorely needed the ladies room, followed by a stroll about the ship.

As I turned to Katy to bid her *bonne soirée*, she linked her arm through mine and invited me to tea the next day, to which I agreed without hesitation. I believe the large amount of wine I consumed was the cause of my easy acquiescence. Tea tomorrow with Katy it would be.

After finding my way to the ladies room, I inquired of a steward where on the ship might be most conducive to a stroll. He suggested the promenade deck on this, the first-class level, where I could then easily make my way back to my cabin. I wondered if he realized I was rather unsteady on my feet. I thanked him, holding on to the wall to maintain my balance, and proceeded to the doors leading outside.

I knew most of those at dinner would linger on for perhaps some time, and then the men would have their cigars in one of the smoking salons, talking politics and business, while the women were most likely to adjourn to their cabins. As I had hoped, there were only a few passengers on the deck.

The evening air was the tonic I needed to complete such a perfect first day at sea. Breathing deeply and setting off at a leisurely pace, I explored all round the deck. There were lifeboats on each side, secured by heavy ropes with pulleys, and stacks of uncomfortable-looking lifejackets. I overheard at dinner that we were to have a drill some time tomorrow morning, where the staff would take us through the motions to prepare for an emergency evacuation.

More people were coming out onto the deck now, many couples strolling arm in arm looking as content as I felt. I had entered another world on this ship, much of it reminiscent of our idyllic world in Marseille. It actually felt familiar and beautiful. The ship was magnificent down to the fine details, and the passengers inhabited her as though they lived here on the sea. I had to acknowledge that some years had passed since the devastation of the war, and it was obvious people had moved on with their lives. Their lives looked bright and shiny like newly minted coins. But these were the passengers of first class. There were many, I knew, in the third-class berths that were traveling to America as immigrants hoping to start again, and they were not housed in such fine accommodations as the *Paris* offered its first- and even second-class passengers.

I felt I lived a foot in two worlds: lavish opulence onboard this ship and my simple, somewhat austere life back in Meuse. Austerity that was self-imposed. It had been necessary for some time to create a cocoon about myself. I had needed solitude and isolation to heal from my weakened state of body and soul. Perhaps I was ready now to find a balance between those two worlds. I in no way desired luxury, but a modicum of comfort beyond the austerity in which I currently lived might be appropriate. I was eager to plant my feet upon a reality of my choosing, walking in a forward direction toward what was possible. All things seemed possible here on this luxuriant ship far from all reality. And what came to mind when I pictured my future was that pristine clinic waiting at home. I would make it all it needed to be to treat and heal others. With that hope, I headed back to my cabin and to bed, to sleep the dreamless sleep of one with no other care for these few short days than to decide what I might to wear to tea tomorrow with my new friend Katy.

CHAPTER 10

BESEECHING –
APRIL 1923

Hope beyond hope at her words imploring me toward eager self-disclosure. Her wanting to know about my life that morning at the river struck the spark of optimism that caused me to think the fates were conspiring in my favor. That my proposals might be more than just my dreams alone falling on deaf ears.

As you left on your voyage to America, without a final goodbye and having Bernard take you to the station, I felt bereft. I knew that my proposals were at once enticing as well as frightening. Was that not my intention? To make one so irresistible that the second would seem plausible as well, possibly even desirable?

And I certainly saw desire in your eyes as you took in the possibilities of the clinic room, an empty space of possibility in which to build your dream. I could not hold your eyes after making the second proposal, for I saw there not desire but astonishment and confusion. I acquiesced, and unable to take your heart hostage, I bestowed on you the clinic, taking in exchange your future consideration of marriage. The importance of our friendship would always take precedence over my desire to make you my own wife.

Still, I heard my voice beseeching you, and I was ashamed of my desperation. I heard the hard turn of my words as I became petulant and demanding and knew I had to immediately take my leave of you, escaping my confusion and inner torment as I walked through the door into my home, separating us from the angst we both felt. You for wanting only the clinic and me for only wanting you.

As much as I know it is better to have a faithful friend than a bitter spouse, my heart continues to ache. I am dreadfully sorry that we parted without a true goodbye. I know that was your intention, to leave things as we stated and when you returned we would begin our arrangement: you in the clinic and me biding my time for six months until your decision.

And for my part, I am making decisions for Félix and myself. I have made plans to buy a storefront in Verdun and run my business almost entirely from there, allowing me to be with Félix each evening as we share this home and become a family. I can wait for you, Marie, but will not sit idle, for I too must move from these times to the next.

CHAPTER 11

TEA IN THE SALON – APRIL 1923

"Marie? Is that you?" asked the caller on the other end of the ringing telephone I just answered.

"Yes, this is Marie Durant. And who is calling?"

"It's me, silly, Katy Levinson. Your friend from dinner last evening."

"What time is it? I must have slept late," I said, stifling a yawn.

"Well, actually, it is quite early. Not much past seven," Katy said in a rather sheepish tone.

Why she would be calling at seven in the morning? "Is anything wrong?" I asked.

"No, all is well, and I do apologize for ringing you at this early hour, but Paul is making a list of all the events he wants us to take part in today, and I wanted to be sure you and I settled on a tea time and it made it onto his list. I was thinking of early tea, perhaps about two o'clock? Paul can fill in his list from two to four with a manly activity. What do you say? Two o'clock in the small tea room?"

"Yes, that sounds lovely, Katy. I'm very much looking forward to visiting with you. I'll see you at two." I replaced the receiver and dove back down under the warm bedding, puzzled to think marriage might include lists of things to be done together and lists of things to be done separately. I had never been one for making lists for anyone but myself, and I wondered if it suited Katy to have her new husband making such for them both.

Feeling well rested after another hour's sleep and my growling stomach demanding breakfast, I regretfully removed myself from the comfortable bed, promising that tomorrow morning I would sleep as late as suited me. Looking out the portholes, the morning sky looked as vast as the sea before us. And that was all there was to see—endless blue sky seamlessly joining the gently rolling dark water at the horizon. Realizing again I was on a huge vessel truly in the middle of the ocean with no discernable land about continued to be rather disconcerting. I needed to get out and walk on the deck to get my bearings before breakfast.

The morning passed quickly, having taken a long turn round several of the other decks in the brisk morning air. I ate more than a substantial breakfast and then sent notes off to the Sisters, Henri, and Félix. Knowing I could not wear to tea the well-fitting trousers I had for my morning stroll, I changed into a skirt and stockings. The blouses Solange sent were so versatile I could wear them with all the skirts and trousers. I tidied my hair, applied a bit of lip color, and off I went to tea.

Katy was seated at a small round table in the elegantly appointed tearoom. Here in this traditionally decorated room there were no elements of Art Deco. The dark wood paneling on the walls, the finely woven Indian rugs upon the floor, and the crystal chandeliers sparkling even at two in the afternoon were all reminiscent both in the colors and style of the lovely home in which I grew up and immediately transported me to a place of serenity.

"I hope you don't mind, Marie, but I ordered a selection of small sandwiches and sweet cakes to fortify us as we chat and drink our tea. Seems I am always hungry these days. My mother tells me that after so much worry and effort spent on the wedding that now I will calm and put back a few of the pounds I lost to ensure I fit into my wedding gown. So eat I shall. How about you? Are you hungry too?" she asked, breathlessly speaking fluent French with her American accent.

"I am never one to turn down food, and what we have been served thus far surpasses anything thing I have eaten in years. We have every reason to assume our tea fare will be just as tasty," I said, adjusting my chair closer to the table.

In short order, two stewards appeared rolling a gleaming silver teacart up next to our table. This cart had two tiers, and both were laden with more food than I think Katy and I could have consumed in two days' time. The teapot, saucers and cups, sugar, creamer, and silverware were placed before us, and my mouth began to water taking in the array so artfully arranged upon the serving platters. Since there was not room on our small table for all the plates and trays of delights, the servers set just two trays of *petit* sandwiches before us and rearranged the remainder of the savories and sweets on the top tier of the cart, leaving it beside our table where we might help ourselves.

Looking at Katy, I could not help but ask, "Did you know you ordered enough food for six people?"

She gave a small laugh. "He asked if we wanted 'the full complement,' and I said 'yes.' Who knew? Isn't this wonderful? Shall I pour?" she asked, smiling as a Cheshire cat.

"Yes, please do, and then I am going to sample one of everything. We can take some comfort as we have a late call for dinner this evening. And we can always walk before then." And with that, we nibbled and tasted for the next ten minutes, "oohs" and "ahhs" our only verbal communication, Katy peppering the sounds of delighted eating with occasional laughter.

This young woman was so carefree and light of heart, so joyous and unrestrained in her *joie de vivre* that I found myself lulled and captivated by her example. How freeing it was for me to be completely anonymous among so many hundreds and hundreds of people, and how fortunate I felt that the one person I did engage with was persuading my spirit to rejoice. Katy and I resumed our conversation much as we had last night, eating and drinking our way toward friendship.

Two hours passed quickly. We talked about our families, our hopes and dreams for the future. How different we were but both of us so sure of what we wanted. She was quite decided that after she had set up her home, which I came to understand was a wedding gift from her parents, she planned on assisting her husband at his office several hours a week in addition to focusing on her own interests.

"Mother insists I must join her dreary clubs and participate in mundane volunteer works, but I tell you, those women seem to only be interested in competing with each other over the silliest of matters. Who will be next year's president? Who will be chairwoman of the Winter Gala? All rather foolish and their pretentiousness shrouded under the guise of 'good works.' I have already made it clear to both my mother and my mother-in-law that I am going to do as I please and please who I want, and it is not going to be hordes of stuffy women. I will help my husband at his office, papers and filing and such, but the remainder of my time I will devote to women's rights."

"But women in the United States gained the right to vote in 1920. What an accomplishment, Katy."

"Yes, we have won the vote, but that does not mean we have equality. And after all the fighting and suffering in the war and all that women as well as men sacrificed," she said through a full bite of pastry, "to think women in France still do not have the right to vote. It's an outrage! I certainly hope you are doing your part in the suffragette movement in your own country." Her voice was getting louder, her face turning rather red as enthusiasm for her subject grew.

I was not yet ready to divulge all my plans, since there was still much to be worked out. It also seemed bad luck to discuss my dreams only to have them fall to pieces. No letter had arrived before my departure, and I was quite anxious to hear from the hospital. If their answer to my request for additional training and observation was accepted and I passed the diploma exams, then my plans for the clinic were much more likely to become a reality. Avoiding Katy's pointed questions about my future, I continued commenting about hers.

"Although I have no idea what is involved in your wifely duties to your husband, I would hope he supports you in your desire to be useful and fulfilled in your own right," I said in a low voice, hoping she might also lower hers.

"I love Paul and he loves me. We have known each other since we were very young. He is only a few years older than myself and would tease me mercilessly when we were children. Which he still does whenever the opportunity arises, but now I pay him no mind. Our families have been friends for ages, and we all get along quite well. Paul knows how I feel. I made it quite clear before our engagement that I was to truly be a helpmate and not a servant, that I was my own person, and just as he had the law as his occupation, I would have my own interests in seeing justice served." She was attempting to keep her voice at a level that only myself and a few tables close by might hear.

"And children, do you and your husband want children?" I asked quietly.

"Of course! Who would not want children? But we are still young enough to wait perhaps a few years, till we become accustomed to married life and living together in the same house as well as establishing our own interests and deciding where we might want to participate within the community, both as a couple and as individuals. Those will be our priorities and that will all take some time." She said this all in a single breath and with such keen intensity that I knew Paul would find his new wife making her own lists of what she wanted to do and accomplish. I estimated Katy's age to be not much past twenty. Although I was six years older, I felt we were kindred in our spirits.

It was after four when we said our goodbyes and that we would see each other at dinner. Regardless, we also decided to meet for tea again tomorrow but would order only two pots of tea, speak only in English as a help to me, and hopefully explore more of the ship. Katy shared my interest in the art so prominent on the vessel. I told her I would ask my valet if he could arrange a tour particular to the art throughout the ship and, if so, I would let her know.

Leaving Katy, I took a circuitous route back to my room by walking the deck one level above. There I found people playing shuffleboard and having bicycle races. Those watching the events were chatting as they ate what smelled like fresh popped corn from small paper bags stained with the evidence of melted butter. The atmosphere was one of hearty congeniality, everyone acting as though we had all been friends for years. I smiled and nodded at greetings sent my way but continued my walk about the deck, making my own observations.

A few women were in stylish trousers similar to mine. I also noticed that only the older women, and by that I mean women ten years my senior or more, wore their hair as I did, pulled back in a chignon or pinned up on top of their heads. Many of the younger women, whom I still counted myself among, had hairstyles similar to the ones so prominently featured in the fashion magazines. I watched the women play shuffleboard, noting their hair was cut primarily of one length all around the circumference of the head, the "bob" hairstyle. Some wore colorful bands round their heads, which settled in the front on the middle of their foreheads. The style was simple and must be easy to care for. It was very appealing, and I made a mental note to ask Katy about it tomorrow. She wore her own auburn brown hair in much the same style. I suddenly wanted to retire to my room, pick up my small scissors, and begin cutting many inches off my long and rather dreary hair. Perhaps they had a salon aboard.

How free I felt! How unencumbered by worry or fear that I would be besieged by frightful memories. Here on this luxurious ship, surrounded by art and beauty, my soul felt refreshed to be among people who seemed happy and joyous. People who were animated and excited about living. I wanted to experience those emotions as well. I didn't need or want to carry anymore the weight of guilt and sorrow that had burdened me for so long. The war was over. I did the best nursing that I knew to do. Those that were lost, millions upon millions of sacrificed men, I needed to remember with appreciation without sacrificing the rest of my life feeling shame that I survived and they did not. My guilt did not honor their sacrifice. There surely was no greater legacy to leave in their remembrance than to live a life as courageously as they had given theirs.

CHAPTER 12

PLANNING – APRIL 1923

R ather than call Maurice from my cabin's phone, I went in search of his room. He had told me it was close to my own, and I soon came upon a door bearing a placard with the word *Valet*. I assumed this room to be his and also assumed he would be elsewhere. By coming to his cabin I indulged another motive besides asking for information. I was curious as to how it might be furnished. Did the "help" in the first-class section also have elegantly appointed rooms or only the passengers they served? To my surprise, Maurice answered my knock so quickly one would think he was standing ready to open the door immediately and answer any request one might have.

"Bonjour, Maurice. I hope this new day finds you well."

"Oui, Mademoiselle Durant. And a good afternoon to you. How might I be of service?"

"Mrs. Katherine Levinson and I are hoping to take a tour of the ship and are wondering if there is staff on board that does such tours and could talk with us regarding the interior design elements along with the objets d'art throughout the ship." I stated this while attempting to nonchalantly peer past him to see something of his room.

"Of course, Mademoiselle. There are two ways to accomplish this. The stewards are very familiar with all aspects of the ship; therefore, I would be happy to escort you and Mrs. Levinson on a tour. Or, for the convenience of our guests, we have a very detailed pamphlet including photographs of all the works of art on the *Paris*. Should you choose the first option with myself as your guide, I can schedule one hour, and although we would most likely not be able to see all that might be of interest, you could go back through later on your own. Choosing the self-guided option, you could stroll the entire ship viewing all the art, using the pamphlet's map and detailed descriptions, at your leisure. And, of course, you may ask me any questions afterward."

It was obvious that he routinely recited this long informative speech many times throughout each crossing. "Merci, Maurice. I believe Mrs. Levinson and I would find it very enjoyable to tour the ship on our own. Would you have two of the guides in your room that I might have at this time?" I was still hoping for a better glimpse into his cabin.

"I certainly do," he said. I sensed his relief that I had made the second choice. "If you will remain here, I shall get those for you." As he turned back into his cabin, I reached my arm forward to ensure the door would remain open and his room visible.

I was somewhat aghast at what I saw. His cabin was in such disarray that I could hardly believe it belonged to this impeccably dressed and highly articulate young man! Clothes and articles of personal toiletry were strewn about almost every surface. There were books in stacks and papers of all sorts covering much of the floor and disheveled clothes discarded across most of the furniture. Obviously they did not have the luxury of having their rooms cleaned and tidied each day. It caused me to smile, seeing the contrast between how Maurice must constantly portray himself as able valet versus how he lived when alone in his cabin. Surely it was the single space onboard that he was free to discard his public role and just be his young self.

He reappeared shortly with the guides, and I was on my way. Returning to my cabin, I telephoned Katy's room. She answered, and we agreed to meet at eleven the next morning and conduct one another on our tour.

I had also meant to ask Maurice if there was a salon onboard, but in my eagerness to peer into his cabin I had forgotten. It could wait till morning. I yawned through this thought and then slipped off my shoes, laid across my bed to rest, and immediately fell asleep.

Two hours later, I awoke not knowing for a few seconds where I was. Once I remembered I was shipboard, I lay surveying the lovely living space that was mine for four more days. Knowing that once I arrived in New York I would be surrounded by the frantic activity of disembarking, collecting my belongings, and finding Solange and Papa, I reminded myself to not feel any twinges of guilt at taking time to rest, here upon the expansive sea between leaving my comfortable home and sailing toward the completely unfamiliar. The anonymity of traveling with virtual strangers I was very much enjoying. There were no expectations on my part. I was free to do as I pleased, keeping my own counsel during this short interval out of time.

I had not an idea as to what awaited me once I was in my sister's world, although I knew she would want to show me all of the city in her adopted state and country. From her letters, I understood she had made a number of friends and that she and Papa entertained frequently. They had always loved the hosting of dinner parties, and I was happy for them that they had made friends for whom they could continue such events. I would be taking part in as much of their life as they could fit into my two-week visit. But I was both looking forward to and somewhat dreading the time, my greatest fear being they would spend our precious days together coaxing me to come live with them.

Aside from my apprehensions, I did hope there would be opportunities for just the three of us to visit and regain our common ground. I also planned to find time to sit and talk alone with Papa, telling him of my plans for the clinic and all that had transpired between Henri and myself. Of course, I would share all of this with Solange as well, but time alone with Papa assured I would have his sole attention and that his words were for me alone. I missed our talks and his wise counsel, and it had been many years since I had been able to sit in his presence and bask in the aura of his fatherly love. And I wanted him to give me a full report regarding his health. Solange would understand, as she always did, that I needed time alone with each of them as well as time spent with the three of us, when our conversations tended to be lighter.

Four more days by myself at sea. No chores, no patients, no animals to tend to; it was a luxury I hadn't anticipated. And thus I bathed at my leisure and finished my *toilette* with great care. I then put on the sage-green gown of *crêpe de Chine*. Looking in the mirror, I again admired the liquid flow of the luxurious material along my trim form. The heeled shoes added to my already tall stature and seemed to elongate the lines of the beautiful gown even more. The matching cape I would not wear to dinner but carry over my arm and wear later as I took another evening's walk about the decks.

What I did not look at in the mirror this evening was my hair and face. Both did not seem to do justice to the lovely clothes I wore each day. I would make a point of seeking out Katy this evening at dinner to ask her opinion. The more I had time to think about such things, the more I felt I needed an update. I smiled, thinking this would certainly be a wise thing to do, as I did not want Solange to think I did not know how to appear as the cultured young woman I was brought up to be. It was very true that I did prefer my much simpler life in Meuse and not having to worry about such mundane things. However, if I was to resume my role as a professional nurse, it would certainly be necessary that I present to all the look of one who knew what she was about—a competent and confident nurse and independent woman. Perhaps a visit to the salon that I hoped was aboard ship would at least be the beginning of truly embracing all that I wanted to become.

Dinner was another extravagant event, offering numerous courses of exquisite food and wines. Katy and I made eye contact from across our several tables of separation, and by way of simple hand gestures, she let me know that she wanted to take a walk after dinner. I gestured back that they were to take their time and I would leave when they did.

The fellow diners at my table that evening were all French, and there was lively conversation sharing why we were traveling to the United States. One couple, most likely in their mid-twenties, were immigrating to America with plans to travel as far west as possible to find fertile farmland on which to build their homestead. They stated firmly their belief that Europe would be embroiled in another war before the end of the century, and they did not want to raise a family in the midst of such conflict. The husband said he had lost his father and two older brothers in the war, and he was not willing to sacrifice his own life, being the only living person to carry on his family's name. Several at our table raised their glasses in a salute to his wisdom. There were, however, older gentlemen at our table telling the young husband his leaving France was almost traitorous; they were absolutely sure there would not be another war.

"Not perhaps in your lifetime but certainly in my own and perhaps in that of my unborn son." With this he draped his arm around his quiet wife, who blushed and placed her hands on her abdomen.

"Here, here!" hailed all the men, raising their glasses once more.

Once again, I saw personified evidence that people were moving on, and some, such as this young couple, were moving to an entirely different country in order to build their future. But I could never consider leaving my beloved homeland. If there were to be another war in my own lifetime then I would be ready once again to serve as I had done before—as bravely and as capably as possible. And if I were an old woman and could not nurse, then I would sit by my river Meuse and pray for all the nurses and the wounded they were tending. But leave my native France? Never!

Out of the corner of my eye, I saw Katy and Paul begin to take leave of their table. I too said my goodbyes and gathered myself and my cape and made for the foyer. There I found Katy maneuvering her arms into what appeared to be a rather complicated affair with a large loose coat. As Paul helped her into the garment, we again exchanged laughter. What was it about the two of us that whatever we were doing was cause for joviality? I was not going to question it. I wanted to shed the intense conversation at the table, which would probably be taken up again by the men along with cognac and cigars. We both bid Paul adieu, and off he went to join a cadre of men and off we went for our walk.

I told Katy of my visit to Maurice's door, and when I described the state in which I found his room, she came to a sudden standstill, the couple behind us almost colliding into us.

"Really? Just a shambles? How delicious is that! Poor boy, his mother would be so ashamed of him!"

And again our laughter welled through us. I do not think I have had as many occasions to laugh in the last six years as I had since meeting Katy.

"I do not feel the least bit sorry for him," I said. "It was obvious he was quite content with the state of his surroundings. And why not? As a valet, he must be stifled in the confines of such formality all the day and night and must find it a great relief to retire to his own place, take off those trappings, and be his own person."

Katy draped her arm through mine. "And that is how I feel at the end of the day as well. In my own home I plan to dress in a very relaxed manner, perhaps even wearing your beloved trousers and only dressing more formally when going out. And how about you, Marie? What trappings do you bear in your daily life?"

"I actually live the life of what would most likely be considered a farmer, and a very cloistered one at that. I wear baggy men's trousers by day as I tend my animals, my lavender fields, and beehives. I only dress myself a little better when I visit my friends or tend patients. But perhaps I am ready to reclaim my role as an actual living breathing woman who cares about herself as much as she cares for the lives of others.

"I have plans, Katy, to open a clinic when I return to Meuse. A friend is renting me a good-sized clinic space just south of Verdun, and I am expecting that it will be quite busy. Especially if I can obtain my Certificate of Nursing diploma and hang my shingle saying so. My greatest challenge is finding a physician to be my supporter—my supervisor, so to speak. A nurse can only treat superficially and administer a few mild medications without the underwriting of a physician to review her work and sign off on documentation as well as scrips for medicines that might be needed."

Katy stopped again mid-stride. "And here I thought you had no ambitions. Now you have laid out quite an elaborate plan for when you return home. And where will you attempt to gain your diploma and find this physician you need?"

I was as surprised as Katy that my intentions should come spilling forth. In all the hours of dreaming and planning, this was the first that I had verbalized things so succinctly to anyone. Yes, Henri knew of my hopes to work in the clinic, but neither he nor the Sisters knew that I desperately wanted to hear from the hospital, telling me that they would welcome me once again. I wanted to return to Meuse as a nurse of the highest order.

"I wrote to the hospital in Paris where I did my original training and where I nursed for three years till the end of the war. I sent this letter of request to hospital administration in late February and gave them my timetable, asking that they either respond to me before I left France or later at my father's address in New York. Since I did not hear from them before I left, I admit I am worried that they have denied my request. If so, then I must rethink my plans. But I have great hope that their answer will be yes. I worked very closely with many of the physicians and nurses who are still at the hospital, colleagues who know me well and, I believe, would be pleased with my intentions to continue nursing."

"Then we will think good thoughts and assume that there will be a letter waiting for you when you arrive in New York. You and I must exchange addresses and keep in touch. You be my champion and I will be yours. I promise I will share all my trials and tribulations as well as triumphs and joys of marriage, should you one day embark on that particular adventure," she said with her wily smile. "And, of course, keep you abreast regarding my pursuits in the name of feminine equality."

It was becoming quite late, and Katy needed to return to Paul. We parted, promising to meet at the grand staircase the next morning at ten to take up our tour. I strolled a little longer, realizing I had not articulated my worry about not hearing from the hospital until the conversation with Katy. And I was not going to let doubt consume me now. I had overcome much in these last few years and discovered that humans, myself included, are incredibly tenacious. If they were to tell me no, then I would go to Paris anyway and present my request in person. One did not live through the blood and death of war, the complete defeat of the spirit and loss of self only to climb back into the light of hope to be told no. There was no way that was going to happen.

CHAPTER 13

SHIPBOARD TOURS – APRIL 1923

After having had tea and a croissant in my room, I arrived at the bottom of the grand staircase promptly at ten, eager to begin our self-guided tour. Katy appeared ten minutes later, slightly out of breath, with an apology explaining she'd had difficulty breaking away from breakfast with Paul.

"And in my haste I left without my brochure. Drat! May we share, Marie?"

"Of course. Take a few moments to catch your breath while I read to you. 'Passengers will notice at once that aspects of the interior spaces, including some first-class cabins, the first-class dining room, and this grand staircase before you, reflect a new style of design referred to as "the style moderne" or "Art Deco." The craftsmen and artists, together with the architects and builders of the ship, have used materials not usually seen in a ship's decor. Here you will see the use of metals, such as stainless steel, glass, and aluminum, as well as colored tiles and chrome to create spatial art that is highly functional yet represents a new age of post-war industrialization.'"

The pamphlet's directions, with accompanying pictures, led us through the first-class dining room, and I again read aloud from the guide. "You will notice the geometric configurations within the works of glass in the lights of the dining room and terra cotta tile inlays upon the floor, in addition to the more free-form design of the tables and chairs."

Coming upon the last viewing listed, we found a group of people gathering close by, all of them men. At first I thought that perhaps this was one of the valet-led tours to view the modern art, but I was puzzled that there were no women among them. Katy was also curious. We moved close to the group as a uniformed, middle-aged man was introducing himself as Second Officer Moreau. He would lead "a riveting tour of the vessel's mighty inner workings." Katy and I exchanged a look that confirmed we were both interested in seeing the "mighty inner workings," and thus we joined the tour.

"Excuse me, mesdemoiselles," the second officer said, looking at us, "but I do not think this is the tour that interests you, for we are going down into the belly of this ship. To the engine rooms."

"Yes, this is exactly the tour we were wanting to join. We are eager to look at the engines that power this ship," Katy said with her ever-present smile and affable way of getting, I thought, most anything she desired.

The gentlemen had now turned round to look at us as Second Officer Moreau said, "Well, if these fine gentlemen do not mind two ladies in what appear to be comfortable footwear accompanying us, I should count it a privilege."

After the second officer agreed to our inclusion, there was not too much the fine gentlemen could say, and other than a general grumbling of consent, the men turned back round as one, and we all proceeded forward and through a door to stairs that I assumed would take us into "the belly of the ship."

The deeper we descended, the louder the noise grew and the hotter it became. At the bottom of the metal stairs the second officer turned to us and, in a voice barely loud enough for Katy and me to hear at the back of the group, gave us a brief history and overview of the vessel.

"The SS Paris was built by the Penhoet shipyard in Saint-Nazaire. She was laid down in 1913 and launched on September 12, 1916. Her maiden voyage was June 15, 1921. She weighs in at thirty-four thousand five hundred seventy gross tons, is seven hundred sixty-four feet in length, with ten decks, a draft of sixty feet, and a cruising speed of twenty-one knots. At full capacity the ship can accommodate a total of two thousand five hundred passengers, including crew. There are accommodations for five hundred sixty in first class, five hundred thirty in second class, and eight hundred forty in third class." Turning round again, Second Officer Moreau led us forward.

We stepped into a room so hot I literally lost my breath. Katy looked as though she might faint away. The gentlemen barely blinked an eye, and they all wore over-jackets. They must have been at least as hot as we were, but they were not going to show it. At this point we were introduced to the chief engineer who was, we were given to understand, in charge of all we saw here below the decks. He was wearing a thin shirt with an *SS Paris* logo and did not seem in the least overheated as he began speaking with loud enthusiasm to this group of interested passengers.

"This is the real brains and brawn of the ship! She is powered by four Parsons turbines, producing forty-six thousand shaft horsepower that drives the four propellers. The electric plant, which is abaft of the engine room, holds three turbo generators of four hundred fifty kilowatts each with reserves. These generators are driven by oil engines," he said and led us farther on into the bowels of the massive undercarriage of the ship. I was beginning to feel claustrophobic and could not imagine working here amongst so much gigantic machinery producing ear-shattering noise. It was magnificently intimidating!

The chief engineer went on. "Adjacent to the engine rooms are the feedwater heaters, evaporators, filters, pumps, and other auxiliaries. Beyond that there is a separate room for the refrigerating machinery. We are in constant contact with the captain and officers up in the pilothouse and can make immediate course corrections if needed. They know they can depend on us down here to ensure things run smoothly up top, and we all stay on schedule."

My sense of claustrophobia was increasing, and I tugged on Katy's sleeve to motion I was going back up. She nodded in agreement, and as we turned, trying to unobtrusively take our leave of the group, the chief engineer shouted to us, "It was nice to see some ladies interested in what really makes this vessel operate. Good day, mesdemoiselles!" Only a few of the men turned in our direction, and none bid us adieu nor in any way acknowledged we had been part of the group. So much for a stealth-like departure.

"I will have to tell Boskey about going on the next tour down under. He would find it as fascinating as I did," Katy said, fanning herself with the pamphlet we shared.

"And who, might I ask, is Boskey?"

"That is Paul's name given to him in college by his fraternity brothers. I have no idea how he came to acquire such a rather obtuse name. Although I know there is a story behind it, he refuses to tell me. Most of the time, at least in the company of people we do not know well, I call him Paul. And I always call him Paul when I am irritated with him, which I am happy to say has not been often." I thought I saw a slight blush to her cheeks as she said this.

"Well, I shall be sure when in his presence to always refer to him as Paul. I do hope I am able to at least have a short conversation with him before our voyage ends. I too would think most anyone would find a tour of the engine rooms quite educational. It certainly gives one pause when we realize what is happening behind the scenes. Up top there is certainly the illusion that we are just moving forward with no great effort. I hope those men working below are provided with as much food and drink as they can consume." I was beginning to cool down, and my feelings of being closed in had abated. We agreed both of our tours of the day were equally interesting.

"I am rather parched and definitely hungry. Let's do go have tea and talk about our adventures this morning," Katy remarked, setting off at a quick pace toward the nearest tea salon.

Once settled with our tea and a "small complement" of food, I broached the subject of perhaps wanting to visit the ship's salon.

"Each time I dress and see these lovely clothes upon myself, I feel quite chic. My dear sister certainly chose well for me. However, if I then look upward into the mirror, I am quite distressed at what I observe of my head and face. My hair is severely out of style, and my skin looks dry and plain. I do notice how well put together the other women are, and certainly yourself, Katy. I thought perhaps if there is a salon onboard, you might consider accompanying me and providing some guidance concerning what I might do about updating myself."

Without a word, Katy put down her teacup, transformed her face into a very serious expression, and pulled her chair closer to the table in order to reach across and take my chin in her hand. She then moved my head from side to side and tilted it back and forth. I allowed her to do this, knowing she was examining me to see if I was at all a good candidate for a salon visit.

"You actually have good skin, Marie. It is somewhat surprising since you led me to believe you spend much time out of doors in all types of weather. Do you use any face creams at all?"

"Actually, I am part owner of an enterprise that utilizes the oil from the lavender grown in my fields to infuse lotions and medicinals. When my face is dry, chapped, or sunburned, I do apply a generous layer of the lotion. It is very soothing and leaves my skin feeling quite nice. I use it on all parts of my body, actually, and if I used it regularly, my skin might not be as dry." I could not quite believe I was discussing such subjects, as I had never talked with anyone other than Henri and the Sisters about my business ventures. But then again, I had never had the opportunity to do so, and it felt very natural to trust Katy and share aspects of my personal life with her.

"Your own skin creams? You continue to amaze me, Mademoiselle Durant! These lotions of yours are most likely what has kept your skin looking so well. As soon as you return to France you *must* send me some." At this she smiled and I assured her I would.

"And your hair, Marie, take it down and loosen it so I might see the length, texture, and color."

"Here? Right now?" I asked, glancing round the formal room. True, there were only a few others at a table some distance away but it seemed improper to take my hair down in the middle of tea.

"Yes! Right here, right now! If you don't take it down I'll come over there and do it myself," she retorted.

"Alright, alright." I removed my pins and combs, placed them on the table, and ran my fingers through my thick hair until it lay out across my shoulders.

"Your hair has some wave to it, which can be a good thing. And it is certainly quite thick, and I detect no hint of gray. I am certain some days I can spy a gray hair or two on my head," she said as she again reached across the table to take up a handful of my dark blonde hair.

"So, Katy, do they have a salon aboard or not, and if so, would you go with me to have my hair cut and styled? And perhaps just a small amount of makeup would be in order?"

"Of course they have a salon, and be assured it is a *très chic* bastion of beauty. Let's finish our cups and go right over and see if we can make you an appointment for tomorrow morning. My, I am having such fun on this trip! Spending my mornings with you and the rest of the day with Boskey!" And with that, we finished our tea and cakes and did indeed find the salon.

I should have known Katy had already surveyed this "bastion of beauty," as she called it. She appeared to be on a first-name basis with the woman in charge, and I let Katy make all the arrangements. She booked a "full consultation" (sounded much like the more-than-enough "full complement" of food in the tea salon) for me at nine thirty the next morning. I truly did want to arrive in New York with my family finding me looking my best, but I must admit, I was more than a little nervous yet equally excited by the idea of updating myself.

Katy and I parted company for the remainder of the day, she off to Boskey and me to my cabin to have a serious look-through of all the fashion magazines Solange had sent. I planned to clip pictures of some of the hairstyles and even examples of makeup that might be appropriate for a woman my age, with tendencies toward what was simple and easy. Certainly there would be times in New York that might call for more of an effort at looking one's best, and I would try to do so. I knew I would be in good hands with Katy but also knew I might need to restrain her enthusiasm. I was enthusiastic enough for the both of us.

CHAPTER 14

THE BASTION OF BEAUTY – APRIL 1923

Eleven the next morning found me anxiously pacing back and forth in front of the salon's door. Katy was late again, and I didn't want to go in and begin my beautification experience without her. The salon's supervisor had been giving me surreptitious glances, and after another five minutes of waiting, I entered the salon.

"Ah, Mademoiselle Durant! I have acquainted your personal stylist, Madame Sylvia, with your request for a full consultation and provided her with your general coloring and overall features. She is preparing now for your appointment and will be with you shortly. Please, take a seat.

"And please, do not worry!" she said, noticing my continual glances toward the door. "I am sure Mrs. Levinson will be here soon."

She then dashed off behind highly hung curtains of ivory sateen to the secret netherworld of the salon. I could smell both the strong odor of ammonia and a sweet fragrance effervescing from what I assumed were the shampoos and magical potions needed to create a more beautiful self.

Sitting down, I quickly looked through the pictures I had torn from the magazines' pages last evening. Where was Katy?

A few minutes later, a very tall middle-aged woman of significant girth, wearing a green apron with the ship's logo embroidered onto the center, dramatically parted the folds of the curtains and walked commandingly toward me with a face full of expectation.

"Bonjour, Mademoiselle," she stated heartily as she paced slowly round me twice, assessing in person, I assumed, more of my "general coloring and overall features." "I am Madame Sylvia, and today you and I will become great acquaintances, for this day will be one you will long remember. You have entered our salon as one woman and in a few hours you will depart as another, a more confident creature arrayed in the finest beauty products available in Europe. It will be a transformative experience! Shall we begin, my dear?"

Without waiting for my reply, she turned and motioned me with a flip of her hand to follow her as she walked to a chair whose back leaned up against a sink, which I gathered was where my "transformation" would begin. If Katy didn't arrive shortly, I fully intended to escape quickly from this bastion of beauty. But sit I did, and as Madame Sylvia wrapped a rolled warm towel around the back of my neck and then draped a cloth the same color green as her apron over my person, Katy entered the salon, panting and apologizing.

"I am so very sorry, Marie! Boskey was ever so effusive in his regards toward me this morning that I found I truly lost track of the time. But here I am, and I see that you are in the extremely capable hands of Madame Sylvia." Still breathing rapidly and with a slight flush to her face, Katy sat across from me in a chair from where I hoped she would supervise all of Madame Sylvia's ministrations.

"I was becoming very concerned, Katy! I thought perhaps you had forgotten or were otherwise occupied and unable to be here with me." Even to myself I sounded rather pathetic. A grown woman unable to maneuver herself through a salon experience? Nonetheless, this was only slightly less frightening to me than my first experience riding Horse and holding on for dear life when he took off at a wild gallop. It was the same feeling—that I was not the one in control.

"Katy, do you not think that after my hair is shampooed we might all pause in this process and discuss together what, if any, changes I might want made to my person?" I knew this sounded stodgy and stuffy but I was trying for reason here and attempting not to be rude at the same time.

"Well, of course, Marie," Katy chimed with a wave of her hand. "We will all three study you in the mirror as Madame Sylvia combs out your wet hair.

Did you bring the pictures, and if so, may I see them?" She exchanged knowing glances with Madame Sylvia. I was fearing a conspiracy here.

I handed Katy the five pictures and watched as she looked at each one while making comments under her breath. "Perhaps, but . . . Oh, I don't know about this one. . . . This is a possibility. . . . But definitely not this!"

I could stand it no longer, and with my head bent backwards and water dripping down the back of my neck despite the rolled towel, I inquired, "Please tell me which picture goes with each of your comments, Katy. Really, it is unnerving when I cannot see what you are looking at."

"We are almost done here, Mademoiselle. Just the cream rinse and we shall move to my style area where we can discuss what would suit you best." Madame Sylvia wrapped my head in a fluffy green towel, which I assumed was also embroidered with the same logo.

We all moved as one to the chair Madame Sylvia indicated with another wave of her hand. I climbed into its black leather seat, and she began pumping a foot pedal, raising the chair in jerky spurts until I was nearly a meter off the ground. Madame Sylvia was a very tall woman.

As Katy's arm extended toward Madame Sylvia to hand her the pictures, Madame Sylvia shielded her eyes with one hand and held up the palm of the other, refusing to take them. "I do not want to contaminate my creativity by looking at pictures from a magazine. I would rather stab myself with my cutting scissors than look at pictures. They won't be needed here."

"I brought them thinking it would be helpful to see what my choices might be should I decide to have my hair cut," I quickly explained.

"And that is the first mistake, Mademoiselle! You limit yourself by thinking those pictures are the only choices you have when, in truth, we do not know what is best for you until we study your hair and facial features. And we never think about color until after the cut is decided."

"Color! I do not plan to have my hair colored today. Is that what you are assuming?" I did not succeed in keeping the panic from my voice.

Madame Sylvia bent close to my ear, whispering, "Oh my! It sounds like we really need to rid ourselves of limitations and open ourselves up to the possibilities of what can be created." She began running her fingers through my wet hair. Why wasn't she using a brush for that?

"I first use my fingers to get a true feel for your hair's unique properties, such as texture, volume, and the thickness of each strand. Only then do we brush."

I realized I must have asked that last question out loud. Truly an indication of my own rising apprehension with this entire situation. "Perhaps I just needed a good shampoo, and we can leave it at that." I began to remove the green cloth from my lap.

"Marie," Katy said, pulling the apron back over me, "we are here because you definitely need an updated hairstyle and at least some minimal skin care and makeup recommendations. Madame Sylvia, might you possibly serve a nice *coupe de champagne* as we continue our full-compliment session? It may help us all to relax."

"Oui, Madame. You both take a deep breath, and I will return momentarily. I realize how exciting and frightening this must be, Mademoiselle Marie, to someone who has never before experienced such a life-changing process."

I rolled my eyes at Katy as Madame Sylvia retreated beyond the sateen curtain. "Katy, I think this is a mistake! I do not want a 'life-changing process.' I just want a haircut." I tried to rise again from my chair but realized almost too late how far it was to the floor.

"Marie, calm down! You are in a fabulous salon on a fabulous ship! Nothing here is an ordinary experience. Do you think I would ever allow anyone but the best possible hairdresser to cut and style your hair?"

Katy leaned forward and patted my arm, giving me her sweetest smile. "You really need to relax and enjoy being pampered today." I felt like a child being cajoled by her mother. "Madame Sylvia is highly sought after and could see you today only because another passenger canceled *and* because I begged and used Boskey's name."

"I have never been someone comfortable with pampering, and I'm not going to start now. When the beautician returns, let's please just get down to business,"

I said as firmly as possible. Katy merely patted my arm again and nodded her head. I realized I had lost the battle before it even began.

"Here we are, my lovelies, and not only champagne but some *petit* sandwiches as well. We will all feel better if we sip and nibble while we chat about Mademoiselle Marie." She handed us each a glass of chilled, bubbling white wine and a small plate of food that really did look appetizing.

Madame Sylvia turned my chair toward the mirror once more, and with our mouths full and chewing our food, we just stared for a time at my reflection. To me, I looked like a wet animal draped in a terrible shade of green that made me look rather seasick.

I took two large swallows of wine and said, "All right. Let's proceed with discussing my hair. I know it is long and dreadful and my usual chignon certainly does not reflect the style of these times. Madame Sylvia, I would like you to cut my hair in the bobbed fashion. Many ladies onboard are sporting such a style, and I find it attractive, and certainly it must be easy to care for. I am a minimalist in most regards and do not want to spend time fussing with my hair any more than necessary."

Madame Sylvia nodded as she downed her remaining wine with a large swallow, her plate of food already consumed, and began brushing out my hair. When she finished, she took my hair in her hands again and folded it upon itself, making it look short.

"Your hair has a natural wave, Mademoiselle, which will be more evident when it is cut and has less weight. Natural curl can be a curse and a blessing. If you are not diligent about using a cream rinse after shampooing, it may curl too much and even frizz. Nothing is worse than frizzing and must be avoided at all costs! Do you understand what I am saying?" Madame Sylvia was very serious about this.

"No, I don't really, but what is my hair's blessing?"

"The natural wave, if not too wavy, will allow you to easily make finger waves, which is very much in vogue. Most women must use a hot iron and clips to create such an alluring effect, but I am thinking you may be one of the few fortunates that need only clips. Hot irons are very hard on hair, very drying, and can even cause breakage and burning if not carefully used. I could tell you stories!" Madame Sylvia lamented as she shook her head back and forth at the terrible memories.

"All right, then it's settled! Please begin cutting my hair in a bob."

"But of course! However, before we begin I need to recommend that you consider bangs. You have a great deal of hair and a rather high forehead—it's actually quite prominent. Certainly wearing bangs will not detract but compliment the bobbed style in addition to minimizing your forehead. We will leave the bangs slightly longer. That way you can still wear them to the side and even wave them if you so choose." Madame Sylvia then reached for a long narrow comb and short scissors.

"Wait! I have never had bangs and don't know if I want them!" I said rather loudly.

"Marie. You must remember Madame Sylvia cuts and styles some of the most glamorous women in the world. Actresses and socialites go back and forth from the States to Europe on this ship, and she is the one who cuts their hair and does their makeup. Would you want Madame Sylvia to tell you how to bandage a patient when you are the nurse? Of course not! And you must trust her as your patients trust you." And with that, Madame Sylvia and Katy smiled at each other as only conspirators can do. I gave myself up to them, sinking a little lower in the chair, and the cutting began.

I found that Madame Sylvia's movements and the cutting off of many inches of my hair was actually very soothing. And I am sure the wine contributed to my calming down and just letting them have their way. None of us spoke for the many minutes it took to cut the sides and back. When she combed the hair down over my forehead and face, I knew the bangs were getting ready to make their appearance. I shut my eyes tightly.

Madame Sylvia splayed her fingers through my short hair, which was almost dry. "Open your eyes, Mademoiselle," she said brightly. "There is nothing to see that will frighten you."

I opened my eyes and looked in the mirror. Who was this person looking back at me? She looked totally different than the woman I saw just thirty minutes ago! Now, she had short, slightly wavy hair—and bangs. I was rather startled and could not look away from myself. I already looked younger and certainly more stylish.

Neither Madame Sylvia nor Katy bothered asking if I liked what I saw. Their confidence in this transformation was so assured that it wasn't even a question as to whether I approved.

"One more thing, Mademoiselle, before we move on to your skin and makeup. I would recommend now, before we actually style your hair, that you consider a henna rinse, which would give your rather mousy blonde strands a boost of gentle color for brightness and shine. Henna is not permanent but washes out after many weeks and then, if you liked it, you could go to your local stylist and have her reapply. By that time, you will need your hair trimmed again as well."

After some hesitation, and seeing Katy's head nodding up and down in total agreement, I said, "Be my guest. If I'm going to do this, let's do it all the way. I do like the cut tremendously!"

I realized I was beginning to sound like Katy as both of my accomplices exchanged knowing glances again, and without a word, the chair was released to floor level, and I was once again escorted to the sink.

Katy was extremely interested in the measuring and mixing and stirring my mad stylist was engaged in and followed her every move. "How much lighter are you thinking of going?"

"We must not be too drastic. But certainly, lightening to match the golden strands already in her hair would highlight her eyes and brighten up her complexion."

In the hour we had been in the salon, I had become used to being only an object of their ministrations, just a head on which to conjure their magic. How I hoped their potions proved beneficial to my person.

Once the henna was applied, I sat upright in the sink's chair while it processed and glanced through the magazine Katy handed me. Were they trying to distract me from their next maneuver? They were looking intently at charts of makeup; colors abounded on pages labeled "Lips" and "Cheeks" and "Eyes." And while I was happy thus far with the changes, I knew I would only agree to very minimal attention to makeup. I did not like the look of a woman who treated her face as a canvas that arrived in the room before she did. I was more concerned with caring for my changing skin. Other than applying my lavender cream, I took few pains to protect myself from sun and was curious as to what would be recommended on this auspicious day of change.

After some time, the henna was rinsed out, and Madame Sylvia and Katy exclaimed mutual delight over results I had yet to see. Katy instructed me to close my eyes as they led me back to the styling chair. Sitting me down and turning me around to face the mirror, I found I was once again hesitant to view myself in the glass.

Katy clapped her hands in excitement. "For goodness sake, Marie! Open your eyes and gaze upon your lovely hair!"

Oh, it was indeed lovely! Golden and soft and the curls were more defined. Whatever magic Madame Sylvia practiced, I knew she was a good witch. For who could have known a person's appearance could so drastically be altered with just changes to their hair?

Madame Sylvia began massaging my head as she rubbed yet another elixir into my scalp and hair, and I became so relaxed I thought I might doze off. She then placed long thin clips into my hair at the sides and back. These would make finger waves, she said, and she would let them dry naturally as we began the discussion of my skin.

By now, I was completely at their mercy and almost gave away my entire free will to these two conspiring women. Distracted by lingering misgivings going round in my head, I almost didn't hear what was being discussed. But the words *cheek* and *eye color* cleared my dulled mind and brought me round just in time.

"Mesdemoiselles, before anything is applied to my face, I want you to know that I am only interested in what creams might benefit my complexion. I haven't taken proper care of it in many years, and I recognize that it could benefit from suitable ointments. I truly am not interested in makeup, but if you must, I will allow you to experiment, if you promise to make it minimal and in good taste." Knowing I really had not a say in the matter, giving them "permission" left me with the feeling I was still somewhat in charge of my own fate.

"Why, Mademoiselle, we always want our ladies to reflect good taste, no? It is only the very young or the very unsophisticated that paint themselves to attract attention—such as *flappers* are doing nowadays! You are a woman of an age when your best features are to be enhanced with such subtlety no one suspects that you are wearing makeup at all." Madame Sylvia, leading the three of us to an elegant vanity table covered with a great variety of tubes and pots, looked very forlorn, thinking I would for a moment doubt her best intentions toward my visage.

I began apologizing as I took my seat in front of the mirror. That is, until she brought forth a palette such as a painter would use, seemingly out of nowhere, in which she had little pots of many colors alongside brushes and sponges of different sizes. This did not look minimal.

Katy came to my side again. "Remember what we said, Marie? And certainly you can see that Madame Sylvia is an artist. Look at what she has done with your hair." As a trio, we all looked in the mirror at my face. They smiled and I grimaced.

"You say, Mademoiselle, that on occasion you use a lavender cream. That certainly is beneficial and most likely one of the reasons your skin is not in worse repair. I would recommend that you use a light layer of your lavender cream nightly to keep your skin moisturized and looking youthful. As for today, we are going to first apply a rich cleansing mask that will nourish and soften your skin, followed by a refreshing tonic to close your pores and prepare your face."

As Madame Sylvia gently applied the thick mask using slow, circular movements with her fingers, I was transported to a place of relaxed bliss. The cool greenish-brown unguent smelling slightly of mint and somewhat of mud was indeed soothing, and I could almost hear my parched skin thanking me.

After fifteen minutes, she gently washed the mask from my face, and the cool tonic she applied next smelled of witch hazel and made my skin tingle.

"And now we will apply a rich moisturizing lotion followed by a light foundation of color chosen to match your skin's natural tones. . . . Like this . . . And lastly, we add the delicate hint of a blush to your cheeks." Madame Sylvia accomplished these tasks as she spoke them and next picked up a pencil that I knew was intended for my eyes.

"Wait! I don't want anything on my eyes. It seems too much."

"It is only too much, Mademoiselle, if applied incorrectly. Your blue eyes are your best feature, and we must always attend to our best features. We put but a thin brown line above your upper lashes with a complimentary light brown shadow on your lids and just slightly darken your brows with a crayon. Now that your hair is lightened, your darker eyelashes are more pronounced. I do not think we need to add any color to them. And voilà! Look into the mirror, please, and marvel at your vision."

With the subtlety of just a slight amount of contour and color, my face appeared flawless and smooth, and my eyes indeed looked bluer and bolder. The artist in me was very much enjoying this experience of a human face becoming the canvas on which to create such startling changes using only minimal color and shading.

"And now, the last two important elements for a completed face: rouge and lip color." Madame Sylvia produced a small round container—a little compact, really, beautiful in itself, with a lid topped by a pink rose made of taffeta. She said it was rouge paste and took out only the slightest amount to color my cheeks. She dabbed it on each and then blended it up along the ridges of my cheekbones. My cheeks bloomed the color of a pale pink rose.

"And now, *la touche finale!*" Madame Sylvia first outlined my lips with a thin colored pencil and then, after removing the top of a gold tube of rose-colored lipstick, she gently applied the warm, rich color to my mouth.

"A light powder to set the makeup and you, dear Marie, are ready to light up any room." She removed the clips from my hair, and there appeared the finger waves.

I must say I looked astoundingly similar to the women in the fashion magazines. I actually felt giddy and did not quite know what to make of it all. I stood, admiring myself from all angles.

"At dinner tonight you must wear colors that will bring out the beautiful blue of your eyes. And Madame Sylvia, do you know if one of the shops onboard would have headbands for both day and evening wear? I think Marie will need several," Katy added as she linked her arm through mine and gave it a squeeze.

"Of course the shops carry them and in great variety, for I choose them myself. Now, for our last discussion, we need to decide which of the products you might wish to purchase so you can create this look yourself."

"I don't really know. Katy, please help me here, and I will purchase whatever you recommend. But again, I do not want a complicated beauty regimen!"

"It won't be complicated, Marie, once it becomes routine. Madame Sylvia, please put together a face cleansing cream and the tonic, and the moisturizing lotion as well as the foundation cream. I believe I saw that you carry in the salon the Bourjois compact, containing the rouge, lipstick and powder? Having that in such a convenient case will help make it easy for Marie. Oh, and add the eyeliner, shadow, and brow crayon . . . and I think that will be all my friend needs at the moment!"

I was slightly overwhelmed but resigned to the list of items Katy felt I needed, wondering how I would ever remember in what order to apply them all.

"I will leave the new me intact the rest of the day and past dinner. But Katy, you must review all of this with me tomorrow. Will you come to my room after breakfast and help me recreate this on my own?"

"Of course! By the end of the voyage it will be second nature. And remember, you only need to add the liner and shadow for more formal occasions, such as dinner parties or outings to the theatre."

Well, that would mean I would never use the eye makeup, as I seldom, if ever, had an occasion at home in which I would need to appear très chic. But I definitely wanted to purchase the entire array. I did have New York City to consider.

Thanking Madame Sylvia effusively as I handed her a grateful and generous gratuity, I then paid the woman at the front and left the salon feeling confident, knowing I looked my best. Who knew subtlety was so powerful—and maybe a little magical? Katy again slipped her arm through mine, and with both of us smiling broadly, we took our fashionable selves off to a celebratory lunch.

CHAPTER 15

ARRIVING IN NYC –
APRIL 1923

For the remainder of the voyage, I spent the mornings in relative quiet, either in my cabin or on solitary strolls about the ship. I had brought from home two copies of recent medical journals on loan to me from Dr. Benoît, the physician in Verdun. These, I decided, would at least give me a glimpse into the current state of medicine and would bring me up to date with some of the medical advances I knew were taking place throughout the world. One journal reviewed the most recent developments in pharmaceuticals and the other described technological advances. I had saved them for such a time when I would have hours to spend in quiet reading.

Afternoon tea with Katy and dinners each evening in the dining room were the exceptions to my last days of quiet aboard ship. I actually looked forward to the lively comradery of my fellow tablemates and was pleased that my conversational English, between talking with Katy and the nightly dinner conversations, had much improved.

Each day before tea I set about doing my hair, which did not take more than a brushing; however, applying my makeup continued to cause me some consternation as I attempted to make my face resemble what Madame Sylvia had so effortlessly created. By the voyage's end, and with some continued guidance from Katy, I hoped to become quite proficient at quickly putting myself together, and felt assured that upon disembarking in New York I would appear to Solange and Papa a woman of style and confidence.

The day before our arrival, Katy appeared mid-morning at my cabin door with a teacart laden with all the delicacies we had come to enjoy with our afternoon tea. We exchanged addresses, me giving her both Papa's in New York and my own in Meuse. We promised each other we would keep up an exchange of letters, and I heartily encouraged her to visit me in France. She had readily become a dear friend, and I so appreciated her helping bring me into the twentieth century. I would miss her liveliness and quick wit as well as the pure joy of having another woman with whom to discuss matters both simple and serious. I was sure we would keep up our friendship, if only through our letters, and hoped that there would be opportunities for future visits.

That evening, we all enjoyed a final dinner—*le dîner du capitaine*. Katy had arranged that we would sit together, and I didn't arrive back at my cabin until almost one in the morning. I hastily began packing my trunk, keeping out only the skirt, blouse, jacket, and cloche hat I would wear when I went ashore.

Solange had sent a wire this morning letting me know she would be meeting me at the ship's dock. I knew they too must be excited we would be together again. I had visited once more the shops on the Lido deck and purchased for Solange a set of pearl hair clips and a colorful scarf much resembling the ones I saw many women wearing as they strolled the decks or played shuffleboard or ping-pong, sporting informal attire such as the wide-legged trousers, which were certainly my favorite mode of apparel. Rather than wear a hat, they wrapped the scarves round their heads, tucking in the ends and securing them with lovely pins. The final effect was much like a turban and made quite a statement. Knowing Solange would be up on all the latest trends, as these fashionable shipboard women were, I felt sure such a scarf would appeal to her. For Papa, I purchased a lighter of gleaming brushed silver and a cigar cutter. It felt good to be bringing them gifts, a token of my thanks for giving me this adventure of renewal.

After stowing all my lovely clothes and various *articles de toilette*—excluding my arsenal of lotions and cosmetics, which I would place in my valise and use in the morning—my trunk was again packed to overflowing. In addition to the gifts, I also bought a few items for myself, including two scarves, a pair of the softest gray leather gloves, and several hair clips. By sitting upon the trunk, I was able to latch it closed. The clock said 2:07 a.m., and thus I donned my pajamas, took one last look out the square windows of my cabin as the lights of the ship reflected far out onto the dark, still waters, and slid for the last time down among the silky linens of my comfortable bed at sea.

I awoke at seven and was much too excited to have any breakfast in the dining room. A knock at my door at eight found Maurice with a morning cart offering coffee, tea, and croissants.

"Merci, Maurice! You must have read my mind. I really couldn't go to breakfast," I exclaimed as the fragrant aroma of the pastries wafted toward me.

"You and many others, Mademoiselle. We will disembark in approximately one hour. Are your belongings packed and ready to be collected?"

"Oui, my trunk is ready. How will I find it once we have left the ship?"

"I will be with the luggage of all passengers I have personally served during the voyage. Find me and you will have found your trunk. I will be looking out for you and have never lost a passenger, so please be assured that you will be reunited with your trunk without delay once you walk onto the macadam." With this, he tipped his hat and rolled his teacart to the next cabin. I immediately consumed the still-warm pastry and tea, wishing I had taken another of the delicious, flakey croissants.

An hour later, a loud knock proved to be another of the ship's men, this one seeking my trunk. As I opened the door wide for him to pack it off, I in turn picked up my valise and, with a last look about my familiar cabin, followed my trunk into the corridor.

The trip up top was slow going since everyone, and their luggage, was making for the departure area. The mood was festive, though. My fellow travelers seemed as excited and eager to disembark as I was. Many of the passengers, those immigrating to America, would now spend long hours making their way through immigration procedures. I wished them all well.

A sudden sense of nervousness invaded my thoughts. What if I could not find Papa and Solange or we missed one another in passing? Would they even recognize me? I looked quite changed since my sister and I last saw each other two years ago in Meuse.

It took nearly another hour to pass through customs before I stepped outside, into another new experience. Throngs of people jostled one another, eagerly seeking family and friends and making it quite difficult to see any distance ahead. My limited view of the reception area revealed a great mass of people waiting to catch a glimpse of the passengers they were there to retrieve. And the sunlight, though welcomed, was blinding, the brightness of the morning causing my eyes to water and blur. I found myself rather unsteady on my feet as I held tightly to my valise and attempted to shade my eyes. Looking about for familiar luggage or persons, I immediately saw Maurice standing a short distance off to my right as he loudly called out my name. I was extremely grateful at the moment to see a familiar face and to know I had at least found my belongings.

I began to hurry through the crowds, trying to make my way to Maurice, when I felt a tug on my arm. Not thinking much of it, as we were all still bumping into one another, I continued to walk posthaste to my trunk. But then someone grabbed me firmly by the arm and stopped me in my tracks. I turned to loose myself from this person only to find it was Solange who had taken hold of me!

"Bonjour, Marie, and welcome to New York City!" My sister held both my arms as she kissed my cheeks and we began to laugh.

"Oh, it is so wonderful to finally be here and even more wonderful that I have been found! My trunk is here as well, with Maurice. Maurice, this is my sister, Solange Chagall. Solange, this is Maurice, my efficient valet from the voyage." Maurice and Solange cordially greeted one another while a man I assumed to be Solange's driver collected my heavy trunk and departed through the mass of people now greeting each other with great enthusiasm. With a hasty wave to Maurice, Solange maneuvered us away from the joyful exclaims of welcome filling the air. I gave up trying to get my bearings and just held fast to her.

Soon, we came upon a vast number of automobiles and horse-drawn carriages lined up waiting to transport people to their next destination. Solange stopped beside a large black-and-deep-maroon-colored automobile, its shine so bright in the sun that I could see my own reflection. The brilliant metal was warm to my touch as I ran a finger over one glossy fender. Climbing inside, it smelled of fine leather and polish, the matte black upholstery soft and supple. I did not think this was a hired vehicle that transported customers throughout the day. Perhaps the car was Papa's. I would inquire later once we were settled at their home.

"Oh, Marie! I cannot tell you how excited we are that you have come! I have so much to tell you that I hardly know where to begin. And look at you! You have become a paragon of style!" Her eyes were wide and bright and her face slightly flushed as she held my hands, looking eagerly into my face.

"And I am equally glad to be here. I cannot wait to hear all you have to share. And the magazines you sent were certainly put to good use." We continued to exchange little pleasantries about my trip as the motorcar eased slowly through the crowds of people and vehicles of all kinds until we were away from the docks and onto the road. I looked out one window and then another to take in all I could see.

Solange was fidgety and full of mirth and laughter and seemed hardly able to contain herself throughout the drive. There must be more than enthusiasm over my visit that was responsible for such high excitement. What on earth she was bursting to share?

I realized suddenly that Papa had not come to meet me. "And Papa? I had expected him to be with you. Isn't he well?" I was concerned, as his letter to me in December indicated he was not his usual vigorous self.

"Papa is in good form. His health has much improved over the spring, and I am relieved that he is nearly himself again. He remains at home overseeing preparations for our lunch. He has made the rounds of all his favorite eateries throughout our neighborhood and gathered every kind of meat, cheese, bread, and New York delicacy he could find, all to lay a feast before you. I do not exaggerate when I say he is beyond the moon that you are here. He has missed you terribly, and your coming is a great salve to his grief at having left you in France."

"I am more than relieved to hear his health is improved, and since I am quite famished, it will be easy to show him his efforts at lunch will be more than appreciated. And Solange, it truly is wonderful to see you, dear sister." I gave her hands a tight squeeze. "Is this your and Papa's car? It is quite elegant!"

"Well . . . I don't really know where to start. So much has happened in such a short time so I will just begin my story. This car belongs to my fiancé, Philippe DeVore."

"Your fiancé! When did you acquire a fiancé?" I was stunned by her announcement.

"Philippe and I met six months ago through mutual friends of Papa's. Philippe came to New York from France shortly after the war. He served as an officer stationed at Normandy. He and his family are from the south of Paris, and that is where he returned once he was discharged. He had a wife and a young son and daughter. All four of them contracted the Spanish flu during the horrible outbreak, and he was the only one to survive. He felt there was nothing left for him in France, and he left to begin again here in America."

Solange took a deep breath and held tightly to my hands. She continued, "He is a wonderful man, Marie. Slightly older than myself and financially secure. He and his brother, who remains in Paris, have an import-export business—wine and textiles. He is a quiet, introspective person, very caring and kind. I love him dearly and cannot believe my good fortune to have found such a man who loves me as well. And he and Papa have become great friends. We have planned to marry while you are here for your visit. The ceremony will take place at his estate."

Letting loose my hands and sitting back against the seat, she turned and looked out her window. "And there is one more piece of news I have shared with no one, Marie, but I must share with you."

She looked at me and said in a whisper, "I am expecting a child. It has only just happened. I have missed but one month's menses, but that is a first occurrence. I have never missed one since my thirteenth year. And I am so excited and happy! I felt I was to burst until you arrived and I could tell you." Tears were in both our eyes as she leaned forward, taking me into her arms.

"I can hardly take this all in, Solange! Marriage . . . and a child? Do you say *no one* knows of your pregnancy? Not even Philippe?"

"Not even Philippe. I have decided to tell him the night of our wedding. It will be my gift to him. I know he will be beside himself with joy as I am. We both want children, and in nine months we will have our first. But you must keep this quiet. Philippe and I will tell Papa after the wedding. I do not want him to think I am scandalous. Oh Marie, how thankful I am you came!"

I was speechless. No words could convey my surprise at Solange's news. She was to be a maman and I was to become Tante Marie. My only thoughts were ones of joy and excitement.

It wasn't until the automobile pulled up in front of a large multi-storied building that I remembered they lived in an apartment. Even knowing this, I was still caught by surprise at not finding them in a single-family home. I had pictured a house rather like the one we had in Marseille. But this was their new life in New York City, and I must not be surprised by anything. Certainly nothing could surprise me more than knowing my sister was soon to be married and, shortly after, a mother. Anything else would pale in comparison to her news.

CHAPTER 16

THE OTHER HENRY –
APRIL 1923

O n Monday morning at breakfast, Solange informed me she was having Philippe's lawyer over in the afternoon to discuss her change in status from a single to a married woman, and she needed to make changes to her accounts.

"François has become a friend to both Papa and myself, and once our business is conducted we will have a social visit over tea. François is bringing his American friend and colleague Henry with him as both men would like to meet you."

"That sounds lovely, Solange. I am quite eager to meet your friends," I said and looked forward to the afternoon.

The two men, looking to be close in age to Solange, who was six years older than myself, arrived at the apartment promptly at one o'clock. While François and Solange sat at the dining table in front of a stack of legal documents, quietly discussing the changes she wished to make, Henry and I sat in the small parlor and attempted to make conversation. It was quite obvious by his comments that he had been told a great deal about our family, including myself, to which he was paying particular interest.

As I continued to be rather strongly queried by this stranger, I felt myself becoming quite uncomfortable. Dressed in what was obviously a finely tailored summer suit of lightweight linen, with his dark blond, pencil-thin mustache waxed to a sheen that matched his meticulously parted blond hair, he was quite the dandy. He sat with his legs crossed and his hands folded casually together in his lap. Noticing his well-manicured nails, I realized I was attempting to hide my own hands, which were beginning to want to run themselves up and down over my thighs, always a sign that I was becoming agitated.

But what did I need to worry over? Certainly not this man, who kept smiling at me and asking a great number of questions about my voyage from France, my work as a nurse, how did I like New York, had I ever considered moving here, and on and on he went. My sudden longing for Meuse, for my home and for my friends, found me briefly overcome with tears in my eyes as I attempted to answer this other Henry's questions with some measure of comportment.

Then, glancing at Solange and seeing a look on her face as she met my eyes, my longing transformed into suspicion and flew quickly to anger. Why were her eyes wide and her smile frozen across her lips as though she had a stomachache? I realized this was her face of complicity. She had orchestrated this ruse.

Solange had arranged this teatime as more than just a meeting with her attorney. This was a planned introduction, for my sake, to an eligible man! How could she be so insensitive, so rude to think I might find this skinny, pale-faced youth someone of interest? And realizing Papa might even be in on such a scheme!

Them thinking such a plan might result in my moving to New York should they find me a husband caused me such a state of distress that I found myself rising quickly from the divan and explaining in a voice loud enough to be heard above François and Solanges's conversation that I was suddenly feeling ill from the heat and must go lie down. With that, I excused myself and made quickly to my room.

The day was indeed stiflingly hot, and I threw the window open with such force it slammed loudly against the casing above. I hoped Solange heard and interpreted the sudden noisy jolt correctly. I flung off my dress, slip, and stockings and threw myself across the bed. Matchmaking indeed! She was not dragging me before a line of would-be suitors that I might be matched as she was.

I must have drifted off to sleep. The light from the window when I opened my eyes was waning, and the breeze blowing through caused me to shiver. It took me several seconds to realize where I was and to remember once again to take up my anger. It would be close to dinner, so I dressed and went to find Solange. She and I needed to talk this out before Papa arrived home. I assumed she had checked in on me earlier and, finding me sleeping, thought it possible I had indeed not been feeling well. But my sister and I knew each other above all others, and I had no doubt she guessed my flight from tea for what it was, and it had nothing to do with the heat. She would have realized I was terribly upset by her ploy but most likely would not be aware of the degree of my discountenance.

I found Solange in the kitchen preparing our evening meal. As she heard me enter, she asked without turning round, "Are you feeling better now? You had a nice rest."

"Yes, I feel rested but also greatly disappointed in you, Solange."

She turned to face me but avoided my eyes, saying, "I am sorry, Marie. I just thought it would be nice for you to meet a man your age and chat for a little while. I heard how pushy Henry was and, of course, I saw your great discomfort. I truly am sorry. I realize now it was extremely presumptuous on my part. I assure you there are no other such surprises in store. That was to be my only attempt at what I thought might be perhaps a pleasant time for you." She walked across the room, knowing better than to touch me. I was still very much insulted by the incident as well as embarrassed.

"I will forgive you but not today. I do appreciate the assurance that nothing like that will happen again while I am here. I'm going to take myself out for a walk and leave you to finish dinner. We won't talk of this again and especially not to Papa. If he did know about it, you can relay my feelings to him when you two have a private moment, as I don't want it discussed in my presence. While your intentions may have been of the most innocent sort, Solange, you know me well enough that even those good intentions were not needed or appreciated."

She did not respond but watched me as I took up my hat and proceeded out the door. I found an hour's walk in the twilight round the busy neighborhood did much to allay my anger and soothe my wounded pride.

Returning to the apartment, I found the table set and Papa reading the paper in the parlor. He stood, and although we greeted one another as warmly as we had yesterday when we were reunited, I saw in his face that Solange had indeed related the afternoon's events. I gave him my kindest heartfelt smile, assuring him in that way that all was forgiven and not to be mentioned again.

Although dinner was somewhat stiff and the conversation rather forced, I felt great relief that I had been able to stand up for myself, hoping that these two I loved most in the world saw that I was capable of steering my own passage through my own life. The next day, the waters had all calmed, and we were once again our same selves.

CHAPTER 17

THE MARKET AND SHABBAT – FRIDAY, 13 APRIL, 1923

riday morning, I awoke to the comforting and familiar smell of baking bread. I quickly slipped into my light robe and shoes, and, running my fingers through my tousled hair, left my bedroom following the intoxicating aroma of yeast.

Solange was standing at the dining table humming softly to herself while fitting white candles into the *bougeoirs* given to her by Henri when she came to Meuse. The matched set was made of fine rose-colored glass soldered together by a thin line of lead. The lead outlined the shape of tulip petals, each of the four petals scalloped to a point where the candle was centered within and held securely in place. Solange had placed the two candlesticks upon a table runner that she and I embroidered together so many years ago in Marseille. Between the candles she had also placed a silver chalice, one I had not seen before. It was tall-stemmed and simple in design. Alongside the glimmering chalice were four very small silver cups of a similar design. The silver gleamed with recent polishing.

"Solange, how lovely," I said, making my way to her with morning greetings upon each cheek. "Surely this is not our table setting for breakfast."

"Today I have another surprise for you. But this one will not upset you, I promise. Philippe has been taking me to synagogue for almost a year now, and I am learning much about the rituals of our faith. He was raised observing many of the holy days and Friday Sabbath. Once a week, we have been meeting with the rabbi, and I am taking instruction so Philippe and I will have a home in which we celebrate the aspects of Judaism that are most meaningful to us. It is sometimes overwhelming, the number of holy days, prayers, and blessings, but the one Philippe, myself, and Papa faithfully observe is Shabbat. This evening, Philippe is coming, and we will all celebrate together. Papa and I wanted very much to share this with you that you might know you are especially remembered each Friday as we prepare for the Sabbath."

I sat myself down in a chair, breakfast forgotten. "I only vaguely remember the ritual of Shabbat from our religion studies. You are going to need to refresh my memory regarding its significance."

"Preparing for Shabbat on Friday is my favorite time of the week. Philippe is going to explain this Jewish ritual, as he so beautifully does, leading us through the prayers and blessings. You and I, we must have all of our chores and work completed for our meal before sunset. You surely remember that Sabbath is a time of rest and remembrance, and there is to be no work done from nightfall on Friday until nightfall again on Saturday. Each Friday morning I bake challah, the bread used in the ritual of Shabbat, and then take myself to market to buy what we will need for our evening meal. Let's have our breakfast and then hurry to the markets."

Her eyes were shining, and I could see how important it was for her to share this weekly experience with me, her sister who was unable to practice in France any semblance of our faith. When I moved alone to Meuse, because of Papa's concerns for my future safety, I had reluctantly relinquished living as Marie Chagall and faithfully kept my promise to him. I took my maman's family name and lived as Marie Durant, a woman all would assume was a Catholic. I looked forward to discussing with him if he still harbored the same fears, that life for the Jews in Europe would, in the future, become extremely difficult.

Once the challah finished baking, Solange had me remove it from the oven and place it atop the counter onto a heavy towel. The loaf was thick and lightly browned, the top crowned with a golden-baked braid. While the bread cooled, we drank our tea with a croissant and shared an apple. I cleared our few dishes as Solange gently tapped the sides of the bread pan. She tipped the loaf from its confines and set it upon a platter ornately decorated in different shades of blue and silver.

"What a beautiful dish, Solange, and the goblet and matching cups on the table. Did you purchase those here?"

"They were Philippe's and have been in his family for generations. He brought very little with him when he left France but the Sabbath goblet, cups, and platter he thankfully carried with him to New York. I was deeply touched when he brought them to be used at our first Shabbat shared with Papa here at the apartment. We have used them every Friday since and will continue to do so in our own home," she said softly as she lightly laid both hands upon her abdomen, reminding me of the child who would be so very welcomed and so greatly loved.

Solange explained that this area of town was populated by many Jewish immigrants, and Washington Square Market, where we were headed, was always bustling and never more so than on Friday mornings. From spring into fall, farmers and merchants from outlying areas came with their food and wares, catering to women preparing for the Sabbath meal. She eagerly described all manner of foods and goods the market would display. She planned to gather what we needed quickly and then stroll us through the throngs of merchant pushcarts and vendor stands to peruse the array of fine fabrics and linens, kitchen items, clothing, and jewelry.

Leaving the apartment, I was surprised to find Philippe's car sitting in front of the building.

"Good morning, Benito. Marie, I'd like to introduce you to Philippe's driver, Benito. I apologize that I did not introduce you to one another when we picked you up."

Holding open the door of the auto for us, Benito tipped his hat to me and said a polite and formal, "Good morning, miss," in a heavy Italian accent.

Solange asked him to first take us farther north, to Manhattan, that I might see something of the grandeur of the city. We drove by many newly constructed buildings that towered high above us. Solange said that there were plans in the works for buildings that would stand much taller. I could believe this as there was construction going on all around. We drove past the stately, white-marbled New York Public Library and along the crowded streets of Times Square. Solange asked Benito to pull the automobile over to the curb as we came alongside Central Park. She and I stepped out and walked briskly through the park for fifteen minutes before returning to the car and heading again toward our final destination of Washington Square Market.

Benito dropped us some ways from the market itself. I could hardly keep up with the pace Solange set for us, walking rapidly the quarter mile or so to where the market was set up. Coming closer, I could see a great number of vendors of every age and gender with pushcarts, wooden boxes, and crates teeming with fresh fruits and vegetables of every color and shape. The smell of fish tinged the air and chickens newly dead hung from their wrung necks along ropes above the meat vendors' stalls. Women were already busy haggling, arms waving and hands stuffing large bags and woven baskets full of their fresh purchases. There was a frantic excitement in the air, and as the commotion increased, Solange and I found it hard to hear one another. I followed closely behind her, making our way through the ever-increasing throngs of purposed women.

Apparently my sister knew many of the vendors, familiar with them, I assumed, because she purchased from them weekly. Hearty greetings were exchanged everywhere one looked, between both shoppers themselves and with vendors in a cacophony of languages. I soon found myself caught up in the exhilaration of this busy marketplace and joined in greeting those my sister cheerfully insisted on introducing me to, in addition to those that just happened across my path.

I strolled a little ways off from Solange to a stall selling honey, soaps, and lotions, wondering how they might compare with the ones we made at home.

Perusing the bottles and baskets of the sellers' wares, I found no products made with lavender, but I purchased many bars of lovely rose-scented soaps and a few jars of the local honey that I would take home to the Sisters. I felt a sudden pang of homesickness but quickly tucked it away, knowing I had many weeks before I would return to Meuse. And I wanted to enjoy all of the sights and sounds of this growing city so very different from the solitude of my home. I reminded myself to not worry about what might await me on my return to France.

Solange eventually found me and steered us toward vendors displaying cheeses of every variety. The smell was almost overpowering. "Choose some cheeses that interest you, Marie. We will buy several kinds."

I tasted many samples that were thrust at me by eager sellers and selected two: a creamy white Brie and a sharp-tasting orange the seller told me was a cheddar. I placed the paper-wrapped rounds in the brown woven basket I had just purchased to hold my gifts for home. The basket, already full to overflowing, would be my gift to myself. I seemed to never have enough baskets, and I had to admit I might purchase another or two before we left the market.

It was almost noon before we returned to where Benito left us, and we both walked to the automobile much slower than we had to the market. I was now carrying three baskets of varying sizes—yes, three—and Solange had woven and cloth bags over each wrist and in both hands, with additional wrapped parcels tucked securely under each arm. Most of what we purchased was food, including sweets, but we did manage to find lovely hairpins and each a scarf. It was easy to get caught up in the frenzy of the market, and I wondered if, when we returned to the apartment, we might find ourselves remiss discovering we had made frivolous purchases. Solange did not seem to share my concern but expressed only excitement at our great finds.

"What a wonderful market," I said, settling myself into the welcome confines of the car. "Seeing and sampling all those wonderful foods has made me hungry. Why did we not think to buy something for lunch?"

"We did think of lunch. Or rather I did, and it is waiting for us just a few blocks toward home." And off we sped, Benito seeming to acknowledge our desire for food and the importance of getting us there as quickly as possible. Again, I was amazed at how rapidly all things moved here in this bustling city. And there seemed no time between one event and the next. Having walked for so long in my relatively new shoes, I had barely removed them from my sore feet before I had to fit into them once again as we pulled up alongside the restaurant where we were to have lunch.

"But Solange, we have a carload of food and goods that need attention. Why aren't we going home to put it away?" I asked, still attempting to wedge my swollen feet back into my shoes.

Coming around to my side of the car, she took my arm and helped disengage me from the cozy cocoon of the vehicle. "Papa is home, and Benito will deliver everything to the apartment. He and Papa will deal with it. Then they will most likely have a coffee. They usually spend one morning together each week; Benito helps Papa perfect his Italian while Papa coaxes his friend to speak a more decent French. Papa and I planned all this well in advance, and he is going to prepare our supper while we spend this day together. Philippe will not arrive till around seven, so we have plenty of time to relax and enjoy lunch together."

I reminded myself I was in Solange and Papa's home now, and I needed to but follow their lead. It was obviously important to them that I experience pieces of the daily and weekly events that made up the whole of their lives. I only hoped I had a wellspring of fortitude to keep pace with all the happenings. I had not realized until leaving the car and entering now another new environment that I had experienced no moments thus far of anxiety nor had any feelings of claustrophobia where I needed to quickly seek quiet and solitude. I could truly relax and just delight in all that was going on around me.

Stepping into the restaurant, we were escorted to a small table at the back of the quaint establishment. Through an open back door close to our table I could see a kitchen garden had been planted with a great variety of savory herbs, which I assumed they used in their cooking. The breeze blowing through the door was much welcomed, and although I wanted badly to once again remove my shoes, I kept them on, following the decorum of a well-mannered woman of

New York City. Solange did remove her hat, weaving the pins back into the fabric before setting it upon the extra chair at the table. I followed suit and we both straightened our hair. Between the pleasant wafting of air from the doorway and the smells from the kitchen, I soon felt refreshed and hungrier than ever.

"Am I wearing you down to the bone, Marie? I know the market is frantic but it is wonderful all the same. I usually go right home and begin preparing the meal, but this day I want to spend as much time with you as possible. Papa often helps me on Friday and was more than happy to do so today. Your absence in our lives is difficult to bear for both of us. And it seems even harder now that we are an ocean apart. At least in France we were still living in the same country."

Taking my sister's hand, I assured her, "Even an ocean apart we are never separated, Solange. Nothing can break the bonds of family. Certainly not our family of three, soon to be expanded to five."

Solange smiled, squeezed my hand, and struggled to compose herself. Tears shimmered in her deep brown eyes, and with a quick whisk of her handkerchief she wiped her nose and eyes before focusing on the menu now placed before her.

Over the next hour we drank our tea and savored a lovely rich onion soup followed by a tart overflowing with fresh strawberries topped with thick cream. How sleepy I felt afterwards and silently hoped that there might be time for a nap, however brief, before Philippe arrived and we began Shabbat. Solange must have read my mind. I forgot how readily she was always able to do so, and as she paid for our lunch, she told me through a long yawn we would both rest once we were home.

Papa had set the table and dinner was roasting in the oven. The apartment was filled with the fragrances of the challah bread accompanied by mint and roasting meat, and the candles and cups on the dining table were now joined by china and silver. Oh, how heavenly this day was, I thought, walking with heavy legs to my room. I dropped down upon my bed and immediately fell into a restful sleep.

I woke refreshed from my short nap and looked forward to celebrating a ritual I had only read about in religious studies many years ago. Solange had told me that it was customary in Judaism that we dress well for Shabbat out of respect. This was her way of telling me I wasn't to wear my trousers but a skirt and blouse. I understood that this was a part of their lives, but the reality that they could freely practice their faith here in this country placed some weight of anxiety about my shoulders. Did Papa feel that I should practice the same rituals in the solitary confines of my own home? I again reminded myself I was but to meld into my family's experiences, ones that I had pleaded Papa to allow us to celebrate when I was a youngster. To be truthful, I harbored no expectations that this ritual would hold any meaning for me, but I certainly could respect that it was important to my family. And it would provide me an opportunity to become familiar with Philippe, for we had not as yet met.

Philippe arrived promptly at seven, dressed in a brown lightweight wool suit and carrying a bottle of wine under his arm. Upon removing his hat, I saw his almost-black hair was longer at the top and neatly combed in a side part. His lightly scented pomade gave a deep shine to his hair, which matched the glow of his dark brown eyes. With a kind smile about his mouth, he greeted Papa and Solange and then turned to me as Solange made introductions. Papa then motioned him into the kitchen to open the wine. There was an air of excitement, a spark of expectation in the air as we all gathered in the kitchen and shared our day's events.

Philippe, I noticed throughout the next hour, was a man of few words, a keen observer and one who listened most intently, and what he did say was insightful and kind. He asked if I had enjoyed the voyage from France, and we talked a few minutes of that, sharing our stories of life aboard an oceangoing vessel, he having traveled for business several times to and from Europe on various ships. He was well spoken and there was a sad kindness in his manner.

As twilight approached, Solange told me that the Shabbat candles must be lit no later than eighteen minutes before sundown, at which time we would all be seated round the dining table. Philippe, in his rich baritone voice, said he would explain each step in the observance of Shabbat and then speak the blessing. Not knowing exactly what that meant but eager to participate, I nodded assent and felt a calmness settle over me.

Philippe began the ritual with these words: "Shabbat calls us to remember that on the seventh day following creation, God rested. Shabbat also calls us to remember that God rescued us out of slavery in Egypt. Each Friday just before sunset we remember, and we celebrate Shabbat in commune with all Jews throughout the world. The woman of the household begins by completing the mitzvah of lighting the candles."

We all turned to Solange. She lit the tapers, waving her hands twice over the flames, and on the third passing, she brought her hands up to cover her eyes as she recited, "Blessed are you, Lord our God, Sovereign of the universe, who has sanctified us with His commandments and commanded us to light the lights of Shabbat."

Papa and Philippe said, "Amen," followed a second later by Solange.

Philippe then poured from the silver chalice a small amount of red wine into the individual cups. He handed one to each of us, saying, "Kiddush follows the lighting of the candles and ushers in the Sabbath. I will say each blessing in English and then in Hebrew.

"And there was evening and there was morning, a sixth day. The heavens and the earth were finished, the whole host of them. And on the seventh day God completed his work that he had done, and he rested on the seventh day from all his work that he had done. And God blessed the seventh day, and sanctified it because in it he had rested from all his work that God had created to do. Blessed are you, Lord our God, Sovereign of the universe, who creates the fruit of the vine."

Papa and Solange said, "Amen."

Philippe continued, "Who made all things exist through His word. Blessed are You, Lord our God, King of the universe, who sanctifies us with his commandments and has been pleased with us. You have longingly and willingly given us Your holy Shabbat as an inheritance, in memory of creation because it is the first day of our holy assemblies, in memory of the exodus from Egypt because You have chosen us and made us holy from all peoples and have willingly and lovingly given us Your holy Shabbat as an inheritance. Blessed are You, who sanctifies Shabbat."

Solange looked over and smiled at me as we all said, "Amen," this time in unison.

Philippe picked up a pitcher of water and explained that we were each to wash our hands in preparation for the Sabbath meal. Into a small basin, he poured water from the pitcher over the top and bottom of his right hand and then the left. Before he wiped his hands dry, he recited, "Blessed are You, Lord our God, King of the universe, who has sanctified us with His commandments." Philippe passed the pitcher to Papa, Papa to Solange, and then she to me as we in turn repeated Philippe's words. When I faltered, Papa chimed in with me.

Philippe smiled warmly at me, indicating with a nod of his head that I was to set the pitcher in the middle of the table, and then said, "The head of the household, your papa, now removes the cover from the challah and recites the last blessing before our meal."

My dear papa rose from his chair, his brown eyes glistening with tears like Solange's had earlier in the day, and recited the blessing as he pulled apart the braided bread, passing it round the table. "Blessed are You, Lord our God, King of the universe, who brings forth bread from the earth." Papa said the blessing again in Hebrew. It flowed eloquently from his tongue, and I realized that Hebrew was the language of his youth, the language of his faith. All those years and I never knew. All those years, out of his sheltering concern for his daughters, he did not tell us he had grown up in a home speaking Hebrew. His eyes full of love met mine, and I felt all the world in this place, all our history brought to life in this singular space, united with my loved ones and to all who came before us in a mystery that I could not explain. I felt perfect peace.

CHAPTER 18

THE WEDDING – SUNDAY, 15 APRIL, 1923

The day arose heavy with low-lying gray clouds and no breaks of blue in the sky. But this day would have no shadow of gloom despite the weather. We had all spent the night at Philippe's lovely home, the better to help with whatever was needed to prepare for the wedding. I had thought Solange might share a room with me, it being her last night as an unmarried woman. She would henceforth share a bed only with her husband. But when we arrived at Philippe's, it was obvious that he and his housekeeper, Mrs. Somers, had prepared with great thoughtfulness a room each for Papa, Solange, and myself. Any thoughts of sharing a room we may have had were quickly put aside for the greater plan.

The bedrooms were luxurious, at least to me who lived so simply. My bed was a large wood 4-poster with a cream silk canopy, and the thick down duvet was so comforting on this cool morning that I propped myself up against the headboard with three fluffy pillows behind me and pulled it up close under my chin. I was in no hurry to rise; it was still early and barely light.

This day of Solange's wedding would be so very special, and here in Philippe's home it was easy to bask in the welcome expansion of our family. And knowing that my niece or nephew would be brought into this house gave me such joy I could not help but smile. I wondered how Philippe would take the news tonight when Solange sprang such a wedding gift upon him. I would venture to guess that he would be both stunned and thrilled.

And Papa would be the happiest *grand-père* in the world! Solange would not share her news with him for another month, since she did not want him to think ill of her. That too made me smile. The presence of a grandchild would most likely be all the coaxing needed to have Papa move in with them.

A knock on my door brought me awake. I must have dozed again as some time had passed and it was daylight out. "Come in, please."

The door opened slowly, and an unknown young woman entered carrying a tray. A morning tea tray. Yes, this was luxury indeed, and I was having all of it. It amazed me that all of my apprehensions and concerns regarding this visit to New York had been dashed away with the news of Solange's wedding and pregnancy. I was also aware that all the attention was focused on Philippe and Solange and not on me, and that significantly added to my ease.

My greatest fear when contemplating my visit to New York had been that Papa and Solange would wage a war to break down my resistance, hoping I might acquiesce to their persistent efforts to persuade me to move to America. It was obvious that was not the case. It was but my own insecurities and perhaps a sense of guilt at living so far from my family that caused me to harbor such intentions on their part.

Another knock at my door that didn't wait for my "come in" found my sister barreling into the room and jumping into bed beside me.

"I don't believe I slept all night and yet I feel extremely wide awake and well rested!" The words poured out of Solange with a wide-eyed look of excitement spread across her face, yet perhaps there was a measure of apprehension also.

"I would think it common that most women would not sleep well the night before their wedding," I replied, hugging her about her shoulders. "Philippe has made me feel so welcome, and his home, Solange—your home as well, I should say—is wonderful in all ways. Does it remind you as it does me of Marseille? The dark wood floors and the paneling of the living and dining rooms? There are more rooms here and they are more spacious, but the high ceilings and the overall ambience of the house is so much like our house in France."

"From the moment I stepped across the threshold of this lovely home, I felt the same, Marie. It is entirely familiar and comforting."

"It must also remind Papa of Marseille. Do you not think he will come live with you once the baby arrives?" I whispered.

"Of course he will! I have no doubt that he will find living here with the three of us and Mrs. Somers much more enjoyable than living alone. And besides, I won't have it any other way." She gave a fierce tug on the duvet and pulled it up to her chin as I had done. And with that, she closed her eyes and drifted off. She obviously needed more sleep after all. I would watch over her for just this little time before all things changed.

A short time later, knocking ensued once more, startling me out of half-sleep. Solange did not stir, so I got carefully out of bed and hurried to the door before more pounding woke her up.

Mrs. Somers, Philippe's congenial friend and housekeeper, stood in the doorway, assuming Solange was with me. In her lovely Irish brogue, she let me know the florist had arrived with the flowers, and she had him waiting downstairs. Solange had asked to be informed of his arrival so she could take stock, making sure all the flowers were accounted for and as she ordered. I assured Mrs. Somers we would be down promptly.

I woke my sister as gently as I could, but still she sat bolt upright. "Oh, I've overslept! What is the time, Marie!"

"It is the time the florist and flowers arrive. Mrs. Somers says he's waiting for you downstairs. I told her you would be right down."

She flung herself from the covers, saying over her shoulder as she hurried out the door, "Meet me downstairs in ten minutes. I want you with me for all things today!"

And so this day of new beginnings began in earnest as I quickly changed into a pair of comfortable trousers and a blouse and ran out the door finishing the buttons. My fingers quickly foraged through my sleep-tousled hair, attempting to coax it into place. Halfway down the stairs I remembered my shoes, but not wanting to go back to my room, I hurried on. I could fly faster in bare feet.

Solange was already talking with the florist, ticking off the first item from a long list of all that was to be accomplished today. As he pointed out each fragrant offering, Mrs. Somers leaned down to inhale the sweet scent of roses, going from one beautiful creation to the next, as though she wanted to ensure all were equally potent. Every bouquet and boutonniere was accounted for. There was also a pink satin pillow decorated with a single white rosebud and two sets of white satin ribbons, and a small white wicker basket filled with pink rose petals.

"Solange, how are the basket and pillow to be used?"

"Philippe's dearest friends have two young children, a son, René, and daughter, Camille, who are so excited about the wedding that I wanted them to feel especially included." She fingered the soft pink petals as she spoke. "Our rings will be tied on the small pillow, and René will carry it down the aisle followed by little Camille strewing the petals before her as Papa and I begin our walk."

Efficient as always, Solange completed the inventory of her flowers and thanked the good florist. He excused himself to see to the finishing touches of the chuppah, and we three began to once again inspect each understated and lovely arrangement. Solange had brought the rings she and Phillipe were to exchange with her when she came downstairs. Mrs. Somers and I admired the matching gold bands. Narrow, simple, and plain with no marks or engravings, adhering to the Jewish tradition, their circled brilliance represented an untroubled life that would flow smoothly. The three of us became misty-eyed contemplating all this day would hold for these two families coming together, Mrs. Somers and I wondering, perhaps, what it meant to each of us as we pondered our own futures.

Watching Mrs. Somers with Solange, I realized these two women, one Irish and the other French, had come seeking from America what they had lost in Europe: a home safe from war and an opportunity to build a family. It was obvious by the sincere exchanges and warm smiles they gave one another that they had grown exceedingly fond of each other. Solange had said that Mrs. Somers had accompanied Phillipe when he immigrated and that she intended to become an American citizen. This stout, robust woman had been Philippe's housekeeper in his home in France. She lost her husband early in their marriage, and they had not the years together to have children. A close family friend recommended Mrs. Somers, recently come from Ireland to France, when Philippe and his wife were looking for someone to help manage their house and help with the care of their two little ones. Loyal, trustworthy, and obviously deeply attached to Philippe, she would be of great assistance to my sister as together they would run this great house with efficiency and goodwill. Their relationship reminded me of my own bond with Sister Agnès, the prioress of the convent, whom I had come to love and who was often my confidante and always my good friend. How fortunate were Solange and I to have these two maternal women in our lives filling that missing piece of our hearts.

The flowers were to be situated in various places both inside and outside the house. The men—Philippe, his good friend and best man Xavier, and Papa— would each wear a simple boutonniere, a white rosebud set on a pillowy sprig of bright green fern. A small box contained the long straight pins that would be used to secure the flowers to the men's tuxedos. Mrs. Somers and I had corsages in much the same fashion but comprised of a small spray of five buds with ferns.

Solange had yet to open the large white box containing her bridal bouquet. She motioned us over as she walked to the chair on which it sat, hesitating for many moments as she gazed down at it.

"I don't know why I should feel nervous at laying my eyes upon my own bouquet. Perhaps because it will make it all seem entirely real."

She slowly lifted the lid, and we gave a chorused sigh as we inhaled the fragrance emanating from the beautiful pristine flowers. These roses were in early bloom with their centers all a pale pink. There were no ferns here, but variegated leaves of green holding exquisitely small clusters of delicate lily of the valley encircled the center's larger roses. Solange did not pick up the bouquet but rather bent down to it, deeply taking in the scent once more before reverently replacing the lid, letting her hands linger on it.

I found myself thanking la Vierge Marie for this brief interlude that allowed the three of us to acknowledge these symbols of the ceremony that would take place in a few hours. I sensed it was important for Solange to have this time with Mrs. Somers and me, the women who formed a loving bond of support about her on this special day and who would always share with her these memories.

"I will take care of the flowers from here, Mademoiselle," said Mrs. Somers, picking up Solange's list from the table. "You need to eat something. Breakfast is laid on the side buffet in the dining room. And then you both should adjourn to your rooms to bathe and dress. There is no need to worry about anything below. All is in order."

Solange still had her hands on her bouquet box, standing as if in a daze. She seemed not to hear Mrs. Somers's directions. I moved to my sister, gently put an arm around her shoulders, and guided her from the room. "We both need some breakfast, Solange."

The chef had prepared the meal early, keeping it warm in the chafing dishes set atop the buffet. He and three assistants had been hired to prepare the lavish dinner for twenty-eight and, according to Mrs. Somers, had been in the kitchen since dawn.

I walked Solange to the dining table and helped her into her chair. She sat quietly, deep in thought, staring at nothing in particular. I felt famished, although I'd had tea and toast a mere two hours ago, but I assumed that Solange had consumed no food as of yet today. I put together two plates with small samplings from each of the warm dishes along with pieces of bread, set them down on the table, and took my place beside her.

She seemed only slightly aware of the food before her but ate with coaxing, an absent look about her eyes. My efficient sister had entered another place. Was this behavior typical of a bride on her wedding day? I thought perhaps so and perhaps even more so of a pregnant bride who had not eaten and was possibly somewhat nauseous.

"Solange, drink your tea and eat a few bites of egg with your bread. You must eat something!"

"What time is it, Marie?" she asked, her fog apparently clearing.

It was almost ten thirty, and the guests would be arriving in a scant two hours. We needed at least that much time to complete our *toilette* and dress. And I was to assist her with it all.

"Time for us to finish eating and prepare for your wedding." We consumed the rest of our food without further comment.

Solange had us take the circuitous route to the stairs, past the doors now open to the back lawn where preparations for the ceremony looked to be complete. The morning was still overcast, but regardless of the threat of rain, optimism reigned. Thirty chairs, fifteen each left and right, had been set up facing the chuppah on the freshly manicured lawn. Strings of white satin were wound round and round the wooden poles that secured the wedding canopy in the ground. Within the strings were set small bundles of pink rosebuds tied with slender pink ribbons. Tall dense shrubs of pungent boxwood enclosed the expansive back lawn. Flowering trees whose blossoms were still falling from the branches, making way for the growth of new leaves, stood tall in each of the four corners of the property. In the flowerbeds under the trees, hyacinths bloomed and tulips were poised to make their appearance. It was an exquisite setting for a wedding.

We stood looking out onto the lawn, and Solange explained how she and Philippe would stand under the chuppah while the rabbi from their synagogue performed the ceremony. They wanted to acknowledge and honor their Jewish heritage with elements signifying tradition and respect. Solange said she also deviated from tradition by planning the cake cutting to take place in the library, where champagne and coffee also would be served. The old and the new—this couple who had survived so much would chart their own way.

Reassured all was progressing in order, she linked her arm through mine, and we proceeded up to our rooms. Once bathed, I would go to her room where we would dress, do our hair, and apply our makeup. Solange told me when I first arrived that she had worked with a very talented local dressmaker who had come highly recommended, and together they designed her wedding gown. She had this same seamstress design a dress for me as well. And although I coaxed her several times, she would not allow me to see either of these creations until we were ready to dress for the ceremony. My curiosity was certainly piqued!

We had decided earlier to wear our hair as we did on every other day. Hers was bobbed in much the same style as my own and had been trimmed a few days ago at her salon. Mine still looked fine in the week since my adventures in the Bastion of Beauty. I thought of how much Katy would enjoy our preparations today. She would be much better at assisting Solange than I, as I knew so little regarding the styling of hair or application of makeup apart from the basics I learned in the ship's salon. But this was my own dear sister, and between us we would do fine. And truth is, we were always uncomplicated though stylish in our dress and *toilette*, never inclined to the ostentatious even when we were younger.

Solange was just lifting our dresses from her closet as I walked into her room. Laying each side by side across her bed, we stood admiring the beautiful gowns. She had chosen for me a lavender satin, the same soft color of first blossoms as they appeared in my fields at home. The exquisite gown was overlaid with delicate lace of the same color. The top of the bodice was lace only, as were the sleeves, which extended halfway down the arms and ended in a wide band of shimmering satin. The cut of the gown was a flowing chemise in style; the front hem looked as though it would extend to my mid-shin, then rounding down on the sides with the back hem ending almost to the floor. I could not wait to feel the cool richness of the material against my skin.

"Thank you, Solange. It is beautiful. I will feel like a princess next to my queen." Feeling tears coming to my eyes, I said quickly, "Let's get you dressed first." She had on her stockings, undergarments, and slip, and as she raised her arms, I slid her exquisite gown over her head and down her body.

Her gown was the same chemise style and the fabric the very palest blush of rose-pink satin with matching lace overlay. The neckline was scalloped lace and formed a heart-shaped pattern lying softly against her chest. The lace sleeves were slightly gathered, ending just at her elbows, the scalloped ends matching the bodice of the dress. Her front hem reached nearly to the floor before rounding and lengthening to the back, which fell into a lovely short train of the lace overlay.

I turned her round and round as we admired her reflection in her tall mirror. She had chosen the perfect color for her dark eyes and hair. She then helped me on with my dress and together we gazed, somewhat amazed and thoroughly delighted, at our images before sitting at her vanity bench to attend to our hair and makeup. She wore as little makeup as I did; however, we did add a spot more rouge to our cheeks and a thorough coating of lip color in a shade lighter than what we applied to our cheeks. With an application of mascara to our lashes, our faces reflected all the happiness we felt.

Solange had chosen to wear a short veil made of the same exquisite lace covering her gown. The veil was attached to a pencil-thin silver headband with combs that fit securely into her hair. She decided she did not want to have to fuss with gloves when they exchanged their rings and had the night before filed and polished her nails.

"One more accessory and I am ready!" She took from her vanity table a narrow black leather box and opened it to reveal a slender diamond bracelet.

"It is a Jewish tradition that the groom give the bride something of value. In a traditional Jewish wedding, the groom would present this during the ceremony. But Philippe gave his gift to me the night I accepted his proposal. Would you work the clasp for me?" I placed the glimmering stones round her delicate wrist. The fit was perfect, the brilliant diamonds lying just below the fine bones of her wrist.

"What is the time now?" she asked, walking to the closet and returning with our shoes. I was stunned as she held forth beautiful heels of peau de soie dyed to perfectly match the color of our gowns.

"It is just after noon," I said, putting the elegant shoes on my stockinged feet. "Your guests should be arriving shortly." I watched a look of nervousness pass across her face. "How are you feeling, Solange?"

"Most of our guests are friends of Philippe's that I am coming to know also. I have met them all, including their wives and children, and find them to be quite nice. We often go to dinner or the theatre with one or more of the couples.

"Papa invited a few of his acquaintances as well, and Oncle Antoine told Papa he would be attending. You will find our uncle a younger and livelier version of Papa. He still has never married after abandoning his family in France, and it is never talked about. I do not know if the marriage was ever officially dissolved. He seems as immersed in his shipping enterprise here in America as Papa always was with his in France. They spend much time together, and I am very glad that Papa has his brother and friends to keep him engaged in life."

She paused, sighing once before continuing, "I know I am avoiding your question, Marie. How I feel is overwhelmed by all the changes that are about to take place. Marriage and moving to Philippe's estate would be change enough by itself, but now with a baby coming along as well, that only you and I know about, I feel such a staggering sense of having to make it right for everyone. I somehow feel it is my responsibility to mesh us all together seamlessly into one family, living together in harmony for the rest of our lives. What if I cannot do it? What if it cannot be done? And what if I do not make a fit wife and mother?" Tears welled at the edges of her eyes.

"No crying, Solange! We don't have time to redo our faces," I said with a smile and a setting aside of my own emotions. "You will have a husband who adores you, who follows your every move with love in his eyes. You are bringing light and joy to this man, to this house. Even Mrs. Somers is ecstatic with love for you. You are not going into this new venture alone. If you are to truly be a family, you must allow others to tend to you as well. I realize all your life you have been the primary caretaker of myself and even Papa. And how very wonderfully you fulfilled that role. But do not deprive your husband of fulfilling his role as your caring and dutiful husband and partner. You are one half of a whole couple, and soon you will have this little one who will have an attentive father and a loving and capable mother.

"Think only on the joy of this day, Solange. Let that be your gift to yourself. Let yourself receive it. And you will not be taking care of tomorrow alone. Tomorrow will take care of itself, as they say." With those words, I hugged her as she nodded and wiped her eyes with the *mouchoir* I gave her to carry, in case there were tears during the ceremony.

During the days leading up to the wedding, before I settled into my bed each evening, I had taken the time to lovingly sew and embroider the delicate wedding handkerchief with her new initials surrounded by an array of small pink rosebuds. I made a nearly identical one for myself to carry, one with my own initials, *M. D.*, including a *C* just after. Anyone looking even closely at the *mouchoir* would assume the *C* was but a fine line of vivid green embroidery, the curled stem of a rose. But I would be this day and during this visit with my family my true self, Marie Durant Chagall.

The windows of Solange's room provided a fine view out over the lawn, and we now stood watching guests arriving, greeting one other with laughter. "You see the happiness that is created here today? These friends of Philippe's I'm sure are thrilled to see his joy, thrilled that he has made such a wonderful match. And Papa and I love Philippe. There is nothing here today that does not bode well for a wonderful tomorrow."

"When did you become so wise as to the ways of marriage and family, my little sister?" she teased.

With the mood lightening, I said, "I read all of those fanciful romantic novels and magazine articles you sent me. Quite informative, I must say." I squeezed her hands and added, "Remain here at the windows, enjoying the scene below of your beautiful wedding venue for a few more minutes as you take deep, happy breaths. I will go down and check with Mrs. Somers to confirm that all is on schedule."

"Marie, look! There is Philippe! That wonderful man is to be my husband. How could I be anything but happy?"

I left her dabbing her eyes once again but with a look of enchantment upon her face as she stood gazing down at her handsome groom, one hand gently laid across her middle. Soon Papa would deliver her into the hands of Phillipe. I just needed to keep both of us in one piece a little while longer.

Mrs. Somers was at the bottom of the stairs talking with Papa. I noted they were close in age and briefly wondered if they might become friends. How handsome they both looked in their finery. I had never before seen Papa dressed in a tuxedo, and as he turned to watch me descend the staircase, I quite literally caught my breath at how dignified and attractive a man he was. Once again I felt thankful I had overcome my fears and doubts and had come to share this day with those I loved most.

"Oh my, and here is my beautiful youngest daughter," Papa said as I reached them. "You are stunning, my dear!"

"Thank you, Papa. You cut quite a dashing figure yourself. Solange is in her gown and is ready for the ceremony."

Mrs. Somers gave me a tight hug, whispering in my ear how happy she was that I was with the family today. She then gave both Papa and me final instructions. He was to remain there at the bottom of the stairs, and I was to have Solange come down to him at ten minutes to one. Together, Solange and Papa would then wait just inside the doors leading to the lawn, where the violinist would be waiting for her nod that the ceremony was to begin. As the musician began the music, I would walk down the aisle followed by the ring bearer and the flower girl, and the three of us would stand at the front on the left side of the chuppah with Phillipe and his best man on the right. The wedding processional would begin as we all awaited Papa and Solange. Assuring Mrs. Somers we both knew our roles, I hurried back to the bride, who was still watching her wedding unfold before her through the windows of her room.

True to Mrs. Somers's instructions, at twelve fifty I told Solange it was time. With a tentative smile on her lips, we held hands tightly, each taking a deep breath. I then followed her to the top of the stairs.

The French doors to the garden were swung wide open, and through them and the adjacent windows one could see the guests all seated in eager anticipation. The air remained heavy and close, the strong fragrance of roses wafting even into the house, and the beautiful ambience of all I looked upon gave the setting a fairytale quality. The ribbons of the wedding canopy were blowing gently in the breeze as were the ends of the tallit, the prayer shawl Philippe wore about his shoulders. I guessed his yarmulke was pinned securely to his hair, as it remained steadfast atop his head. Philippe kept glancing expectantly at the door, eagerly anticipating the emergence of his betrothed.

Papa was waiting expectantly at the foot of the stairs, and his eyes found his daughter as she appeared at the top. He gasped and took hold of the handrail to steady himself, overcome at the sight of this exquisite bride, his own Solange. This oldest daughter who had made our home a place of efficiency, joy, and solace all those years in Marseille. The daughter who seamlessly and gracefully arranged the dinner soirees for Papa's clients and friends, and the daughter who became his trusted accomplice in business. She had willingly accompanied Papa to this new land, and he would now accompany her as she moved into her new life. This beautiful woman whom we both loved and admired was today forging her own journey into a future with a man we all held in high esteem. The man who was the father of her child. I watched in awe as my beloved sister stepped confidently down the stairs to take the arm of our papa.

Although the sky remained veiled, the air humid and warm suffused with the smell of the gardens and flowers, the rain seemed held at bay and hopefully so for the duration of the ceremony.

We stood ready in our places, just inside the open doors. Solange gave the attentive violinist her nod and the processional music began. With measured steps, I made my way to the front where I would give witness next to Solange as her maid of honor. Reaching the chuppah, I turned and watched the children with their rings and rose petals make their way down the aisle, accompanied by the single violin playing a song that was not familiar to me. The occasional atonal notes of what was possibly an ancient melody suited the mood perfectly.

The violinist stopped and looked to where Solange and Papa were waiting. The guests all turned as one and stood, acknowledging the beautiful bride accompanied by her proud father. The music began again, a song that seemed to sing of hope and happiness, and Papa began the walk to escort his daughter to her groom. She looked strong and determined, her head held high with eyes looking forward, gazing only upon Philippe as he awaited her under the marriage canopy. Philippe wiped once at his own eyes as he beheld Solange, and in a show of solidarity with his bride, he too held his head high, and with love and pride accepted his betrothed from her beloved papa.

The rabbi's words were in English with short intermittent passages in Hebrew. Young René, holding the gold rings, stood attentive and serious throughout the short service, ready at his cue to present them to the rabbi for his blessing. With a pang of my heart, I realized this dark-haired child reminded me much of Félix and that I missed him terribly. It would be many weeks before I was home again, and I quickly reminded myself with some lingering sense of sadness, as I had with Solange earlier, that this day was the only one that needed attending to at this moment.

With a look from the rabbi, the young ring bearer presented the pillow from which the rings were removed. The rabbi led Solange and Philippe in the words to secure their union, and they placed the rings onto one another's waiting fingers. After the final blessing in Hebrew, Philippe gathered his wife into himself for a kiss.

The violinist struck up what sounded like a jubilant gypsy folk song, and we all stood and applauded the newly wedded couple. Solange and Philippe were both beaming as they made their way back down the aisle, stepping together across the threshold of their home. As if heaven were bestowing its own blessing, light drops of rain began to kiss the tops of our heads. A loud clap of thunder, perhaps applause too from the heavens, sounded in the near distance. We all made our way into the house where servers awaited the guests with crystal flutes of bubbling champagne.

Everyone had an opportunity to chat and say a few words to the couple before being guided into the dining room for the wedding dinner. I kept a close eye on Solange and was relieved to see her engaged with her guests, smiling as she affectionately greeted those who came to celebrate their happiness. I also noted that she and Philippe stood close to one another, Solange's arm linked into his as though they were really one body. As long as these two held onto each other, this day would continue to find them both enjoying themselves. Mrs. Somers and I exchanged smiles frequently, and I was so pleased to see that she was an honored guest today, with no other duties than to enjoy the remainder of the festivities, now that the ceremony was completed.

The elegantly laid table gave evidence once again to Solange's superb sense of style. The thin silk cloth gracing the formal table was a very deep shade of rose pink that beautifully complemented Solange's gown. Small clusters of white rosebuds were scattered down the middle of the table, accented with fronds of fern, and tall crystal candelabras with white candles were placed among the flowers. I was touched that among the candelabras Solange had placed the lovely small *bougeoirs* from Henri. The flame of every candle, both short and tall, was reflected in the mirrors on the four walls of the spacious room, and although the skies outside were growing dark and threatening, this room was aglow in candlelight. My sister had attended to every detail. One look at Philippe told me he too was proud of his wife's careful and loving hand in creating such a perfect day for both them and their guests.

Philippe directed Papa to sit at the head of the table, representing all of the parents: Philippe's maman and papa, Solange's mother, and my own who were no longer among us but were to be remembered and honored today. Solange and Philippe sat to Papa's right with Mrs. Somers and I to Papa's left, just across from them. The guests, ten couples and the two children, sat where they desired around the table as the young, liveried servers began to pour the first of many fine wines from Philippe's well-stocked cellar. I suddenly realized that Oncle Antoine had not made an appearance. I had sincerely looked forward to meeting this mysterious relative and would have to ask Papa later of his absence.

As in France, the meal consisted of many courses, the food French and rich, accompanied by lively conversation. All was consumed with much time between dishes to allow for the many toasts that were forthcoming. As the food and wine was enjoyed at a leisurely pace, these toasts by the gentlemen at the table became longer, more eloquent, and gave cause for both laughter and tears.

Solange, while obviously enjoying herself, drank little wine and nibbled only a few bites from each course. I had meant to ask days ago if she was, perhaps, finding herself nauseous at times. She might also be contemplating sharing with her husband later this evening that shortly their new family of two would be three. Although she assured me Philippe would be overjoyed, it would still most likely be a daunting surprise on one's wedding night. But I caught her eye now and then, she very much aware that I was keeping watch on her, and she assured me with a soft smile that, indeed, she was well.

As I gazed round the table, observing the joy reflected in each face, I was overcome with conflicting emotions. Feelings of both outrage and sorrow gripped me so tightly I thought I might explode in anger or dissolve in a pool of tears. What might have been, what would have been had the war not torn us all apart, rupturing the very soul of our lives? Here I sat among loving people, including my own precious family, and yet I would never be a part of this world. Since arriving, I had been surprised by the atmosphere of general goodwill among people everywhere I went. I was stung and amazed that so much was new or under construction, evidence of affluence and prosperity.

I tried and failed to not compare the tall, sleek facades of downtown New York City with the devastation still evident in Verdun, the French citizens still struggling toward renewal in the aftermath of the war. Our meager attempts to forage optimism with every wagon and truckload of concrete and charred wood that we hauled away from the bombed edifices of the town were carefully tended. Each time ground was cleared in hopes of a new building begun or a site repaired that might again house a shop or café, we believed it a sign that our recovery was continuing, that these efforts gave evidence of life righting itself again. The war was past, never to wreak its havoc again, and we somehow continued to pull hope up from our souls.

But there was so little money or help from the government. Everything was in short supply and difficult or impossible to find. It was left to us, the local populace, to devise and execute our own recovery, searching for materials, bricks, mortar, lumber, nails, and all that was desperately needed to patch the trappings of life back together.

Here in America, however, in this large, vibrant city, there was no carnage, no neighborhoods or entire towns shelled and bombed into oblivion. There was no evidence that the cruelest war in the history of mankind had taken place merely an ocean away. I saw only an almost frenetic energy everyplace I went. Everywhere you looked people seemed in a hurry, on their way to something of great importance and seemingly oblivious to the needs of those they had fought beside such a short time ago. Theirs was *la belle vie*, the good life.

Were people here not aware of the stagnation that permeated much of Europe? Yes, many countries, including America, had helped us to remain free, but what now of the cost, confusion, and worry as a continent struggled in these years after so much conflict? Allies and enemies came and killed and maimed, leaving us stripped and bare among the ashes of our loss. And in that moment, just for a breath, I felt indignant and isolated from those I sat in company with. All present at this table had fled their countries to come here and bask in peace and prosperity while those back in their homelands were left to struggle. Me. They all left me.

But I would never leave France. I would go to Paris to study and return to Meuse stronger and more capable than ever, determined to contribute and foster strength and health in all ways to forge a bright future. I would not go lightly tripping through life believing we had nothing to fear. I knew life wasn't just or fair but often cruel. Humans so cruel to one another that though we remained alive the essences of so many souls were forever damaged.

Only here in Phillipe's home did there seem to be a measure of times remembered. Of a slower pace, as if embracing what was lost and what was left behind. Phillipe and I were the two who had been witness to the horror of the battlefields and the resultant carnage. The utter chaos in the aftermath of the war, countries decimated and societies ripped apart. He lost his young family, and his sorrow must be so very deep. He was regaining his life footing by creating himself anew with a new family in a new country.

Philippe and I hadn't spoken of our mutual experiences, but I saw his grief and shared the same. It was like no other and beyond explanation. I knew Solange had told him my story as she had told me his, and I felt a kindred compassion that instantly drew him to my heart. I also knew it most likely that while he loved Solange deeply and would be a wonderful husband and father, there would be a piece of him inaccessible to anyone else. There were many of us, I was sure, that would live out their lives hoping one day, miraculously, that the unspeakable memories would somehow expunge themselves forever from our consciousness. But we would go on day-to-day, year-to-year throughout our lives, making peace as best we could.

I was lost in my emotional reverie for perhaps many minutes. I knew I must attempt to calm myself, stilling my hands that had been running themselves over and over across my lap. My napkin had fallen to the floor, but I dared not move to pick it up for fear of completely falling apart and fleeing the room. I slowed my breathing, taking small sips of water, and attempted with all my forbearance to bring myself back to the present moment.

I did not want my feelings obvious in any way and certainly did not want to tarnish the resounding joy for my family and Philippe. This wedding proved that hope could be made manifest and new life was possible, and I was not to judge how others chose to find their peace. My beloved family was here now, safe and secure in this land they had chosen as home. My family in Meuse was as dear to me and much more in need of what I had to offer, and that was where I was longing to return. Where I would return.

At half past five, Solange and Philippe left the table. Fifteen minutes later, the rest of us were directed into the library, where the cake was to be served. I thought how those fifteen minutes had been their first alone as man and wife and was sure they enjoyed even that brief respite from the day's events. I certainly would have welcomed fifteen minutes to myself. A semblance of control had eased back into my mind and body, and I was fully back to the present as we all moved into the other room.

As we entered the library, the couple was standing behind a stunning three-tiered wedding cake positioned upon the long reading table. The cake was decorated in white icing and topped with pink sugared roses. Bottles of champagne, half-filled glasses, stacks of small crystal plates, silver forks, and napkins were arranged on either side of it. Hot coffee and tea in tall silver urns with china cups, spoons, cream, and sugar waited on a side table.

We all gathered in front of the cake, and Philippe invited each guest to take a glass of champagne. Looking quite serious, he met the eyes of each person, saying, "My wife Solange and I would like to thank each one of you for sharing this most special day with us."

As we each lifted our glass, many responded with a hearty, "*Santé, bonheur, et prospérité!*"

One by one, Philippe handed Solange the crystal plates as she cut pieces of the delicate white cake filled with a chocolate cream center and handed them to her guests. The confection was divine, not too sweet, with delicate hints of cherry that went well with a second glass of champagne.

Philippe soon thereafter led Solange to their front door where they gave each guest a personal and sincere adieu as they departed. Papa and I stayed but a few minutes after the last guests had gone before Benito drove us back to the apartment. I assumed that shortly after enjoying her piece of cake Mrs. Somers had taken charge once again of her kitchen, and when that was put in order, she too would retire.

Exhaustion made me numb and wanting only to drop into oblivious sleep. I sensed Papa felt the same. We exchanged no words on the way home but several times gently touched each other's hand for a few seconds. We both needed the deep sleep of those who had held themselves together for the sake of those they loved.

The only voice in my mind as I drifted off that night was a prayer to la Vierge Marie that my new brother and much-loved sister would rest peacefully in joy, their secret tucked between them to be shared when they were ready.

CHAPTER 19

DISCUSSIONS WITH PAPA – APRIL 1923

Although I slept late the next morning, I arose before Papa. I was grateful for this time alone to settle my thoughts from yesterday's events and take measure of my own emotions. I wanted to be completely present with him, these being our first moments together, just the two of us.

Taking the teapot to the dining table, I could not but think the apartment seemed too quiet, as if it were already lamenting the loss of Solange's presence. I felt her absence as well and wondered how it might affect Papa. Sipping my tea, I surveyed the home from where I sat, small rooms with mostly bare white walls and a sparse assortment of furniture that was obviously of poor quality and construction—mismatched, random pieces so unlike what Solange preferred. She always wanted her environment to exude warmth and good taste. A few color-filled paintings I had done in Marseille hung on the walls, attempting to relieve the stark, barren look about the place. Solange's lively essence had created the illusion of stylish ambience that made this small apartment a home.

I saw little of the furniture from Marseille. When I asked Solange about this, she replied that although they did ship most of the pieces to New York—the tables, chairs, beds, armoires, and *chiffoniers* that had graced our home—nearly all were too large for the apartment. They were storing the furniture and other household belongings in Oncle Antoine's warehouse at the harbor. The intent had been to live in this modest space while becoming familiar with New York, choosing after some time an area of the city where they might want to purchase a home. However, her relationship with Philippe had progressed quickly from friendship to engagement, and talk of her and Papa relocating was put aside, knowing Solange would move into Phillipe's home. Solange's intention now, as Papa had suggested, was to place most of the furniture from Marseille into her and Philippe's home, while Papa mentioned repeatedly that he was perfectly content to remain here. And I believed that to be completely true on his part. However, that was before we had a baby coming.

Papa had traveled so much to so many destinations throughout our growing up, and I assumed sleeping aboard any one of his ships was a rustic affair, considerably close and sparse and furnished with only the rudiments of comfort. But he never complained about any aspects of life aboard ship; it most likely had not bothered him in the least. He allowed Solange and me to decorate our spacious home in Marseille to our liking, assuring us it was also to his liking. He certainly wanted his house to reflect well upon the clients that almost weekly sat round our large dining table as they ate and drank and talked of business.

As I sat alone with these thoughts, Papa quite literally burst into the room, dressed and spruced for the day.

"Did you sleep well, Marie?" he asked, pouring himself a cup of tea and looking quite pleased with life.

"I did, and you certainly look as though you did. You appear ready for the day, Papa. Do you have an appointment this morning?" Papa's countenance surprised me. It radiated pure happiness and also some sense of relief, stemming, I assumed, from the fact that the wedding had gone so well and Solange was now married and settled.

"As a matter of fact, I do. I have plans to spend the day with my youngest daughter, showing her all of my neighborhood haunts and how I spend my days. And we are certainly going to pay a visit to Antoine, to hear why he was absent from the wedding. Usually when he doesn't make a promised appearance he at least rings later with an excuse he calls a reason."

We talked as I made some toast and eggs and another pot of tea. I had been longing to spend time alone with him, and this morning provided us with the quiet and leisure to do so.

"Why do you think Oncle Antoine was unable to attend the wedding?"

"He is someone who always says yes to an invitation to avoid having to say no and then does what is convenient or most comfortable for him when the time comes. My guess is that however much he wanted to be there, any group of persons over the count of three causes him distress. And weddings are not an eagerly anticipated event for a longtime single man." Papa kept eating as he spoke and really seemed, on the whole, quite unconcerned about Antoine. I was glad we were going to seek him out today, as I wanted to see for myself if this mysterious and elusive uncle actually existed.

"I keep thinking, Papa, about all of us. So much has happened to our family since those placid days in Marseille before the war. And the changes seem to have all been to everyone's benefit. Are you content here in America?"

Papa contemplated that for a moment. "As content as an old Frenchman can be who leaves his country, his home, a beloved daughter . . . and who daily misses her. But I know absolutely that immigrating here was for the best. The wedding yesterday was testament to that good decision. Although France is my heart, it was unable to beat freely. My greatest joy here is the freedom to embrace our culture and faith and to move about life without worry of what might become of us. Of course, there is prejudice here, as there is everywhere, toward anyone perceived to be different than oneself, but I am finding most people here attempt to be tolerant and allow one another to do as they wish, giving each other a wide berth. That was not the case in much of Europe during and after the war. I still very strongly believe another war will be fought, and once again countries, including France, will find their citizens at risk and none more so than the Jews. You must continue to adhere to your promise, Marie, that you will never divulge that you are a Chagall but continue always to live as a Durant," he said with a piercing look, as if to forge it into my mind this was to be so.

"In France, I do think of myself as a Durant, and it seems very natural not allowing myself to think any other way. I have seriously taken to heart your caution. It is, though, amazing to me that here you, who were always so reticent about displaying any religious practice, seem now to have completely embraced your heritage. I would be lying to you if I said I did not envy that part of your life. I was the one who always begged that we celebrate our holy days and follow our customs, and it is ironic that now I am the only one not doing so. But since it is not an option for me in Meuse, I do not desire it anymore. Perhaps my need for the spiritual has been somewhat filled by the presence of the Sisters and their sure reliance on their Catholic rituals. And I seem to have made a connection to the Virgin Mary. Do you think that is odd of me, Papa?"

"Absolutely not. We are all spiritual beings, and we all pray to the same god, whether we acknowledge it or not. We seek out what meets our needs or allow what becomes familiar to satisfy our spirit. I am greatly relieved that you have found friends and other sisters among those at the convent."

He paused and leaned toward me. "And what is worrying you, Marie? I see it moving around the edges of your mind."

His question was so unexpected my breath caught in my throat. I took a long moment before answering. "I am sincerely glad you saw this concern in me and have asked about it. I was not sure how to bring up what is consuming my thoughts of late. I need your counsel regarding a rather delicate situation that keeps me awake at night.

"You know of Henri and how he has been my kind benefactor since my first difficult days in Meuse. He has become, like the Sisters, a very dear and congenial friend."

"Oui. Solange and I have spoken often of Henri and the Sisters and their kindnesses to you. And for that we are most grateful. Has something changed in that regard to cause you concern?"

"Henri tells me, Papa, that I have become more to him than a friend. Before I left for New York, he presented me with two proposals. The first was an offer to use the vacant clinic room attached to the house he just purchased. The home belonged to a physician who lived and practiced there, but he left to serve in the war and never returned. Henri contacted the doctor's family and learned sadly that the young man died from wounds he sustained, and the family was more than willing to sell to Henri. The house is less than a five-minute walk from the convent and lies between my home and Verdun. The location and the large room are more than ideal and perfect for caring for patients."

"And isn't that what you want? A clinic space in which to practice? It sounds an excellent situation, but I can see you obviously have reservations about the arrangement."

"Yes, I have grave reservations, because Henri's first proposal came with a second. He has asked me to marry him. He assured me that the offer of the clinic was not tied to becoming his wife, although, while that may be true, I know he hopes very much I will accept both proposals. It was as if Henri meant to tempt me with the one, knowing how enticing the clinic would be, hoping his second proposal might then seem a palatable addition."

"Did you and Henri discuss these offers of his and did he know of your suspicions regarding his intentions?"

"I was quite distraught and, as I have frequently done in the past, sought advice from Sister Agnès. She basically told me to be honest with Henri, to not make any rash judgement as to his intentions, and to trust myself to make wise decisions. So, before I left I accepted Henri's offer to use the clinic space, for which he would receive a percent of my monies earned, but that I could not at this time accept his proposal of marriage. That I needed six months in the clinic, giving us ample opportunity see each other often, before I would even consider marriage."

There, I had shared all of it. I sat back with a great sigh, keeping my eyes looking into the swirling waters of my now cold tea that I had been stirring furiously as I related all this to Papa.

"He sounds like a compassionate banker who knows how to present what is certainly in his own best interests while making the proposal as enticing to the customer as possible." I saw that Papa wasn't kindly disposed to this talk of marriage to Henri. I needed to tell him what hadn't yet been said.

"And Papa, he knew Maman."

A look of startled puzzlement froze on his face. "Your maman? How can that be? How could he possibly have known your maman?"

Steeling myself, I told him the story. How Henri met Maman when they were both youngsters, and he had seen her only occasionally during summers when he came to the house with his uncle, my house now, to sell or barter with Grand-Mère. That Henri had been greatly taken—infatuated, I believe—with Maman, her light spirit and loveliness being so different from his own more reserved nature. That it was he who kept up the house all those many years as a testament to the memory of his childhood friend.

Papa gazed into his own teacup before saying, "So now I too understand his attentiveness to you and the house. It seemed so curious—the house so well looked after when you arrived and his always seeming to be there when you needed assistance. I cannot deny that after Solange visited you and felt Henri was an honest and well-intentioned man I was greatly relieved that you had someone who seemed to be looking out for you."

Looking into Papa's eyes, I said, "He assures me that his fondness for me has nothing to do with Maman but that he loves me for myself."

"I think it more likely a complicated set of feelings and intentions on his part and hardly altogether separate from his long-ago feelings for your maman."

"I don't know what to think or feel toward him beyond gratitude. A sense of obligation, perhaps, after all he has done to be helpful. And possibly something more that I cannot define. It may be love but how am I to know? I have never experienced it with any man before."

"Does passion enter into any of your feelings for this man?" Papa asked.

"Passion? I have no idea. I doubt I would know passion if it stood directly before me."

"Yes, you would know, my dear. It does not frequently occur, but when it does present itself it is demanding, overpowering, and makes the fool of many of us." His gaze drifted out the window, as if remembering. "It can also make for great love, Marie."

"It sounds altogether frightful. I am certain that is not in the least what I feel for Henri. He is so familiar and reliable as well as exasperating sometimes. And most of the time I feel only thankful and occasionally frustrated by all of his plans and ideas regarding what I should or should not do." I smiled. "Sounds rather more like a papa than a potential husband, does it not?"

"Many in a marriage, one or both of the persons, often want exactly what you just described: a marriage with someone familiar and reliable. And many settle for that because they have never experienced passion."

Feeling somewhat uncomfortable with our conversation and a great need to get up and move about, I stood and walked over to the window, looking down on the street below as people bustled about their day under a morning sky, blue and brilliant.

"I am not seeking any relationship with any man. I have absolutely no feelings of need or longing for a husband." I paused before sharing further. Barely speaking the words aloud, I went on, "I have wondered often if perhaps I am broken from the war—that I might be unable to feel such desires." This was the first time I had given voice to these thoughts, and saying the words were easier with my back to Papa.

"Not desiring marriage or an intimate relationship does not equate to brokenness, my dear. I felt the same when Solange's maman passed—no need or desire for another companion or wife. And then, unexpectedly I met your mother and there it was, unannounced and urgent."

"What was?" I asked, wanting him to go on.

"Passion. The overwhelming necessity to be in the presence of that person. A drive toward union so strong it dislocates all the senses and defies logic. It was maddening, the strength of it. And the joy of it was beyond anything known to me before. There is certainly something to be said for the comfortable and convenient, but there are no words to describe a love lit by passion. Neither is easy and both require you give more of yourself than you ever thought possible."

Papa's words were frightening to me. I had never heard him talk of such things as love and passion, and I could not ever believe myself caught up in such a turmoil of emotion. "I have no intentions of falling into either experience, Papa! What a lot of trouble it all sounds."

"Oh yes, loving is a lot of trouble, but not loving is little better than dying by lonely degrees each day."

I moved back to the table, exasperated by this talk, and began quickly clearing the dishes to the kitchen. I washed them in hot soapy water and laid them to the side to dry. Papa followed me and, taking up a towel, began to dry the plates and cups, after which we returned to the table.

After some moments of silence, I said, "So you have not given me your opinion regarding Henri's proposals."

"I can only counsel that after much contemplation on your part you choose what is truly right for you, Marie. You said he was agreeable to rent you his space without marrying him, and that is what you told him you wanted. If that continues to be your truth after six months, then that is what you must convey to him. Never acquiesce to another's wishes for yourself unless they are your own desires as well. And you are doing fine seeking your own answers."

"That is largely what Sister Agnès told me. Having both of you give me permission not to accept Henri's second proposal makes it easier to accept the first and forge ahead with my plans for the clinic."

"That would seem to be your desire and passion, dear: your nursing and opening your door to patients. I must say, though, that while I do not think this man is the one to stir you to strong emotions of love or passion, do not close off your heart to the possibility of either. We seldom get to choose whom to love or what evokes our passions. Rather they affix themselves to our hearts with a fierce desire that we are seldom prepared for. But I would say that if you are content with the plans you are making, then you have my blessing. Remember to trust your own good judgement and to have courage in all things, *ma chère*."

"I am certainly excited about opening and operating the clinic. Hopefully any day now a letter will arrive from the hospital in Paris granting my request to study there. And the last hurdle to overcome will be finding a physician to oversee my treatment and care of patients. By first going back to la Pitié-Salpêtrière and obtaining my Certificate of Nursing, I hope to convince and assure the physician in Verdun that I am highly qualified and capable of assisting him in his practice as well as managing my own."

"*Mon Dieu!* How forgetful of me, Marie. Please forgive me," he said, pulling from his pocket a letter. "Saturday's late mail was here last evening when we returned from the wedding and you had already gone to bed when I saw it."

It was the long-awaited letter from la Pitié-Salpêtrière. I stood up from my chair, took it from Papa's hand, and looked at it for many moments before carefully opening the envelope. I continued standing as I read it quickly through a first time and then sat as I read it again, slowly, word for welcomed word.

• • •

5 April 1923

Mlle Marie Durant

C/o M Michel Chagall

152nd Street and Riverside Drive - #25

New York City, New York

United States of America

Dear Mademoiselle Durant,

We have received your request to further your nursing studies at l'Hôpital universitaire Pitié-Salpêtrière for a period of six weeks. We have reviewed your records from your initial training here during March and April of 1916, your service during the war in Verdun, and your recovery here and continued service as a hospital floor and surgical nurse from December 1916 through December 1918.

You have an outstanding record of nursing service, and after a thorough review of your file by our committee of physicians and nurse instructors, we are happy to offer you a six-week program of instruction, to include mandatory participation in grand rounds and assisting physicians in the surgery theatre.

I shall meet with you in my office on 27 April at 09:00 to discuss your courses of study and your schedule during the period of training. We have also noted your request to attend specific classes and surgeries and will make every attempt to fit that into what will be a very intense program. At the end of the six weeks, if you feel you are adequately prepared, you may sit for your Certificate of Nursing exams on Friday morning, 8 June.

We look forward to having you continue your nursing instruction here at l'Hôpital universitaire Pitié-Salpêtrière.

Cordially,

Sister Jeanne-Claude

Sister Jeanne-Claude

Registrar of Nursing

• • •

Relief flooded my senses, followed by a swell of expectation. My plans were coming to fruition, and I could move forward with purpose and intent.

"Marie, *ma chérie*, what is your news?"

"Good news, Papa. Great news! I have been accepted at l'Hôpital de la Pitié-Salpêtrière! I am so stunned I can hardly think. I do know I will need to send Henri a telegram letting him and the Sisters know that indeed I will be in Paris until early June, and reminding him once again that I want to rent the space. I cannot believe you had this in your pocket all this morning."

"Again, my sincere apologies in addition to my congratulations. I am so pleased for you, my dear! And once you return to France and your clinic, is it fully equipped and ready for patients?"

"Actually, the clinic is completely empty other than a plinth table, numerous empty drawers, and an apothecary cabinet full of stale, half-filled jars. The doctor must have taken everything with him, although I can't imagine how or why. I was told he served in field hospitals, as I did. I think a better explanation is that he boxed it all up and sent it to his family for safekeeping, as though he had a premonition he wouldn't be returning."

"Since you will be needing supplies, equipment, medicines, and such, I would very much like to provide the monies for you to purchase whatever you need to make your clinic all you hope for your patients. I have several physician friends here with whom I have shared your story. They are most eager to meet you and assist in what way they can. They would also be able to provide you with the names of companies and suppliers where they purchase their own equipment and whatever else one puts into a clinic," Papa said with a smile.

"Oh, Papa! That is wonderfully generous of you! I was hoping to speak with you about the clinic and what would be needed, and here you are offering your assistance. When can you set up a time to talk with these friends of yours? I am sure they have catalogues that I might look through, and perhaps they would afford me the benefit of perusing their medical offices to see what they have stocked."

Ah, I was greatly relieved that we had moved on to the comfortable topic of medicine and away from matters of the heart. My letter of acceptance appeared at the perfect time. And how exciting that Papa was willing to help fulfill my passion—yes, my *passion*—to create a truly first-rate clinic. Having up-to-date medical provisions should also reassure and hopefully help to further convince a physician of the benefits of entering into a collaborative arrangement with me.

"I can call them this morning, and I am sure we can visit their offices later this week. Thank you for letting me be a part of your world that I have known very little about. It will give me the greatest pleasure to listen as you talk to them about your plans." Papa seemed almost as excited as I was.

"And now, I have one more question to ask. I realize it is delicate in nature, but I find I must, as you are so constantly in my thoughts, and I have spent much time worrying over your welfare.

"Are you well, Marie? Did going to Meuse allow you the solitude you needed and the time to heal and find yourself again?" he asked gently.

I looked into his caring eyes and told him honestly, "Yes, Papa. Going to the house in Meuse was the most expedient thing I could have done, given my state of mind. The quiet of the setting, the healing fields of lavender, the kindness of the people I have come to know, and even knowing that my own maman and grand-mère lived there before me provided a sense of tranquility and well-being. I feel as though my family is there still, nurturing me as we share the home together that is now truly mine. I am deeply grateful to you for telling me of this gift from Maman and in your own quiet but decisive way prompting me to have the courage to see if it would be a place I could be. And yes, it is my home now and where I am most content and want to be. I plan to always remain in France but certainly will continue to visit our family here."

Papa took me in his arms and gave me several hearty pats on the back, perhaps so I might not see what I suspected, that there were tears in his eyes as there were in my own.

"Good, that is what I hoped to hear. That is what I have observed since your arrival, but I needed to hear you speak it as well. I'm going to make those calls to the doctors now while you get dressed."

Back in my room to ready myself for the day's adventures, I once more read through the letter from the hospital and offered up a sincere merci to whoever was watching over me. I could hear Papa making telephone calls and setting up meetings with the physicians. This time in New York was certainly continuing to be one of surprises! How fortunate I counted myself! A loving, growing family and dear Papa, still my greatest advocate and supporter. His blessing regarding my plans upon returning to France freed me so and allowed me to pour all of my energies into my nursing and plan for a fulfilling, prosperous, and satisfying future. One with many friends, a multitude of patients, and no husband.

I returned to the dining room, prepared to walk out the door, to find Papa had arranged to meet all three doctors that very afternoon at Dr. Levine's office at one o'clock. We walked to the park and through a number of local markets, and he introduced me to his friends and acquaintances that we happened upon as we sampled cheeses and meats. Back out on the street, he told me about the physicians.

Papa had met two of the doctors at the museum, which offered weekly lectures and discussions of exhibits and both historical and current events. Local authors, artists, professors, and sometimes panels of experts provided lively and interesting presentations. Papa found himself often in the company of Dr. David Whitmore and Dr. Emil Levine, who also attended the museum's offerings. The three men frequently sat side by side and then began to go out after the events for a communal meal to continue their discussions. The third doctor, Terrance Ferguson, joined them for the weekly dinner that had now become a much-looked-forward-to event. The four had become fast friends, and Papa very much enjoyed their company. All but Dr. Ferguson were widowers who, like Papa, were satisfied with their lives being filled with family, friends, culture, much lively conversation, good food, and laughter.

We arrived at Dr. Levine's office, which was attached to his stately brick, two-story home, precisely on time. All three physicians were there, seemingly awaiting our arrival with great anticipation. As Papa had indicated, they were most eager to hear the tales of my days as a battlefield nurse and my life since then. They appeared close in age to Papa; however, they all seemed to still find much satisfaction in continuing to see patients rather than retiring.

I had never spoken before of those long bloody days surrounded by the multitudes of injured and moaning soldiers, of our heroic efforts to keep them alive and so often failing to do so. I shared the degree to which the wounded had suffered and how dedicated the doctors and nurses were to doing all we could for them. As I answered their questions, I realized I could talk of that time now without feeling overwhelmed by the memories, indicating to me that I was indeed healing and ready for whatever lay ahead. And I knew intuitively that I could trust these men of medicine to have a degree of understanding that few outside of the profession could. We spoke for two hours about the war, and I was grateful that they were interested in how the people of France were faring now.

It was easy to entrust to them my memories. Finally, I had met Americans who were conscious and concerned about the state of the world beyond their own.

These kind gentlemen then listened as I told them my plans for the clinic. They spoke at length of what would be required in terms of equipment, instruments, and medicines. As they talked, I wrote a long list of items. Papa once again assured me he would place the orders, the others chorusing in that they would help him as well since they knew what and how much to order and from where, once I decided on what I needed. Papa would have all of it shipped directly to my house.

I could hardly believe my great fortune; I was to be the recipient of all that would allow me to care for my patients in the best possible manner. Scalpels and sutures, syringes and stethoscope, clamps, needles, a microscope, thermometers, bedpans, gauze and cotton—even such items as costly ointments and medications were added to the list. Papa and the good doctors also insisted I would need a desk with file drawers for documenting, making notes, and filing the patients' information. However much I insisted that I could purchase such a desk in Verdun or that Henri could surely find one for me, Papa was adamant that all I needed was to come from him.

"Marie, will you be making any visits to patients' homes?" Dr. Levine asked.

"Yes, I plan to help mothers in labor as well as those who might not be able to travel to the clinic."

"Ah, very good. Please excuse me a moment." Dr. Levine then left the room, returning shortly with a large brown leather doctor's satchel. It looked almost new. "I purchased this bag many years ago but never had much occasion to use it. The great majority of my patients I see here."

He stood before me and with great ceremony placed the fine leather bag soundly upon my lap. Looking into my eyes, he said with a smile, "I would be honored if you would accept this and use it as I could not."

I was quite overcome by his benevolence. "Dr. Levine, I . . . I . . . Thank you! This is a most generous gift! It's beyond my dreams. I assure you, I will do it justice. Thank you for your confidence in me."

I had passed inspection. Papa sat beaming with pride at all of us, caught up in our world of medicine.

Amid hearty goodbyes and the promise that I would keep in touch with them, at least through Papa, we took our leave.

"And why, may I ask, don't you want the inventory shipped to the clinic?" Papa asked before we had reached the end of the block.

"Because by having it delivered to the house I can go through the items individually and take them to the clinic a portion at a time." The real reason, which I did not share, was that I feared Henri might think it presumptuous of me to be moving into the clinic space full bore. Better if I moved in gradually, I felt, and not risk seeming too quick to take possession. I did not want to appear entitled to that space but rather to keep a clear delineation between being a renter only and not a possible future wife. I doubted I would be able to wait the six months before telling Henri of my decision. I did not want to encourage any false hope or lie by omission, hurting him in the process.

We walked many blocks to an area of New York that was busy, loud, and quite crowded, and my head was spinning the entire way as I relived all that had just occurred. My life was moving forward at a heady and welcomed pace.

Having eaten breakfast many hours ago and lunch forgotten by our visit with the physicians, we were both famished. We agreed that we were too tired and filled with excitement to go home and prepare a meal, and Papa declared we needed to celebrate. He was clearly exceedingly pleased with our successful and productive meeting with his friends and the fact that he could provide me support in such a way.

Since we still had time before our scheduled visit with Oncle Antoine, Papa led us to what he said was one of his favorite eating establishments. "The best Italian restaurant in New York City," he stated with enthusiasm.

As we walked through the door of Angelo's, anyone catching sight of us gave Papa a boisterous greeting, telling him they would return to seat us momentarily. The restaurant's decor consisted primarily of red-and-white-checkered tablecloths, and each of the walls held large paintings of the lovely and vivid Tuscan countryside. Couples and families of many nationalities filled the lively restaurant with noise, as though everyone was celebrating as we were. I found myself smiling, feeling as happy as Papa and thankful to be sharing this day in New York with him.

We were given a corner table by the front window, and as we looked over the menu, many people approached us. Papa stood again and again to make introductions. It was obvious they all worked in the restaurant, knew Papa quite well, and were eager to meet this other daughter. He ordered what seemed an inordinately large amount of food, and all of us, including the wait staff were sorry that Prohibition prevented us having a glass or two of good wine with our meal. Everyone Papa introduced me to spoke English with thick Italian accents and was generous in their comments as to what a fine daughter Papa raised. What stories he must have told them I could only imagine as I smiled and, having a hard time keeping up with the Italian-accented English, just vigorously nodded my head when it seemed most appropriate to do so. Papa was grinning ear to ear as we sat back down and waited for our feast to arrive. My Papa was proud of me and my heart was glad.

A basket overflowing with thick crusty bread, bowls of salad with olives, tomatoes, and onions, platters of pastas topped with fresh fish and grilled calamari, and sides of pickled vegetables appeared in quick succession. Mr. Angelo, the establishment's namesake, a large, red-faced, jolly man, kept coming to the table to fill our water glasses and to witness evidence that we were indeed eating and enjoying his delectable offerings.

When we could eat no more, having consumed almost all of every dish, the owner's wife, a waif of a woman, placed between us a great slab of chocolate cake. She patted me on top of the head, saying in Italian something I could not understand. Papa said she had chastised him for having such a thin daughter with no meat on her bones. I thought to myself, she must not have gazed upon her own very slender self of late.

We left the restaurant full-to-bursting, now headed for Oncle Antoine's place of business. Papa hailed a taxi and directed the driver through the various sections of town as indicated. Papa explained to me that New York City was divided into boroughs and how the bridges connected the different parts of the city. The populations in each section were made up of contingents of immigrants from all parts of Europe; the Irish, Italians, Chinese, Russians, and Jews from many nations were as pieces of a great puzzle, distinct in language and culture, pieced together to create this great diverse city. Papa showed me the synagogue he, Solange, and Philippe sometimes attended, and though I wanted to stop and go in, Papa said we needed to move on to Oncle Antoine's. He had told his brother we would arrive there at approximately five o'clock. I also felt that Papa, even here in New York, did not want me seen visiting a synagogue. Sometimes his caution seemed extreme.

When we arrived at Oncle Antoine's tight, disheveled, third-floor office in an aged, rickety wooden warehouse encased by very dirty windows, my evasive uncle was not there. Papa knew many of the men coming and going from the building, and when he inquired, none of them knew Antoine's whereabouts but said he had been in early that morning, conducted his business, and left again before noon. They said he might or might not return but most likely would not make another appearance until tomorrow. Papa thanked the men, did not bother to introduce me to any of these "rough men of the harbor," as he later described them, and we took our leave.

We then walked along a stretch of the harbor, Papa looking, I knew, for his brother, and watched the giant ships being loaded and unloaded with goods for and from all parts of the world. It appeared much more congested and busy than my memories of the harbor in Marseille. It was a scene straight out of an adventure tale: ships of all shapes and sizes flying flags of unknown foreign ports with burly, brusque men yelling to one another in every conceivable language as they directed the frenzied activity.

I would have stayed longer, watching it all unfold, but Papa wanted to be on our way back to the apartment. I could tell he was frustrated and eager to talk with his wayward brother, whom I now believed was but a phantom and not truly a walking, breathing person. I shared my sentiments with Papa, who was not much amused. He was obviously concerned, and I had a suspicion that Oncle Antoine was avoiding his older brother, for reasons to which I was not privy.

CHAPTER 20

PASSAGE TO PARIS –
APRIL 1923

The remaining days in New York found Papa and me continuing to explore his adopted city. We spent several hours at the museum and met up with our physician friends, together attending a one-hour lecture regaling the artists working in the current rage of Art Deco style. They were very interested in my descriptions of the art and design aboard the *Paris*.

Sharing lunch afterwards, they all again wished me the very best, assuring me the equipment and stock for the clinic had been ordered and would soon be sailing on its own journey to France. I thanked them profusely and told them I would remain in touch and keep them informed of the clinic's evolution.

On several mornings, Papa and I took long walks through Central Park and then explored surrounding neighborhoods, taking lunch at places we both found enticing. We enjoyed sampling foods that were new and exotic to us, dishes from Greece and Eastern Europe. We also ventured into Chinatown, where Chinese immigrants had established a large and thriving community reflecting the vivid colors and pungent scents of their homeland. I purchased incense, yards of silk fabric, a puzzle for Félix, and aromatic teas for the Sisters along with fine quality writing paper and pens and gifts for others back home in Meuse.

A few days after their wedding, Solange and Phillipe invited us to their home. Philippe sent his auto round for us and we set off, eager to see them; we had not spoken since that Sunday. We found them exceedingly well, happy and smiling, and sedate Philippe seemed almost animated. This was most likely due not only to the marriage but also to his happiness at the news of their child.

Though Solange had planned to wait a month before telling Papa, they were too excited, and their news spilled out during our after-dinner coffee. I nearly spilled my own cup looking up at Papa, anticipating his reaction and hoping he would not view the announcement unseemly, given the less than nine months till the arrival of his grandchild.

And Papa's reaction when he heard the news? I will remember it all of my days. He looked from Solange to Philippe in stunned surprise and then began laughing through his tears as a torrent of excited Hebrew flowed from his mouth. He went from one to the other and back again, kissing the tops of their heads.

Watching Papa's lively response, the three of us were laughing through our own tears as Philippe responded to Papa in Hebrew. Solange suggested lightly, as if an afterthought, what a fine idea it would be for Papa to move in with them, where he could see his grandchild every day and perhaps even help with the care, if that appealed to him. Papa, still overcome by the news he was to be a *grand-père*, told them he would give it serious consideration.

Before I left, we dined once more with Solange and Phillipe, and when the day arrived for my departure, they and Papa accompanied me to the dock and bid me bon voyage. How sad it was to leave them, but there was undeniable eagerness on my part to begin my studies at la Pitié-Salpêtrière and then return home to what felt like a grand new chapter in my life.

It was a pleasant and welcome surprise to find I was assigned the same cabin as on my voyage to America. And my trusty valet, Maurice, remembered me and seemed pleased that he would again be attending to me during this homebound journey. While I did enjoy the time with the other passengers, and especially Katy, on the previous voyage, this trip I sought only peaceful solitude in which to contemplate, reflect, and plan.

At the back of my every thought was the desire to write to Henri and tell him definitively that I would not be accepting his proposal of marriage. However much I wanted to put those words on paper, I had promised him to think about it for six months after opening the clinic. That seemed an interminably long time, considering I knew what my answer was. I only hoped he would not change his mind concerning the use of the clinic space even though I would not consent to being his wife. I intentionally put that worry aside.

Other than early-morning and after-dinner walks about the ship, I seldom ventured outside of my familiar cabin. I moved the large comfortable chair and oversized hassock, along with the side table and lamp, to face the side-by-side square portholes where I could look out across the vast expanse of water as my mind sailed ahead to Paris.

The first day, I requested of Maurice that he inform whomever he needed to that I would take my meals in my cabin. The weather on this return passage found most days overcast with heavy mist or light rain and only occasional breaks of sun, suiting perfectly my desire to remain inside and relieving me of any feeling of obligation to mingle with other passengers.

"Were your previous experiences in the dining room unsatisfactory, Mademoiselle?" he asked. "If so, I will see to rectifying any concerns immediately."

"No, no," I assured him, "everything was excellent, but I have much work to do on the sailing home." I thought the term *work* covered a multitude of relevant possibilities as to how I might spend my time.

He seemed immensely relieved, and thereafter, breakfast and lunch arrived each day like clockwork. Around eight in the evening, Maurice would check in with me to ask if I would like a dinner tray. He would already have the dinner waiting atop the cart he conveyed, warm under the domed silver cover. I regularly anticipated and enjoyed those elegant evening meals, complete with a carafe of wine. I think he remained puzzled and a bit concerned that I was not participating in any of the onboard activities, although I did occasionally have afternoon tea in one of the many salons.

In my cabin looking out to sea, I felt content and settled, reflecting back on all that had taken place over the last two weeks. Snippets of talk and visions from my time with my family, their friends, and my own new acquaintances traveled through my mind during my days on the ship. I thought upon each remembrance, securing its permanence in my mind.

This time upon the sea held me a willing captive between two worlds and eased the transition from who I was in New York to who I would become when I returned home. My life in Meuse felt much more the real world, the true me. While I had enthusiastically embraced my time in that world of Solange and Papa's, and all that had become their new reality, I was not sorry to embark on my voyage home, eager to begin my studies in Paris.

On the third day of the trip, I once again visited the Bastion of Beauty, placing myself into the competent and eager hands of Madame Sylvia. She was thrilled that I kept up my modern haircut, and yes, I had her apply the henna rinse once again after she trimmed and shaped my hair. She reminded me more than once that the need to find such a bastion of beauty when I returned home was of paramount importance. I did not know of any salons in Verdun but previously I had neither reason nor desire to do so.

I purchased more of the luxurious skin creams and subtle makeup, not knowing if any would be available in Verdun. When I inquired about a salon in Paris, Madame Sylvia wrote on a scented card the telephone number of "an establishment of the highest reputation" where I could make an appointment before returning home. This salon would also ship the makeup and *crèmes* I so liked and the henna color Madame Sylvia used on my hair, as she was very doubtful I would find any of it "in the back-country places."

In jest, I asked Madame Sylvia if she made house calls. That I could not imagine anyone as skilled as she and did not relish the thought of someone else managing my appearance.

She placed her large hand over her generous heart, knowing that my words were sincere, and said, "Oh, my dear Mademoiselle, you flatter me so!" I would miss Madame Sylvia and told her as much when we parted.

Three days later, we arrived in Le Havre. With a sincere adieu to Maurice, as he heaved my trunk out the cabin's door, I left the *SS Paris*, carrying Papa's old valise on one arm and the physician's gift of the fine leather doctor's bag on the other. I took a taxi to the station and boarded the afternoon train headed for Paris and my adventures at La Pitié-Salpêtrière hospital. It wasn't until I was settled on the southbound train that I became anxious, questioning my intent and abilities to assume once again my role as a nurse and the new position of overseeing my own clinic.

CHAPTER 21

L'HÔPITAL UNIVERSITAIRE PITIÉ-SALPÊTRIÈRE – LATE APRIL 1923

After finding an inexpensive room at a small hotel close to the hospital, I spent a surprisingly restful night drifting off with memories of my past experiences at la Pitié-Salpêtrière. I awoke early that next morning, dressed quickly, and hurried off to find breakfast before I arrived at the nurse registrar's office.

As I approached the front entrance of the hospital grounds, I stopped and stood in wonder, admiring the grandeur of the wide, three-story, ochre-colored stone building. The clock tower standing proudly in the center above the enormous domed, slate-roofed entrance told me I still had some ten minutes before my appointment with Sister Jeanne-Claude.

Strolling the familiar grounds, I recalled with fondness, and a lingering sadness, the years I had spent there—the many months of my first training as a volunteer Red Cross nurse before leaving for the field hospital on the outskirts of the Verdun battlefields, and later my time of recovery spent within this safe place of healing and the subsequent years on the nursing staff before returning to my family in Marseille. And here I was again, three years later. My excitement and apprehension were palpable as my racing heart ran ahead of me. I continually glanced at my timepiece and up to the clock in the dome, wondering if minutes had ever passed more slowly than those waiting to talk with the woman who held my immediate future in her hands. I hoped she was kind and flexible and would allow me to attend the lectures and classes I requested.

I walked up the center of the wide cobbled approach to the main building and passed through one of the three tall porticos, round arches supported by four solid columns of the same yellow stone. Heavy, sturdy, indestructible, exuding confidence as only good architecture can do.

Once inside the lobby, the smell of old wood and polish caused me to inhale deeply, a smell I have loved all my life; the smell of my childhood home and one I remembered from my days here. Yes, all felt familiar. I asked directions of the Sister sitting in attendance in the reception area just inside the foyer and was directed to a corner office on the second floor. The wooden stairs creaked with each of my steps, as though in welcome, and I was feeling more composed when I stood outside Sister Jeanne-Claude's office.

The door was slightly ajar, and I knocked a little too heavily, causing it to open wider. After a moment, I was called inside. This office also smelled of rich wax. The wood-paneled walls and bookcases on each side of the small office were burnished to a brilliant shine, illuminated by the morning sun streaming through the room's one window on the east wall. There was really little room for more than two or three people in this cramped space, which was overflowing with books and files. Her desk placed under the window and the two chairs across from her more than filled the room. It was all neatly organized but still the impression was that this person needed a larger office in which to do her job.

Sister Jeanne-Claude stood from her chair but did not come round from her desk. She removed small rimless reading spectacles that sat low on her long, sharp nose and, pointing with them, directed me to sit. She was at least as tall as myself and very thin—almost gaunt. She introduced herself and then sat again, saying nothing more to me as she perused what I assumed was my file.

Remaining silent and still, hands folded in my lap, a small notepad and pen at the ready, I took in my first impressions of this woman. As she turned her head while leafing through the pages, the stark light of the sun fell directly across her aged face. Pale and heavily lined, it looked to be covered by a thin veil of spider's web. After some minutes, she glanced up with a slight smile, her bright blue eyes looking directly into my own. And there in her eyes I saw the vivid life of her.

"We understand from your letter of request, Mademoiselle Durant, that you would like to study here for the next six weeks, the time culminating in taking your exams. Is that correct?"

"Oui, *ma Sœur.*"

"And that you wish to attend the physician professors' lectures and to participate in or monitor classes in medical-surgical, pediatrics, and obstetrics. We would require you to observe in surgery and, with your background, most likely begin to assist the surgeons during procedures. This would allow you firsthand exposure to the new techniques being utilized since your last experiences here as a surgical nurse. Are you in agreement?"

"Oui, *ma Sœur*, and I am extremely grateful for this opportunity," I said as I set in front of her a plain white envelope containing the money for my tuition, books, and room and board. Over the years, I had saved a large percentage of the monies Papa sent me every month and had more than enough to pay for the next six weeks of my classes and lodging.

Laying the papers that contained my past and future upon her desk, she removed her eyeglasses and said with a sigh, "While it is somewhat out of form for a nurse to request such specific courses of study, all to be conducted within such a timeframe, we have taken into consideration your exemplary service record during wartime as well as your years of nursing service here following your recovery. We are making an exception and granting your requests.

"There remain at the hospital several physicians you worked with, including Dr. Geoffrey Renard, and nurses who remember your expertise in surgery and the compassionate and capable care you provided to your patients. We are pleased to welcome you back, Mademoiselle Durant," she said with a genuine smile.

"However, I must caution you that in order to complete all we have arranged for you the schedule will be arduous, with at least two lectures and additional classes each day plus assigned time in surgery and on the wards. Are you ready for such a grueling six weeks, Mademoiselle?" She looked at me intently, all trace of the earlier smile gone.

"I am ready for such an accelerated course of study, Sister," I assured her. "And again, I am extremely appreciative that you have allowed me to return to la Pitié-Salpêtrière."

"I believe you to be sincere in your commitment and am confident that you can do the work required. The doctors remember your abundant tenacity. It will again serve you well," she said, her look penetrating my eyes. I held her gaze and nodded my head. We were both making a commitment, one to the other, and I certainly planned to hold up my end of the bargain.

"You will be living in the House School with the other nurses in training. Since we are full to capacity at this time, we have had to place you in a small ancillary room that I hope you will find tolerable. Although most of the other nurses are younger than you, as they are in their first training, we do have older nurses such as yourself who return from time to time to refresh their skills before they return to a hospital or clinic to resume their work. You will find yourself in good company, I am sure." With this, she smiled again, a new look of kindness in her eyes.

"I have attached your schedule giving specific hours and locations of lectures and classes, including days and times you will be in surgery. The books and papers you will need have already been placed in your room. Since it was specifically noted in your files that you were most exemplary in your skills assisting the surgeons, including the closing of surgical sites, I have assigned you during your first week to observe two of our surgeons, and the weeks after you will be assisting them as they may request. One of them, Dr. Tanvir Singh, will also be the instructor for the medical-surgical lectures. I have attempted to schedule your time in surgery around your classes so one will not interfere with the other. However, you will need to check the posted surgery schedule daily.

"I am sure you remember, things can change at a moment's notice, depending on the status of existing and incoming patients," she said as she stood and held out what I assumed was the schedule of my life for the next month and a half.

I took the folder from her hands. "I understand completely, Sister. I want to express my sincere gratitude to you and the instructors and physicians for allowing me this opportunity."

"Please see me if you have questions or circumstances that you feel we need to discuss. I think, while you may find much has changed since you were last here, most will be familiar."

With that, I left her and walked back outside. A short distance from the main entrance, I found a bench and sat to catch my breath and calm my beating heart. I wasn't sure whether to laugh or cry, so great was my happiness at being here, anticipating once again learning, nursing, and walking the halls of this familiar and esteemed hospital.

Some time passed as I lingered, looking across the wide expanse of the hospital's grounds, admiring the trees beginning to whisper of coming blossoms. Eventually, I became restless and ready to venture to the House School, eager to see my "ancillary room." Strolling at my leisure, appreciating the early spring promise of all things new, I watched multitudes of birds pecking in the greening grass for their own breakfast, their morning flights and songful chatter filling my senses with joy.

The nurses' lodgings were located directly behind the hospital's main building. Passing the front facade, I made my way round to the rear of the building, where I stood poised before what was to be my temporary home. Upon entering the double doors, I found the stern-looking house matron seated just inside.

"Bonjour, Madame. My name is Marie Durant. Sister Jeanne-Claude has assigned me a room here."

She checked her list and after finding my name drew a long black line through the length of it. Her manner was curt and terse, without even a cursory *bienvenue*. "Sign this," she said, pushing a document at me.

I signed without reading it, and she then directed me to the clipboard where I would enter my name each time I left and returned to the house. She took a long minute to look me thoroughly up and down, as if memorizing my person should I be found sneaking in or out. Only after reassuring herself she would remember me by sight did she relinquish into my hand the key to my room.

"My trunk should be here shortly," I said.

She let a short sigh of impatience escape. "It will be delivered upon its arrival, I assure you." Her directions to my room were rather vague, but I didn't want to press her by asking for more details.

I did lose my way several times, but by backtracking and being redirected twice more by student nurses, I eventually found it. Finally, I climbed a set of narrow, steep, bare wooden stairs that were set into a dark corner alcove one would only find if you knew it was there. At the top stood a door, over which hung a single bare, unlit bulb with a long pull chain. Standing in the dark, I pulled the chain, thankful that the bulb did indeed work, allowing me to see the keyhole into which I could place the key. I did so, turning the heavy brass knob, and stepped cautiously into the room.

It was clear that when not needed for a short-term nurse's stay the space was used for storage. Boxes and crates of all sizes had been moved to one side of the room, the side where the ceiling canted down to the floor. On the other side a narrow bed, a small nightstand with an oil lamp, and an old wooden bureau had been placed against the wall under one of the room's two windows. All was clean, including the bright, clear panes of glass, and I could not have been more delighted. The narrow windows looked out directly onto the hospital grounds, and across the way I could see people coming and going. From my third-floor view, they looked small and harried. I would most likely look so myself in a very few days.

The sound of moaning and heavy panting outside my room brought me out of my reverie. I opened the door to find a tall bulk of a man dragging my trunk up the stairs, thumping loudly step by steep step, his cadence matching the steady complaints issued just under his breath. Reaching the top, he pulled in my heavy trunk and placed it in an open space against one wall.

"Thank you for bringing my possessions such a distance. It looked quite a feat."

He took out his handkerchief and wiped his sweating brow. "It would do us all good if you nurses were to leave your fineries at home and just bring a knapsack or two." With that, he turned and headed back down the stairs. It seemed no one was very generous with their welcomes. And it did not deter my enthusiasm in the least.

I opened the lower drawer of the bureau to unpack my clothes and found two neatly folded, starched, and ironed uniforms, complete with cap and stockings. Beside these lay an over-cape. Sister Jeanne-Claude had taken great care to ensure I had all that was needed to begin my first day looking like the nurse I was.

After completing my unpacking, I attempted to study Monday's schedule but was unable to ignore my rumbling stomach. I put on my shoes and prepared to go find something for my dinner. Rather than eat in the dining room among my nursing sisters, still all strangers at this point, I chose instead to walk through the hospital grounds and find a café.

After dining on mussels and clams, I made my way in and out of shops and meandered through a small park, stopping to observe the work of several plein air artists. The evening was warm and fragrant, the sidewalks filled with families enjoying their after-dinner stroll, and the city's colorful ambience made for a leisurely and interesting walk back to the hospital.

Returning to my cozy room, I completed my nightly *toilette*, tumbled into bed, and once again attempted to review my schedule. But twilight lined the edges of my windows, and when I could no longer keep my eyes from closing, I gave myself over to sleep.

My days were tightly scheduled from eight in the morning through four in the afternoon, six days a week. I attended twice-weekly lectures given by each of the two professor physicians. One was a hospital staff physician, Dr. Dubois, and the other a visiting surgeon from London, Dr. Singh. Dr. Singh taught classes on medical-surgical topics, while Dr. Dubois lectured in the areas of pharmacology, research, and new technologies. A senior nurse instructor, Sister Solaire, taught the pediatric and obstetric portions of the classes.

I was fascinated by the extent of medical research being conducted around the world in the years since the war. New discoveries and experimentation had taken place in the area of diabetes with the discovery of insulin, a pancreatic extract that resulted in stabilizing many patients' conditions, often preventing their death from the disease.

Discussions of experimental treatments in the form of vaccines for polio, smallpox, typhoid, and other infectious diseases were presented during Dr. Dubois's lectures. Additionally, the diagnosis and treatment of blood-borne illnesses, the discovery of vitamins—such as vitamin D, which was found to prevent rickets—and bodily chemicals called hormones were continuing to unfold. Ongoing and aggressive research continued in the hope of discovering antibacterial drugs that would prove effective in treating streptococcus bacteria. Should these drugs be developed it would profoundly alter the way patients were treated for infections. The discovery could not come soon enough. If such medicines had been available during the war, how many thousands upon thousands of soldiers' lives could we have saved from the lethal infections resulting from wounds? I could not linger on thoughts of the past but would concentrate on what could be accomplished in the future.

Dr. Singh's lectures, more than any others, were riveting, delivered as though we nurses were his colleagues in medicine, equals in the battle against disease and injury. He spoke enthusiastically of innovations in the areas of medical-surgical procedures, techniques, and the associated technologies that were being invented at such a rapid rate. New devices had been created to conduct electrocautery, and treatments with regard to the use of anesthesia, infection control, and wound management were also discussed. Dr. Singh reviewed outcomes of ongoing experiments being conducted at Harvard University in developing electrosurgical equipment that could be used in conjunction with a variety of surgical procedures. I could not put the words on the page quickly enough in hopes of remembering all that was said. He was a knowledgeable and engaging speaker, and students were completely attentive when he shared his wartime experiences as a surgeon on the front at Normandy. He thoughtfully and often passionately communicated what he had gleaned from the war as a physician and how those years continued to shape his goals and values regarding his practice of medicine.

He spoke quickly, his lilting speech reflecting his Indian heritage while the accent of one educated in London at times made his French hard to follow. Often, when excited about his topic, he would revert to English and other times Punjabi. When he saw the look of consternation on our faces, he would smile, backtrack, and begin again.

He seemed an endless font of information, constantly spilling forth facts and examples from patient cases. If I continually took notes, it meant I could not watch him as he paced back and forth in front of his eager students, his enthusiasm and hope so evident in all of his person. Watching his animated face, arms, and hands gesturing as he drove a particular point home reinforced and validated how correct my decision was to come here for study. This doctor was the epitome of all things one would hope to find in a physician who might one day change the course of medicine.

I traded note-taking for the experience of sitting in his presence, trusting my memory and his lecture handouts that I would absorb most of what he so exuberantly imparted to us. As I looked about the room of nurses, they were as spellbound as myself. It was as much about the persona of this charismatic man as it was about the subjects he was teaching.

During his lectures, I often felt myself transported back to the battlefields of Verdun, re-experiencing my own harrowing events in the field hospital. Those experiences had transformed me as well, and I believed I was a different person than I might have been had I not gone through those years as a battlefield nurse.

As the days progressed, we were given opportunities to examine animal and human tissue, looking through the latest in microscope technology at cells both typical and atypical. Both physician professors allowed us to ask questions and pose hypotheses to which there were not yet answers, and when they spoke about this new age of medicine, the treatments and cures that seemed impossibly miraculous appeared to be within reach.

Following the illuminating lectures from the doctors, our nurse instructors always brought us back round to focusing on our role as the patient's nurse and oftentimes the physicians' eyes and ears. It was obvious that they knew the physicians well and I'm sure saw each new class of students become enthralled with the doctors and their passionate lectures. While the physicians taught all that was new and exciting in the world of medicine and medical advancement, our nurse instructors reminded us that the nurse's place was in the wards with our patients and assisting the doctors with whom we worked. Both doctors and nurse instructors were in agreement that the more the nurses understood about the patients' maladies and subsequent treatments, the better care we could provide, resulting in better outcomes for the patients. And, as we were reminded, good nursing contributed to the good reputation of the physicians and the hospitals in which we served.

I dared not share my own intentions, as I did not want to run the risk of an instructor telling me I could not manage and treat patients in my own clinic. I kept my counsel, feeling somewhat duplicitous but also daring and free, eagerly anticipating opening my practice once I returned to Meuse.

In contrast to the physicians' lectures, Sister Solaire's classes in pediatrics and obstetrics were traditionally formal and tended toward direct instruction and structured weekly exams on topics including the anatomy and physiology of the pregnant woman and fetus, pre- and post-natal care of mother and baby, and breast and bottle feeding. We spent three weeks discussing nurse midwifery practices specific to labor and delivery, what procedures were used to facilitate a healthy delivery, risks such as causes of early labor and maternal and infant infection, complications that could occur during labor and after birth, and how to prevent and treat these most effectively. The cause and prevention of sepsis was a widely discussed topic.

She lectured also on the cautions and dosages of maternal anesthesia, such as ether, and the utilization of forceps during delivery, both of which were now used more frequently by physicians and midwives. In France, nearly forty percent of all babies were still delivered in the family's home, this being especially true in rural areas where a hospital was not in close vicinity or when the cost of a hospital delivery was prohibitive. Sister reiterated over and over the crucial role of the nurse-midwife in helping to ensure both the mother and the infant's survival. During my time of study, we had the opportunity to observe and assist in many deliveries of babies born at the hospital.

I was disappointed, however, that we did not have the opportunity to observe a nurse-midwife assisting a labor and delivery in the family's home. I was certain I would have opportunity to do so once I returned to Meuse and made my availability known, although I would have preferred that home-birthing experience in collaboration with my instructor before striking out on my own. I did find reassurance in knowing that what we learned about the human birth process was nearly identical to the birthing of animals. The experiences I'd had with ewes coming into the world in less than typical circumstances would, I hoped, serve me well when it came to assisting human mothers as they pushed their infants into this world.

My new knowledge of current techniques and treatments available opened up a host of opportunities for patients to receive a higher level of care than I could have provided otherwise and added clarity to my plans for the clinic. But the fact that I still needed to secure a physician supervisor continued to weigh heavily on my mind. There were many medical procedures and treatments that only a trained doctor would be able to provide to my patients.

I especially looked forward to assisting Dr. Singh during surgical assignments. At times, he would most graciously pause, if possible, during a procedure to expound on the patient's underlying concern and what the surgery hoped to accomplish to remediate the medical condition. He would explain why the particular technique was chosen and the steps he would take in surgery. He often took my questions in the moment, and therefore, I found those times added greatly to my understanding and furthered my learning. Occasionally, when the last surgeries were completed, we would continue our discussions as we cleaned ourselves and the surgery suite. We functioned as an efficient team, and he seemed to appreciate my nursing skills and my avid interest in the surgeries themselves.

It was with mixed emotions that I became reacquainted with Dr. Renard. He appeared unexpectedly at the House School one Sunday morning two weeks into my classes, his presence announced by a young nurse letting me know I had a visitor in the reception area below. I closed my book, smoothed my hair, and quickly slipped my feet into shoes before making the passage down the dark stairs to the first floor. Not thinking too much as to who my visitor might be, I was surprised to find him sitting in one of the overstuffed chairs in the lobby. Taken by surprise at seeing once again this physician whom I had met with so often during my recuperation and subsequent years of nursing here, I attempted to recover from all manner of emotion as he stood to greet me.

He more than anyone else was responsible in helping me understand the damaging emotional trauma I had suffered. During my first months of recovery, we met weekly as he gently but purposefully led me through my denial and pain. He assured me that it was typical for those serving in wartime—especially those engaged in the bloodshed of battle and seeing so much loss of life including friends and colleagues—to return deeply scarred and suffering a *crise de tristesse sombre*, a crisis of black melancholy. The horribly vivid memories and terrifying nightmares were my dreaded companions for many years after, and it wasn't until I found the solace provided by my house in Meuse that healing continued beyond the walls of this hospital.

As I stood before Dr. Renard, I had to pause in the moment to fully embrace the reality of his presence before I was able to sincerely return his greetings. Coming here once again feeling strong and capable did much to assuage my fears regarding any health concerns I still harbored.

We met twice more before the end of my six weeks. He wanted to discuss in great detail my life since the war, saying it would help physicians such as himself better understand the journey toward recovery. Initially hesitant to revisit all that I hoped had been put aside, he convinced me that as a nurse, as well as a patient, I could provide great insight into what treatments might be effective. Those long conversations actually proved cathartic for me, and in the end, I was grateful to him for once again pushing me toward acknowledging the progress I had made in the hard fight of coming back after such profound injury. We would stay in touch until his death many years later.

It became my custom that after the day's last class and if the afternoons were warm I would seek out a comfortable place on the grass of the hospital grounds to lay the blanket from my room, eat what simple food I had purchased from the little market nearby, and study until the light faded. I would then gather my belongings, along with the myriad questions and facts trying to assemble themselves within my mind, and walk back to my attic room where I would continue to study until midnight, quickly complete my *toilette*, fall into bed, and often dream of home.

The weeks passed in rapid succession. I had only brief snippets of time to write to Solange and Papa and to send a quick note to the Sisters and Henri to let them know things were going very well and that I would be sitting for my exams the day before my return to Meuse. Now that the time here was nearly at an end, I was very eager to be home and take up my life again. I did think of running the clinic as an adventure, for I would need, as Papa always told me, to have courage if I was to navigate all the changes and challenges I foresaw.

CHAPTER 22

THE INDIAN KITCHEN –
7 JUNE, 1923

It was a Thursday. My last Thursday of training at l'Hôpital La Pitié-Salpêtrière. Tomorrow, exams would be conducted, and if I succeeded in passing I would be returning home with my Certificate of Nursing, the highest level of certification awarded to nurses. Receiving my initial volunteer nurse's diploma here in 1916, from the Société Française de Secours aux Blessés Militaires (SSBM), the French society providing assistance to wounded servicemen, seemed forever ago. These last weeks of intensive study brought frequently to mind all those with whom I trained and served, and those lost. Especially dear to me were nursing friends Jeanne and Annette, and Dr. Bisset, all killed during the shelling of our battlefield hospital. Often, speaking to them in my thoughts these last weeks, I felt their close presence as I moved through the hospital's familiar corridors and passed from class to class.

Although I was eager to reunite with beloved friends, my kind and humorous animals, and to once again sleep in my own bed, I was experiencing sadness at the thought of leaving what I had come to think of as my forever hospital home here in Paris. How wonderful it was to work side by side with other nurses on a daily basis and to learn from the many fine and accomplished doctors. Working in my clinic, I would be with a physician only occasionally. I put aside those daunting thoughts and attempted to focus on what needed to be completed during the final days before my journey home.

And truth be told, my sorrow at leaving was particularly acute knowing I would more than likely never see Dr. Singh again. He was my favorite instructor in the classroom, during rounds, and in the surgery suite.

Dr. Singh exuded a strong, self-assured confidence without the trappings of ego that so many other physicians seemed to wear as a mantle of entitlement. He was also quick to voice his regrets at what he and his follow doctors had not accomplished in those arenas of battle, their frustration at not being able to save more soldiers from their horrendous wounds, and he often cited the lack of appropriate medicines and inadequate supplies as well as the sheer numbers of the gravely wounded that could not be satisfactorily cared for as examples of the realities of practicing medicine in the devastating theatres of war.

At times during his lectures, when it appeared that he was perhaps becoming distraught at the memories that were obviously still so vivid, he would stop his pacing and place his hands upon his turbaned head. The act of readjusting his headdress seemed to bring him back to the here and now of the classroom of 1923. He would heave a great sigh as he completed the realignment of his senses and launch once again, more calmly, into his lecture.

Having experienced such similar situations at Verdun, I understood his deep sense of frustration and also his commitment to now take what was learned on the battlefield and translate it into more effective medical practices. Yes, I would miss this physician, this man I had come to greatly admire and respect.

After my initial two weeks participating in pre-and post-surgical rounds and assisting during surgeries, my last four weeks were scheduled solely with Dr. Singh. I mentioned this to him one day as we were scrubbing to begin the first of several operations. His reply surprised me. After reading my hospital file and the high commendations I received from the surgeons and nursing supervisors, he had requested that I assist him as much as possible.

"I probably should have checked with you first. Please tell me if you would rather rotate in with other surgeons, and you can certainly do so." His brow furrowed into a worried look. "I should not, I now realize, keep the best for my own patients." I could see that he did indeed feel he had perhaps been overzealous by having me assigned exclusively to his schedule.

"I am certainly fine with the arrangement, Dr. Singh. I have a particular interest in amputations, resections, reconstructions, and deep wounds and am honored that you have been requesting my assistance. I have learned more in these past weeks, between your lectures and surgeries, than I have in all my other nursing experience combined. During wartime, all injuries that end up in surgery are critical, and the difference between life and death hangs in the balance of a matter of minutes. Here in the hospital setting there is some opportunity to directly teach or discuss as you perform the procedures, and I so appreciate you taking that time when appropriate."

Those were the most words I had ever spoken to him, and they came tumbling out of my mouth quickly, hoping to convey that I relished the hours in the surgery suite with him. We worked extremely well together, and time seemed to stand still in those moments when a patient's life depended on our skill and efficiency. I knew what instrument or clamp he would need before he requested it and had it ready to place into his palm. There was a fluidity between the movements of our four hands. Eventually, I closed the surgery sites for all of his procedures. We were an effective team, with low post-surgery infection rates and excellent outcomes for patients. I was more than happy to continue this arrangement that was beneficial to us both. From time to time, just before drifting off to sleep, my mind would wander away to a place where I saw myself walking side by side with him as we talked and laughed. I chastised myself each time, realizing the childishness of such fantasies.

As the students and those teaching us became more familiar with one another, informal cadres were formed, made up of six or so nurses, nursing instructors, and sometimes doctors. We would often dine together in small cafés or kitchens for an evening meal once or twice a week. Dr. Singh was certainly the center around which my limited time outside of classes revolved. Two of his fellow physicians, friends of his, and several of the nurses, now friends of mine, ventured out more frequently in those evenings of the remaining three weeks of study. Each time, we would make our way to a different café, suggested by one of the doctors who lived in Paris, and sit for hours eating and discussing new medical breakthroughs and research taking place across Europe and in America. The nurses occasionally talked about what work awaited them at home after their studies came to an end. Some planned to apply for positions at la Pitié-Salpêtrière, hoping to remain in Paris. I shared only that I would begin nursing in a clinic upon my return home and that my patients were primarily rural farmers and laborers.

None of the other students had family living outside of Europe, and none had been to America. They encouraged me over and over to share more of my New York experiences. I enjoyed regaling them with stories from the ship, the frenetic energy of New York City, and recounting memories of the wedding. I did not speak of the New York physicians who helped me equip my clinic or my need for a physician to oversee the facility, and certainly not the fact that my family left France due to my father's concerns regarding another war and possible persecution of Jews and other minorities. These times were meant to be lighthearted; we all needed to ease the heavy load of hospital work and the constant demands of classes and study.

Some nights, I would seek out the company of a nurse instructor from maternal and infant care, asking if I might treat them to tea or a meal. Speaking with them in a less formal setting, I could have my questions answered in a more thoughtful and thorough manner, and the time away from the hospital was welcomed. My instructors knew I planned to educate local women regarding diet and self-care during pregnancy and about what to expect during and after the birthing process. I would also be available to act as a nurse-midwife in the delivery of their babies. Most infants in and around rural Verdun were still delivered in the home, and I was certainly willing to travel to those mothers. Although I found those meetings helpful and informative, I did enjoy to a greater degree the comradery of the group of us that included Dr. Singh.

During our evening forays with our colleagues, Dr. Singh was an attentive and patient listener. He rarely spoke of his life outside the hospital, and if he did it was in reference only to his work, never mentioning his personal life. It occurred to me that those times were restful for him. The good doctor could but sit and listen to the stories of others, the long fingers of his hands folded together on his lap or busy working into the shape of birds the small colored papers he pulled from his pockets, his head nodding attentively. His reticence to talk of himself only increased my curiosity regarding this handsome, turbaned doctor from India.

On this last Thursday before my exams, I assisted Dr. Singh in a below-the-knee amputation. Gangrene had set in, and although extensive wound care had been provided in the weeks previous, the patient's diabetes and concomitant damage to his circulatory system did not allow healing to advance, and hence needed amputation. The man was young with a family, and the hope was that by saving the knee joint, and with the advancement in artificial prostheses, the patient would be able to live close to a normal, viable life. And if his diabetes could be controlled, he would return to work and provide for his family.

It was after four in the afternoon when we stepped out of the operating room to remove our gowns, masks, and gloves, scrubbing our hands and arms for long thoughtful minutes. Dr. Singh and I were at side-by-side sinks, and as always when I assisted him, he thanked me for my work, especially my skill at closing the surgical site.

"You are always welcome, Dr. Singh. Again, I take great pleasure in working with you as I always leave knowing more than when I entered," I said with a smile, feeling my face blush warm as I dried my hands.

He finished scrubbing and turned to me. "Would you consider joining me for a dinner of Indian food this evening? There is a kitchen close by, and I find I am hungry for some comfort food from home. I would very much like to share that with you."

I was caught off guard at the invitation, assuming by his words that it would be just he and myself, but was very happy to join him and told him so.

"Excellent! I won't be more than thirty minutes. Please meet me in the surgical lobby." That said, he made a quick exit through the doors, perhaps concerned I might change my mind. I wondered at his invitation as I quickly gathered my things and hurried to my room to change, slightly anxious as to how the evening might unfold.

He appeared a short time after my arriving back in the lobby and led me out through the grounds of the hospital where we proceeded down the street. He had changed into a suit of light gray tweed. I wore a pastel skirt and blouse and carried a sweater over my arm, as the evening was still warm.

"Do you like Indian food, Nurse Durant?"

"I actually could not tell you. I have not had the good fortune to have ever sampled Indian cuisine. But I am most certainly looking forward to the experience," I said, walking faster than my normal pace just to keep up with him. He walked as fast as he spoke.

"The kitchen we are going to is very small and quiet. I visit it frequently during my teaching stays in Paris and have become well acquainted with the owners, Monsieur and Madame Dhariwal and their family. Their son and daughter cook as well, and the family have had their restaurant for many years."

He seemed so at ease with the two of us walking together down the avenue, as though we had done this countless times before, that I found myself letting go of the busy day and breathing in the fragrant June air. And while it was wonderful to be walking at this time of day to what I anticipated would be a delicious dinner with someone I rather liked, I was keenly aware of my caution, wondering why he had asked me to accompany him. Did he sense my deep regard for him? I found I wanted to smile and to continually look up at his face, remembering my frequent bedtime thoughts of him. He was only slightly taller than myself, although his turban added to his stature in many ways other than his height.

We talked as we walked for at least thirty more minutes, turning this way and that onto side streets here and there. He stopped suddenly, announcing we had arrived at our culinary destination. The aroma emanating from the restaurant was divine, and my mouth was now watering.

We were greeted heartily by a couple I assumed, from Dr. Singh's description, were the owners. The high-ceilinged, narrow restaurant held no more than ten tables, and we were at present the only ones come to dine. Unfamiliar scents of aromatic spices permeated the air. Colorful banners and pictures graced the walls, depicting scenes from India in bright reds and golds. I felt myself transported to another place.

Dr. Singh and the Dhariwals spoke to one another in their shared native language accompanied by cordial bows and smiles. It was very clear from their demeanor that they were quite fond of Dr. Singh. Now speaking in French, he introduced them to me, and after a very friendly welcome they led us to a table in the back of the establishment. I sensed this was the doctor's usual seat, close to the back where he could converse with his friends coming and going through the kitchen door.

"We are honored that you accompany the good Professor Singh this evening. He is a great friend, and we are pleased that he is having dinner here in our kitchen and in the company of a new friend. We have been looking forward to meeting you," said the elderly gentleman graciously before bowing and returning to his kitchen.

At a complete loss for words, I looked over at Dr. Singh, raising my eyebrows in question. He was smiling and folding a small piece of rose-colored paper that appeared out of nowhere and met my look saying, "Well, I might have mentioned that I hoped to bring you here for dinner at some point. Or rather I hoped that you would agree to dine here with me this evening."

"And why would you have mentioned that, Dr. Singh?" I couldn't help myself asking.

"Please, call me Tanvir. I think that our work in close proximity both in class and rounding with patients, as well as all the time spent in the surgery suite together, qualifies us to be on less formal terms. Would you not agree with me?" he asked with a smile.

"Yes, I suppose it might. And you may call me Marie." I also noted he had skillfully evaded my question.

As though on cue and in celebration of our now more informal status with one another, Monsieur Dhariwal stepped through the kitchen door and presented us with a large platter filled with an array of enticingly colorful foods accompanied by a basket of naan. "Please, enjoy our humble offerings. May you eat slowly and savor each bite as you linger long over conversation," he said, setting the food on the table and giving us each a cloth napkin. There were no plates, knives, or forks offered.

"I never ask for a specific food when I come here, Marie. I just have them bring me what is fresh and on the evening's menu. They do know my favorites, and I suspect we will also enjoy some of those this evening."

Tanvir used his fingers to pick up a savory meat skewered on a thin stick of wood. "Please, Marie, help yourself. This is Indian satay, chicken on skewers, and in the small bowl is peanut sauce that you eat as an accompaniment with the meat. These are foods we can eat here with our fingers as we would in Punjab," he said, dipping a piece of the chicken in the sauce and closing his eyes as it reached his mouth. As each dish arrived, Tanvir would tell me its name and the specific ingredients. That evening we shared fragrant dishes including mango curry, aloo gobi, and tikka masala with vegetables.

We exchanged smiles, and my murmurings of "delicious" and "I've never tasted anything quite so good" were answered by, "I am so glad you are finding everything to your liking." Why did I feel that he wasn't just speaking about the food? As succulent courses continued to be presented before us and our appetites became sated, we slowed our eating, allowing us to truly engage in conversation.

"Your classes, Marie . . . Have you found them challenging enough?" He smiled, licking sauce from his fingers. "Were you able to find time to sleep as well as study?"

"I seem to need little sleep and yet feel rested and eager for each day. My time here was so short, and wanting to make the most of this experience, I have not been too concerned about sleep but more interested in studying."

"Ah yes. Indeed. Tomorrow are your exams, correct?"

"Yes, and then I leave Saturday on the five o'clock train. And where will you go, Tanvir, once the term has ended? Do you ever visit India? I know you mentioned you have family there," I inquired with great curiosity.

His lovely hands that I noticed so often in class became still, and with a deep sigh, he leaned back into his chair. He paused and looked at me directly. "I love my profession and relish the opportunity to teach and work in Paris and in London. My work is my life. That is not to say that I don't love India and my family—I do. However, at this particular point in my life I have no desire to return and settle into the daily life as a village doctor in Punjab. That is what my father was and he, as far as I ever knew, appeared completely content with all aspects of his medical practice. He was also a very political man and immersed himself in local affairs. He died several years ago, leaving my mother alone with only her constant haranguing of me to return home as her singular purpose in life."

He dropped his head into his hands, saying, "I apologize for my unkind words regarding my mother. It is guilt taking hold of my tongue. This selfish son wants to continue living life on his terms but knows every year that he neglects his duties to family is another year of sorrow for his mother that she doesn't deserve."

He took another mouthful of food and looked up at me again. "I have two younger brothers, both working in England helping to rebuild the rail lines destroyed during the war. They will return home at some future time. However, the burden to continue our family's esteemed place in the village does not rest with them, but with me—the eldest and a doctor who is to take up where my physician father left off. I am the one to go home and take my place as the head of our family and resume my father's extended community duties within our village." He had wiped his hands and was folding his paper again in quick movements matching the pace of his speech.

Why he would choose to share with me what I felt had been pent up in him and unspoken for ages was beyond my understanding. I certainly related with his wishes to live his own life. Had I not done the same with my own family, choosing to go alone to Meuse, a place I had never seen or set foot in, rather than immigrate to America with Papa and Solange? However, I had done so with my family's understanding and encouragement. I could not imagine living with the sense that I was not living up to my family's expectations.

"I had somewhat of a similar experience," I shared, in what I hoped was a calming and reassuring voice. "I chose to separate from my family shortly after the war and to live alone along the River Meuse in an old house left to me by my mother. At that same time, my father and sister moved to New York City. There has always just been the three of us, and we are very close. Our parting was difficult, but I have never doubted my decision to remain in France nor has my family been anything but supportive. I have not had to live with the guilt you are so obviously struggling with. I am truly sorry for this difficulty in your life." I wanted to reach out to him, this vulnerable, pained man so different from the confident surgeon and eloquent classroom professor of the past six weeks. It reminded me that we never truly understand another's struggles, and we should never assume another's life is easier than our own.

"I apologize again, Marie. I certainly did not intend for our evening to dissolve into a litany of my personal concerns. Thank you, truly I thank you for listening and even understanding somewhat my dilemma. There are many Indians living in Western Europe who are wrestling with these same issues. We are a suppressed people living under the British crown, struggling for sovereignty and independence, both individually and collectively as a country. It has caused us to feel displaced and in conflict in a myriad of ways that are difficult to untangle. My generation desires freedom to chart India's course with her own people apart from the forced servitude as a colony of the British Empire. But I feel my destiny is tied to Europe as surely as it is to India. Here is where I studied and now practice my craft. My friends and fellow physicians are here. Western Europe is where all of the exciting and innovative changes in medicine are taking place, and I want to be part of all that is happening."

With a tone of submission, he went on, "Realistically, I know I must return home in the not too distant future and assume my destiny. I am first a son of India, and that is my blood and bones, and obligations cannot be neglected much longer. And I am a good Sikh and will return to Punjab and my mother and make peace with what awaits me there."

With a sad smile and looking totally exhausted having expelled his deepest feelings, he said, "And now, Marie, please, my new friend, tell me of your plans when you return home. I heard you tell our colleagues earlier this week at dinner that you are going to work in a clinic close to your home in Meuse."

I told him of my plans to set up and run the clinic in the space I would be renting from Henri, that he would receive a portion of the money made once things were operational. I did not share anything regarding Henri's other proposal.

But I did voice my constant concern that I had not yet convinced the doctor in Verdun to act as supervising physician, and knowing I must have such oversight, I was stymied and frustrated as to how to proceed. "The good doctor in Verdun is halfway out the door to retirement and dreaming of the warm beaches of Nice. He wishes to take on less, not more," I confided.

"When I return home, I plan to call upon him once again, explaining that I have had additional training, and hopefully my newly acquired Certificate of Nursing will convince him that I would be able to take a substantial portion of the patient burden from him, and help advance his plans for retirement in a few years to a life in the South. We shall see if his determination to keep me at bay will become more flexible with the little I have to offer in the way of compensation."

I took another drink of the tea our kind hosts served us and continued, "Up until now, I have on occasion provided treatment to our local residents at the convent near where my clinic will be. The good Sisters there are my dear friends and allow me to see patients, tending to numerous ailments and wounds and various other concerns. I also have quite a reputation for coaxing reluctant lambs into the world when their mothers are determined to hold on to them. I hope to extend my services to human mothers and help deliver their babies as well." I smiled with that last remark, trying to lighten the mood of heaviness that had settled about us as we both shared from the deep places that life sometimes takes us. He had listened intently, and I felt we were kindred spirits tentatively finding our way into the future.

Without thinking, I placed my hand upon his at it lay on the table, saying softly, "But we have survived much, you and I. The war is over, and we are free from the torment of those horrid years of conflict. We can overcome anything after that. All will work itself out. My father always says we need to but trust our own good judgement and have courage in all things."

He took hold of my hand and we sat then, quiet and still, finishing our tea and looking at each other, offering occasional smiles of mutual support. Both of us were spent from our tales and lethargic from having consumed such a great amount of food. Two hours had passed, and I could sense a shared reluctance to end the evening. It somehow needed closure, though, and I was happy when he said, "Let's take the long way home, Marie. The night is calm and still, and we can walk away our worries and settle our stomachs at the same time. You are sitting for your exams early tomorrow, and I don't want to keep you up late."

As we made to leave, the Dhariwals would not accept payment from Tanvir, but I saw him leave a large note under the teapot. What a beautiful friendship they shared with one another. I was grateful that I had experienced this evening. Grateful to them for their hospitality, allowing us to linger over each other's stories and grateful for what I sensed was their benevolent watchfulness over us during those hours. I was saddened to think I would not return to see them again. I thanked them sincerely, hoping they truly understood how pleased I was to have met them and how touched I was to see their solicitousness toward Tanvir. I sensed he felt in their compassionate presence something of home in India that temporarily assuaged feelings of guilt and longing.

We meandered through the streets of Paris for an hour and arrived back at my building just before nine o'clock. Tanvir assured me his rooms were close by and within a few minutes' walking distance.

We stood under the soft light of a sconce next to the front door that I should have been hastily going through. I looked into his rich, dark eyes and said, "Thank you for dinner and more so for the conversation. I have not shared such feelings and concerns with anyone other than my family. Although I do not know how I will resolve my problems, it was a great relief to be able to talk with someone so understanding." It was difficult to break away from his gaze, and I found myself wanting to think he also found it hard to say goodnight.

As though the thought had just struck him, he said, "You have indicated nothing regarding any worries you might have as to your exams tomorrow morning. Do you feel prepared? I know you will find out before you depart whether you have passed. I hope to see you before you leave for your train. In fact, might I help with your luggage and escort you to the station?"

"In answer to your first question, I really am not concerned with taking the exams. That may sound overly confident, but I truly have no qualms and have every reason to assume I will pass and carry my certificate home with me. And yes, I would very much appreciate your assistance with my luggage *and* your company to the station. My train leaves at five, so perhaps you could meet here tomorrow just before four?"

He took my hands and smiled, once again the confident man. "Let's meet at two. We will have time for a leisurely meal, and you will tell me all about your exams and the fact you got the highest marks of all," he teased.

I loved his smile, his gentleness. He leaned in to me to say *bonsoir* with a lingering kiss upon each of my cheeks and placed into my hand the two origami cranes he created during dinner. The lovely scent of him made its way to my heart, which skipped several beats, leaving me lightheaded. I wondered if I would be able to sleep at all knowing I would recount over and again our conversations of this evening and attempt to conjure up all I could of him.

CHAPTER 23

THE PASSAGE HOME TO MEUSE – JUNE 1923

The next morning, I awoke eager and anxious. I was not sure if these feelings were due more to taking my exams or meeting Tanvir at two.

Having completed the exams in just under three hours and feeling sure that I had passed, it was still with a great sense of accomplishment that I accepted my Certificate of Nursing from Sister Jeanne-Claude. She wished me great success and exacted from me a promise that I would let her know how my nursing career unfolded. She told me as well that if I was ever interested in teaching to please get in touch with her. I tucked this surprising statement into the back of my mind and hurried to pack up my belongings.

When Tanvir arrived, my trunk and bags were ready to stow into the back of the car he had borrowed from a fellow physician, and off we went toward the train station to find a place for lunch and a final conversation.

"Knowing you would pass your exams, we had to have a celebratory lunch before you left," he said, pulling the auto up in front of a quaint-looking brasserie.

"I do feel like celebrating, but I'm also somewhat in a whirl. After weeks in America and weeks of study in Paris, passing my exams, and now heading home so quickly to begin settling into the clinic, events seem to be pulling me along in their wake rather than me being at the helm."

"While you may feel that way, Marie, remember, it is your drive and determination that set all of these events in motion," he stated, taking my arm as we walked into the restaurant.

During lunch, we talked of all that was inconsequential, keeping the conversation light, saying we would keep in touch however infrequently and wondering aloud what we both would be doing a year from now. I wondered also if he at all shared my sense of regret at saying goodbye. I attempted to memorize his face as he spoke and then as he listened to me speak, observing all I could about his countenance and person. I wanted to remember who he was and who I was when we were together.

Lunch flew by all too quickly, and again, as Tanvir helped me board the train, we wished each other well and agreed to write, having exchanged addresses at lunch. He held my hands tightly as he kissed my cheeks, but his smile was not reflected in his sad eyes. Yes, he would also remember me with fondness.

I dozed on and off during the four-hour ride from Paris to Verdun. Feeling heavy with sleep and dreams of Paris and thoughts of Tanvir, I stepped down from the train onto the platform. The quiet cool of the evening's breeze gently brought me back to the here and now. Setting my heavy bags down beside me, I scanned for a familiar face among the few people waiting for their family or friends.

I had written to Sister Agnès to please make contact with Bernard, asking if he might pick me up at the station and transport me to my home. Not seeing him anywhere on the platform, I went looking for my trunk and found it a few train cars down among the other passenger luggage. I secured a porter who placed it onto a rolling cart, and we moved off toward the front of the station.

There I found Bernard, leaning against his battered old truck, looking for all the world as tired as his vehicle. I gave a little wave, but he stayed where he was until we were close. He then reached down to the cart for my trunk and bags, hoisted them into the back, and got into the truck without a welcoming word or gesture. I thanked the porter, handing him his gratuity, and then climbed in too. My joy at being home was mollified by Bernard's stale behavior.

"Merci, Bernard! I so appreciate your coming and taking me home. I hope it was not a great inconvenience," I said, searching his face for any evidence of such.

"It is not inconvenient, but I do not like driving in the dark anymore. I only have one light on the front of the truck, and it is not very bright."

With this obtuse declaration, he started the truck and off we went through Verdun, heading south to my home. The air blowing through the partially opened windows provided some noise that seemed to preclude making polite conversation. And knowing Bernard was a man of few words, the silence suited us both fine. As we passed the convent and Henri's house—and my clinic—it was already dusk, and I was unable to see either place clearly.

Halfway home, Bernard asked, "Did you have a good visit with your family? I see they didn't talk you into staying."

"Thank you for asking, Bernard, and yes, I very much enjoyed the time with my sister and papa. Solange was married while I was there, and the wedding was beautiful. And my family never intended to persuade me to stay in New York, knowing my home is here, as are my friends."

"Humph. Well, good. Good that you are back."

In the twilight of the evening, the road was familiar in the extreme to us both, and I never doubted Bernard could manage to get us to my house. I did begin to think perhaps he was truly ill at ease driving at night, though, and not just because of the single light glowing from the front of his timeworn truck. He sat stiff and straight in his seat with his head perched far forward on his neck, looking much like a turtle. He kept his eyes looking directly ahead, as if expecting the unexpected round every bend in the road, and drove slower than was needed. He did not wear eyeglasses, but perhaps he needed to do so. Bernard was stubborn in the extreme, and it would take an influence greater than mine to persuade him to have his eyes examined. I found myself watching the road closely, thinking another set of eyes couldn't hurt.

We rode the rest of the way in taut silence until the truck stopped in the road alongside my house. Bernard handed me my front door key, which I had entrusted to him before I left. He unloaded the trunk, and I grabbed up my valise and my nursing bag and hurried to the door, holding it open for him. He deposited my trunk just inside the entry and with a curt nod in my general direction was out to his truck and on his way.

I stood outside looking across the dark road to the river, waiting until his truck was distant enough that I could hear the welcoming sound of the water washing over the rocks. I was home to my River Meuse.

Lighting the lamps as I went from room to room and lingering over each piece of familiar furniture and my own belongings, a peace settled about me. My home seemed to welcome me, and I felt the familiar presence of my family that had lived here long ago. And my family across the ocean was also with me here. Papa and Solange were always close in my thoughts.

I walked through the parlor to the kitchen and stepped out the back door, headed for my little barn. Horse welcomed me with a high-pitched whinny as my cat, Pedro, stretched where he lay in a corner of the hay in Horse's stall. I picked up my sleepy cat, draping his warm, purring body over my shoulder, and went to check on my hens. They were all perched on their roost, soundly sleeping. I would gather whatever eggs were there in the morning.

Laurent was also much in my thoughts this night, and I wished his spirit peace. It seemed forever ago that the young soldier's terrors from the war drove him to end what must have been constant torment. My hand reached up to touch the wall where his lifeless body had lain against the house by the strangling rope. I gave thanks that my own severe depression and angst had not driven me to seek the same relief. Caring for Laurent and the two other young soldiers shortly after my arrival in Meuse had been my salvation. Henri had realized I needed saving and had rightly concluded that by tending to the needs of those wounded boys I tended to my own wounds.

I turned toward the door and to other thoughts but paused. Gazing far across the nineteen hectares of my lavender fields, I saw in the starlight of evening the faint purple hue of brilliant blooms flowing across my land. My heart overflowed with contentment at all I returned home to—this wonderful home in Meuse, my refuge and sanctuary, my peace and joy. In leaving for these past months I had accomplished all I set out to do and had made the passage home again, renewed and confident of my abilities to make of my life all I wanted.

I then walked round the outside of my home and across the road to my flowing river, gurgling softly as the poplars on its banks displayed their summer leaves. In all directions I saw reflected the hope and promise of the days ahead. All seemed fresh and ready for tomorrows.

Having taken the measure of my home and finding all well, I walked back inside, thinking of what needed to be accomplished in the next few weeks. Arriving soon would be a great number of boxes and crates from America, filled with what the New York physicians, Papa, and I had ordered for the clinic. Not wanting to inconvenience Bernard again, I would take my wagon to the station as the supplies arrived and transport them myself. My original notion to bring all of it here to my home rather than taken directly to the clinic now seemed cumbersome and unnecessary. Henri, I was sure, would see the logic in my moving all the boxes straight from the train depot to the clinic.

Seeing Henri tomorrow was utmost in my mind. It had been some time now since we had communicated, and I needed to reassure myself that he was still amenable to my renting the space.

Next on my list of what I needed to do posthaste was to meet once again with the reluctant physician in Verdun. And thirdly, I wanted to enjoy a leisurely meal with the Sisters and share with them my adventures in New York and Paris. I knew they were eagerly awaiting our reunion, as was I. We also needed to discuss whether there was interest and the possibility of an additional garden on the convent grounds to grow medicinal herbs and plants, and I needed to seek confirmation that Sister Dominique would be able to assist me in the clinic. Having a private chat with Sister Agnès regarding the state of her health was also imperative. So much to be accomplished.

These feelings of passionate excitement and defined purpose, charting what I hoped would not be rough waters these next few weeks and months, filled me with great excitement and, yes, some measure of anxiety as well. Forging ahead with this new endeavor felt as though a veil of the old had been lifted and discarded, giving way to a clear bright path before me.

Before settling in for the night, I carried armfuls of clothes from the trunk up to the extra bedroom, laying each lovely garment gently across each of the beds. The clothes could air for a couple of days and then I would arrange them in the closet.

Lying in my bed, it was difficult to quiet my mind. Pedro's burrowing in next to me with his soft, furry body finally settled my thoughts, and I was able to sleep deeply. When next I opened my eyes, early morning sunlight filled the familiar and welcoming room.

There were but three eggs in the coop, meaning Henri, most likely accompanied by Félix, had been by recently to tend the animals and gather the eggs. Making the three eggs my breakfast and hastily finishing my few chores, I hitched Horse to the wagon and headed north to Verdun.

Coming upon Henri's house, I saw evidence of his being home. I also saw a new lean-to and shed he must have constructed in my absence that was occupied now by Donkey who, recognizing me, raised his head and welcomed me with loud braying. I pulled my wagon up beside his new quarters, leaped from my seat, and gave him great hugs and greetings. He and Horse were long due a visit, and I left them side by side as I went in search of Henri.

However, knocking at both the front door and the door to the clinic's entrance brought no response. Perhaps he and Félix, who I was so eager to see, were at the Sisters'. I walked the short distance to the convent and presented myself at their door. Rounds of bonjours and excitement greeted me.

Félix was indeed there and shouted, "Marie, Marie, you're home!" as he threw his small arms tightly round my legs. With tears in my eyes, I swiftly picked up the dear child and gathered him into my arms. "Marie, I've been waiting every day for you. I was afraid you forgot to come home," he whispered in my ear.

"Never, Félix. I would never forget to come home to you and all my friends," I said, setting him down. "And look how tall you have become! Your legs are longer and your pants much shorter," I teased.

"Well, I will be five years old soon, and you are invited to my party. What do you think you will get for me, Marie?"

"I certainly think some new clothes would make good presents."

"Those are not very much fun," he said, smiling as he buried his warm face into my hip, much as Pedro had done the night before.

The Sisters then gathered round me, voicing how happy they were that I had returned. Sister Agnès stood a little distance apart with a wise smile upon her face, taking us all in. I approached her with fond greetings, which she reciprocated in kind.

"We've just finished breakfast, Marie. Now let's all repair to the refectory and have our tea before morning prayers," said Sister Agnès.

Sharing all that had taken place in my absence caused the Sisters' morning schedule to be quite delayed. They plied me with endless questions and I, in turn, wanted to hear every piece of news from them. It was coming up on noon before we felt we had exhausted our many updates. The Sisters then left for chapel, and Félix and I went outside to walk the convent grounds. Félix was excited to show me the baby goat and mother given to the Sisters just days before in exchange for six laying hens, candles, lavender soaps, and lotions.

The gardens had indeed been expanded and the air was filled with the fragrance of herbs. When I asked over tea about the addition of another garden, a topic we had touched on before I left, the Sisters surprised me by saying they had already tilled another space, and Sisters Dominique and Evangeline had planted many healing plants, including aloe vera, arnica, arrowroot, mint, marigolds, garlic, and ginger root and an array of herbs, all that Sister Dominique and I hoped to plant. They all agreed the drying of the herbs and plants would not be an added inconvenience but rather an easy accommodation alongside the drying of our lavender.

Sister Dominique was most ecstatic about the expansion to their horticulture; she was quite knowledgeable regarding the use of herbs in the prevention and treatment of some illnesses, and as I had learned more about the uses of medicinal plants while in Paris, I looked forward to continuing our discussion on this topic of interest to us both. She assured me also that she had been given Sister Agnès's blessing to become my assistant in the clinic. This was all encouraging news.

Taking in the richness of the gardens, evidence of the thoughtful preparation the Sisters had put into the planning and planting, I marveled again at the joy of the comradery and friendship of these wonderful women. We were all filled with a new sense of purpose on this summer morning.

At the sound of a motorcar approaching from the north, Félix released my hand, shouting, "It's Henri!" and began running toward the road.

Henri with an automobile?

It was indeed Henri, driving an open motorcar with a small wagon-like appendage attached to the rear. Whatever it held was covered by a large swath of heavy burlap secured at the corners by lengths of rope.

Catching sight of us, Henri honked the horn and waved. He pulled the auto up alongside us and jumped lightly from the car. I could only assume this was Henri based on Félix's say so. This man was dressed in a smart tan driving coat, a snappy billed cap, and driving goggles. How could this possibly be my worn and rumpled friend of traveling commerce?

But Henri it was. Removing his goggles, he lifted Félix high in the air, both of them laughing at their happy reunion. I but stood in place, certainly happy to see Henri but utterly puzzled at the transformation of his person.

He set Félix down and slowly walked over to me, greeting me without words as he held my arms and kissed each of my cheeks. He stepped away, saying, "Welcome home, Marie. It is wonderful to see you. How are you finding your homecoming?"

Laughing, I said, "Rather full of surprises, actually. Who is this person I see standing before me?"

It was his turn to laugh. "I assure you it is myself. A change of clothes and a different means of transportation does not mean a changed man."

"Félix and I were just on our way to the honey house. Come with us and tell me all your news." I hoped he would provide me with the details I needed to make sense of all these changes.

"It is your news I'm most eager for," he said as we began walking.

"I heard all about it, Henri," said Félix, jumping up and down. "The Sisters and I talked with Marie for a long time. She had a good time and passed her tests!"

"Did she now?" Henri looked up at me with a smile as he ruffled Félix's dark mop of hair. "Well, my congratulations to you, Nurse Durant. I look forward to hearing all about it."

Félix took each of our hands as we walked a threesome together to the large outbuilding. Evidence of the Sisters' preparation for the coming honey and lavender harvest was everywhere. All the implements for gathering the honey from the combs, the clean and shiny extractor, the molds for the beeswax candles and the shears and twine for cutting and drying the lavender were arranged in neat and orderly fashion at their stations on the long work tables. My fingers tingled with eagerness, and I promised myself that even with the new clinic I would still find time to involve myself in our moneymaking endeavors as I had these past few years. Those times provided many enjoyable months working closely together.

It would be but a matter of scheduling clinic time three days a week and Saturday mornings, leaving three days, late afternoons and evenings free for other work. Most days of this coming summer and fall would be spent here, between the clinic tending the patients and then at the convent working with the Sisters in the gardens and making the lavender honey and candles. I could think of no better way to spend my time. I did not intend to sleep in the clinic but would stay whenever I needed to in what the Sisters referred to as "Marie's room": a small, cozy room meant for storage located off the chapel that suited my simple needs perfectly. Returning to my home every second day, the hens and Pedro would be fine, and Horse would always be with me.

Bringing my thoughts back to the present and still curious about Henri, I said, "Please tell me about your motorcar. Are you using it now to travel the roads?"

"Well, Félix and I have made some changes, have we not, my boy?"

"Oui! Henri has a shop in town and hardly travels now. You see, he didn't want to leave me so much because I need a real home every day." The happiness in his eyes was heart melting.

"A shop in Verdun? What does all this mean for your business?"

"It means, Marie, that I am no longer a vagabond. I'm weary of that life and am now choosing to conduct my business at my storefront in Verdun, with infrequent, perhaps just monthly excursions to seek new acquisitions for the shop and my customers."

"Acquisitions? That doesn't sound like a storefront where you will be selling kitchen supplies and staples."

Henri smiled as he removed his driving coat and cap, setting them atop a bench. "The shop is large enough to serve two purposes. On one side is a gallery with fine paintings, some statuary, and new or finely refinished furniture. The other area is for more general household items, small used furniture pieces, and various accoutrements for the everyday living in a home. There are no general "kitchen supplies," as you say. I will show it all to you when you come to town."

I did not catch all that Henri said because I was caught up in admiring his clothes that till now had been covered by his long coat. He wore tailored, tan-colored trousers with a starched and ironed shirt of deep blue cotton and freshly polished brown leather boots. I could hardly look away from his neatly trimmed and combed hair.

He was looking quite the businessman rather than the wagon-riding peddler I had come to know. The transformation was startling, and I was attempting not to stare at this well-dressed and confident man standing before me. Had he changed in other drastic ways as well?

"There is also a display of our lavender soaps, scented lotions, and beeswax candles. I hope you will approve of what you see. For Félix and myself, these changes mean we are together every day in the mornings and evenings. When school begins, I will take him on my way to the shop. At the end of the school day he can return with me to the store until time to close up and come home.

Saturdays I am open till noon, and he can chose to either come with me to Verdun or stay here with the Sisters."

"Now that you are home, Marie, could I stay with you on Saturdays too?" asked Félix hopefully.

"That will be a discussion we must have with Marie once she decides on her clinic hours. She will be busy as well. Is that not correct, Marie? Opening your clinic is still your plan, I assume."

I heard his concern and quickly spoke to dispel any doubts. "Henri is correct, Félix. I have come home with my nursing diploma all current and shiny, and once I find a physician to oversee my treatment of patients I will open the clinic."

"But Saturdays, Marie, what about Saturdays?"

Taking Félix's small hands in mine, I said, "Many people can only come for care on a Saturday, Félix, since they work Monday through Friday. I hope to be available to them three days a week and then early on Saturday mornings until about noon. That way we will be able to have Saturday afternoons and Sundays together. How does that sound?" Giving my legs a big hug in reply, Félix skipped out the door after one of the convent's roaming chickens.

After a few seconds of silence while we watched the boy, Henri said, "You look well, Marie. And it seems as though we have both given some thought to new attire and personal style. Your new haircut becomes you. I think our current undertakings have allowed us to shed the past in many ways and look to the future. And now, I am eager to hear about your family and your adventures."

"I will need many days to tell you of all that happened in New York and Paris and all that has transpired for me to arrive so excited and expectant. While I was worried that my coming home prepared to quickly forge ahead with my plans might somehow upset the Sisters' and your normal lives, it seems we are all ready to begin a new chapter.

"I must admit, Henri, that I am the one finding the changes, especially all of yours, somewhat disconcerting. And whatever must Donkey think of his own more sedentary life?" I was trying to come to terms with the surprising unease

I felt at not finding all things familiar, wondering why I found Henri's presence beside me so disturbing.

"I assure you, Donkey was more than ready for a much-earned rest from all those long hours in all seasons plowing our way over these long roads. During and after the war people needed access to scarce provisions, and Donkey and I were able to assist in meeting that need. Now that life is settling again, folks are eager to get out and travel themselves, confident they are safe to venture to other towns to get what they need. And the men, those that have returned to their families, can now provide for them and reassure their loved ones that life moves on.

"I also was eager for changes. Buying and settling into my house means a proper home for Félix and myself, a shop in town close to my new home and customers, school with new friends for the boy, and the sense of being part of a community." A note of doubt crept into his voice. "I do hope, Marie, that you view my decisions as wise."

"As long as you are still the Henri I know as my dear friend, I can easily adjust. I admire your dedication all these years to the people you served, because that is truly what you did for the many families you looked in on. You tended them as much as I tended the young soldiers. You helped us all bear what seemed unbearable during those meager years after the war. No one is more grateful to you than I. And now we both have much to look forward to."

Henri nodded. "And right now, I am very much looking forward to lunch. Would you do Félix and me the honor of dining with us, Mademoiselle Marie?" he said, granting me a bow. "And following lunch you can once again peruse your clinic. Boxes bearing your name have been arriving at the train station for over a week now. From your letter, I knew they contained your equipment and supplies for the clinic." He gave a sly little smile. "I have taken the liberty as they arrived of moving them into your new space."

My great friend, still bringing to me what he knew I needed. But this time his efforts were not for a grief-stricken, questioning young woman but a woman confident, self-assured, and very excited.

Over a simple lunch of cheese, baguette, and fruit, Henri told me that Dr. Benoît had closed his practice and moved his family to Nice. I was not too surprised at the physician's leaving, for he voiced that possibility the last time we had spoken. However, I was certainly disappointed, my angst renewed regarding the lack of someone to oversee the clinic long-term. But that would not deter my intention of moving forward and opening on 2 July, and I said so to Henri, who thought that wise.

He commented that during my absence, many ill and injured had come to the convent looking for me. The Sisters did what they could for whoever came, but often there was little they could do other than offer simple care, comfort, and tell them when I would be returning. Henri expected I would see many at the clinic's door before July's opening date. All the more reason to unpack the boxes and set up the clinic space as quickly as possible.

Over the next several days, with the help of the eager Sisters, boxes and crates were pried open with hammers and screwdrivers and unpacked. I was occupied with arranging supplies and equipment into cupboards and drawers. The box containing the precious microscope I carefully unpacked myself. The Sisters were so curious that I took the time to demonstrate to my wide-eyed friends the world of cells. Along with the microscope, there were twenty slides, each smeared and labeled with a specific example of aberrant cell growth and a variety of tissue samples. I carefully placed the microscope on the shelf beneath the glass-faced cupboards, which now held clean milk-glass apothecary jars lined up neatly in rows. I had ordered fifty small cards attached to string that would eventually become labels that slipped over the lids of the containers. For now, the jars were empty vessels waiting to be filled with healing tinctures, salves, and dried medicinal herbs and plants.

During the times I was alone in the clinic, my thoughts traveled to Paris and Tanvir. How I wished I could show him this beautiful space in which I would nurse. I so wanted him to meet my friends and see my home and the river. I caught myself many times daydreaming of his being there and entertained conversations with him in my mind. It did little good to tell myself to focus on the present, leaving the pleasant memories to be visited only occasionally, and to acknowledge that what had transpired was in the past.

By the end of the week, most of the unpacking, sorting, and organizing was complete. I took myself to the printer's in town to order single-page flyers announcing the clinic's opening and hours of operation. A local craftsman, recommended by Henri, agreed to create the sign that would hang above the door with the words *La Clinique Meuse*. I hoped to have elements of metal and tile in the shingle and drew a few sketches for him, wanting it to remind me of the beautiful Art Deco stylings aboard the *Paris*. The craftsman said he would think about the composition and present me with samples of materials and a design he thought would suit my intent.

Those two tasks accomplished, I went in search of Henri's shop, where I found him busy with customers, a husband and wife, haggling with him over the price of a very large painting of gladiators engaged in battle. It was difficult for me to comprehend why anyone would hang a picture in their home of battered, bleeding men engaged in violence.

While waiting for him to conclude his business, I took the time to stroll around the store and found several lovely pieces of furniture. I especially liked a desk that could serve quite nicely as Sister Dominique's when she was checking patients in and out and organizing their records. The desk that Papa chose for me, that had yet to arrive, I would place in the rear left corner of the clinic under the large window. How eager I was to begin!

Henri walked to where I stood, my hand atop the desk I was admiring. "*Pardon*, Marie. I must say, I was more than fair with that gentleman, as I had no great love for his choice in art and bid it a fond adieu as he carted it out my door."

"And how much might I barter with you on the price of this desk, Monsieur? It would be perfect for Sister Dominique, as she will need her own workspace. It will be my gift to her for all her hard work thus far."

Henri looked at the tag displaying the price. "I don't think there is much room for haggling on the price but I would deliver it to the clinic free of charge."

"You've just made another sale," I said, reaching into my bag to make payment. I wanted to do so quickly before he could offer me anything else "free of charge."

Henri assured me he would deliver the desk that evening.

"Well, be sure to let me know when you arrive, and I will help you carry it in. I also need four or five straight-backed chairs, Henri, matching if possible, for the patients to sit in as they wait their turn. Might you have those here or know where they could be found?"

"I have a storeroom in the back and there are chairs there, some matching, but I will look to see how many and let you know when I bring the desk."

As other customers made their way into his shop, I bid Henri a good afternoon, and pleased with myself at all I had accomplished I decided to stroll the streets of Verdun, something I had not done in a very long time. Something that until now I had avoided as evidence of the war's destruction to the city had been everywhere. But now, with much time having passed and myself in a much better state of mind and body, I was ready to take in this city in recovery that was to be part of my life.

Walking for hours through the streets and along the river, I noted that, indeed, life had begun to spring up in the form of reopened or new cafés, boulangeries, shops, and a *pharmacie*. There were again lush, grassy places where children played. I found Félix's school, perused a reopened bookshop, and even happened upon a beauty salon. On the spur of the moment, I entered Salon La Lavande and made an appointment for a morning in the last week of June, just before the clinic's opening.

All seemed rather right with the world. Again, I found myself wishing that Tanvir could actually see my life, see the renewal happening in Verdun. I could not describe it adequately or capture in words in a simple letter the hope that was evident everywhere I looked. Missing also my family in New York, I found tears welling in my eyes.

Determined to continue enjoying this day, I settled upon a café for a late lunch along the riverfront. The white-aproned *garçon* seating me at my table suggested I might try the fresh escargot with a *petite salade* and then brought me a glass of chilled white wine, the bouquet reminiscent of ripe apricots with notes of spice. Raising the glass to my mouth, I thought how perfect a day it was in which to reacquaint myself with this city, my city, now burgeoning with new hope. *Santé à la ville de Verdun et santé à la Clinique de la Meuse!*

CHAPTER 24

THE SCENT OF HIM – SATURDAY, 23 JUNE, 1923

Unable to sleep much after first light, I ate a quick breakfast before leaving the convent and walked south along the road to the clinic. The sound of birds welcoming the new day accompanied me as the morning air sparkled with moisture from the night's summer rain and hinted of the coming day's warmth. The pungent smell of the rich, wet earth filled each breath, and I stopped to watch the birds pecking the ground for their own breakfast. As I rounded the slight bend where the clinic came into view, I smiled, seeing the colorful blooms of flowers planted along the front and side of the wooden porch. The smell of the lavender's rich oil, so aromatic in the early morning, welcomed me to my new place of work.

I was eager to take one last account of my supplies and medicines. Today was Saturday, and I was nervous thinking the clinic would open in just a short time. The opening date was July the second, little more than a week away. All of the essentials were here, labeled, shelved, and inventoried, and if I needed anything in addition, I could place an order on Monday. Today, I would take stock one last time, reassuring myself the clinic was ready to see patients.

It was true that over the last days since I had been home, many people arrived at my door for care, word of mouth traveling quickly about the new clinic opening. It was wonderful that I had on hand oil of cloves for a toothache and dried herbs for a poultice to treat a deep cough. I cleaned and sutured several wounds, set a young boy's broken leg, and gave a mother enough lavender salve to ease her little daughter's multiple bee stings. I realized my anxiety stemmed not from any concern regarding my treatment of patients but that not having a local physician with whom I could collaborate and who would provide supervision continued to be of paramount concern. The absence of a doctor in Verdun was all the more reason for me to provide needed care but did not negate the fact that the clinic needed official oversight.

Henri had found six matching chairs. They were abandoned by their compatriot of a dining table, which had been purchased by itself, meeting someone's need for a table alone. The only items I still required were the folding screens that would partition the patient waiting area from the treatment space. Henri left yesterday for Reims and would return sometime Tuesday afternoon, assuring me that he would find screens and they would be in place before 2 July.

I turned my attention again to the chart on my clipboard listing each apothecary jar in alphabetical order as they appeared in the glass-fronted cupboards. Approximately ten of the thirty jars now contained dried herbs, including culinary lavender, and a variety of teas such as chamomile.

I worked through the morning but stopped briefly to lunch with the Sisters, collecting more supplies before returning again to the clinic. I had just opened the far-left cupboard to label and fill three more jars with dried herbs I had brought back from the convent when I heard the clinic door gently open and quietly close. I had placed the "*Fermé*" sign on the front of the door but knew anyone familiar, seeing me through a window, would know they were welcome to enter. My first thought was that Sister Dominique had come to see if she might assist me in any way, and certainly I would welcome her company.

As I turned round to welcome my visitor, I was more than startled to see Tanvir standing tentatively just inside my door. He stood silently, looking apprehensive. I met his silence with my own as I grasped the edge of the plinth table, realizing I was suddenly short of breath, heart racing. I did not want to faint.

We stood looking at one another, neither of us making a greeting of any kind. Slowly, I walked round the end of the table until there was nothing between us but a few unsure steps.

"Marie," he said softly, searching me with his eyes. We both moved together, and I found myself enfolded in his arms. His scent of spice and musk enveloped me as he pulled me tightly to his chest. How long we remained still and quiet I do not know, my head tucked against his heart, pounding as fiercely as my own. After a while, I must have made some sound because he began to murmur, "Shhh, shhh, all is well now." And yes, that is how it was. There in his arms, all was well.

When we moved apart he took a handkerchief from his suit pocket and wiped my eyes. How surprised I was to feel tears on my face. How great was my relief at seeing this man I had missed every hour of every day since my return from Paris. And how incredible was my joy, knowing instinctively that he felt the same—the same sense of relief and joy at our suddenly being together in such an unlikely circumstance as him appearing in my clinic.

"How is it that you are here?" I asked, looking for reasons in his eyes beyond just a banal answer implying nonchalance.

"I am here because I could not stay away. I came not knowing how you would receive me. And if you had merely greeted me as a colleague, I had the ready excuse that, as your teacher, I had come to see if your clinic was in good order and to offer you my services as a supervising physician. I am beyond relieved that I did not have to offer that as my only intention for such an unexpected visit." With these words he took his handkerchief and wiped his own eyes.

I smiled and without thought stood on my toes, reaching up to kiss his mouth. Just a quick kiss, a greeting kiss, I told myself. "I am more than happy to accept all that you offer, and I, in turn, offer you hospitality and a place to stay, at my home just a short distance from here. That is, if are able to stay more than just today."

He put his arms about my waist and picked me up, laughing as he did so. "Yes! I can stay for three days if you will have me."

We just stood there, shy grins across our faces, content to remain looking at each other as our hands sought to reassure us that we really were in one another's presence. He smoothed my hair, his fingers gently caressing the edges of my face. I kept my hands planted firmly on his chest, wanting more than anything to remove his turban and grab hold of his hair between my fingers. How I had wondered about what lay under that covering on his head.

Regaining some sense of time and place, I asked, "Did you just arrive this morning on the train from Paris? Did you bring a bag? Are you hungry? Oh, I am so excited for you to meet the Sisters!"

"Yes to all your questions. My bag is just outside the door. I did not want to appear presumptuous or obvious and felt I could save face if needed, making a quick exit had you found my sudden appearance unwelcome in any way. However, I think it is safe to say that I heartily accept your kind offer and eagerly look forward to seeing the lovely home you described to me in such vivid detail during our conversations in Paris. And how are we going to explain my presence to your Sisters?"

Suddenly I felt anxious, not knowing what to do next and realizing that I had literally allowed myself to fall into this man's arms, my longing obvious and perhaps unseemly in his eyes. He was my professor, an esteemed physician who had taught me for six glorious weeks and with whom I had shared many dinners and conversations as we discussed much that pertained to medicine and much that pertained only to us and what we hoped and wanted for our lives, our world, our patients, and yes, ourselves. But never in those weeks did we become familiar with one another beyond the traditional French greeting of friends, the quick kisses upon the cheeks that had me wanting to linger close to him as he held me just a little longer with each encounter during the weeks leading up to our final adieu.

"Tanvir, I must admit in all honesty that I do not know in this moment what is proper or expedient. This is all completely new to me, these feelings, and you being here and not knowing what next to say or . . . how to introduce you to my friends . . ." My voice fell away into an abyss of confusion.

"Today is Saturday," he said. "Why don't you tell me what it was you had planned for today and tomorrow. Were you going to be here to receive patients on Monday? If so, I would be happy to assist you, and in the time between now and then we can discuss if my filling the role as your supervising physician is one that meets the requirements of your clinic and is acceptable to you. I did take the liberty of writing to Dr. Benoît in Verdun, letting him know that I would be calling upon him sometime on Monday, hopefully along with you, and the three of us discussing how best to facilitate you referring patients to him and he to you as appropriate. However, I did not receive a reply from him. But I assume he will receive us and be reassured of your qualifications and expertise, having your professor arrive to ensure that your clinic's needs are met and such." He gave his hand a fling about the room, a laugh escaping with his last words.

It sounded irreverent, as though our professional collaborations were merely a ruse to allow us to spend time together and not solely devoted to the practice of medicine. We both knew we wanted this coveted time to be spent only in the company of each other and to as quickly as possible dispense with the aspects of running a clinic. By agreeing to act as my supervisor and attempting to contact the now-absent Dr. Benoît, he had already worked out those details, allowing us to spend this weekend without encumbrances. I ventured to guess he had been plotting this since I took my leave of him in Paris. How thankful I was that he did so; how thankful I was that he was willing to help me regarding the clinic, but even more so, how immensely overjoyed I was that he was truly here for the benefit of us.

We decided to go on to my home and spend the rest of the day merely getting reacquainted. We needed time to right ourselves. Possibly to explore if this relationship was to be a new dimension of our lives. Who were we to be to one another?

I drove the wagon slowly, giving Horse his head but tempering his eagerness to be home to eat and settle in for the day. I too was eager, but even this time in the bumpy wagon allowed us to settle a little as well. Tanvir had many questions about the area and asked me again to tell him how I came to be here in Meuse.

The afternoon sun illuminated the trees and my river. The red-roofed house seemed to shine and look intensely inviting, my fields of lavender brilliant blue and expansive. I was proud to be bringing Tanvir to my home and could hardly believe I was not conjuring another of my daydreams.

After driving the wagon to the back of the house, together we released Horse from his trappings and gave him his portion of hay. I then led Tanvir back round to the front; I wanted him to hear the river as he entered through my front door. We set his bag down in the foyer, and grasping hands, I walked him from room to room but hesitated when time came to show him the upstairs. Although I felt I should be shy and reticent, I wanted only to take him to my bed. And taking up his bag, we moved silently together up the stairs, our unspoken desire making it obvious we shared the same intention, shared the same intense need to be together.

I had never held another person in my arms—not flesh to flesh, not soul to soul. I inhaled deeply his intoxicating scent, breathing in all I could of him: spice and musk and male. It made me heady, and I frightened myself at the urgent need to be as close to him as possible, his warmth intensifying the notes of cinnamon and clove, of cardamom and something so uniquely him that seemed to effervesce from his skin.

He lay on his back, sleeping silently and still after our ardent lovemaking. I had no need of sleep. My only desire was to watch him and memorize every detail of this exquisite man. To gaze upon this being, who had captured my heart, my mind, and caused me to dismiss all my good sense. His long black eyelashes lay feather-soft against his rich mahogany skin, his shoulder-length black hair curling about his head, framing his face in glistening waves. Lowering my head, I moved my face into his hair and let it tease my eyes, my nose, my mouth. I quietly moved over him to where his breath fell now on my face, sweet breath of mint and faraway places. I took his breath as my own, matching my rhythm to his, his chest rising and falling in slow, even tides of slumber.

The dark curly hairs of his chest were thick and tight, ringlets of black my fingertips ever so gently lost themselves into. I lightly traced the darker line running through the middle of him from breast to groin until I stopped and marveled at the manner in which he was assembled. I had seen hundreds of naked men, most of whom were screaming and bloody, and I had never had the time nor any inclination to wonder over any part of them except to determine what might be salvaged. And now this man, this beautiful, whole, pristine being without injury or wound lay here before me, and I could linger over him at my leisure.

Unable to resist, I lay my face into the warmth of his groin. His lovely warm parts still pungent and damp made my breath again become rapid and my heart race. The desire to be close to him once more was almost more than I could contain. What wonder was this that merely the sight and scent of him caused me to feel and behave in ways totally foreign to my nature? But perhaps that is exactly what was occurring. These powerful feelings were part of my nature, and it wasn't until now that they had cause for expression and a need for fulfillment. Would he startle if my hands began to fondle him?

Looking up at his face, I was surprised but not embarrassed to find him watching me, a soft smile about his lips and desire in his eyes.

"Do as you please, Marie."

"But I am not sure what to do," I said softly. "At first I only wanted to look at all of you, but now I find I want to be close to you once again. And the smell of you, it is a heady potion making me desire things I have never even imagined. And it is all very bewildering. I had not expected such a sensual experience."

His fingers began lightly stroking my arm. "It is meant to be a highly sensual experience. The most sensual of all experiences and many say the most ecstatic. The coming together of two and creating such bliss is often thought of as a mystical experience."

"Is it always this, this . . . intense? As though you are transported beyond your body?"

With a quizzical look, he raised himself to his side, his elbow on the bed and hand under his chin. "How amazing that you find this first experience of the physical so very intense. I am told it is not always that way for a woman but rather can be somewhat painful."

"Yes, there was an element of pain in the moment and a lingering one as well. But it is the physical evidence of our joining and therefore a joyous discomfort. And you, Tanvir, how do you feel?"

"I feel complete bliss and a longing to stay here with you forever. And a deep despair knowing that I must leave in three days."

Feeling tears behind my eyes, I said to lighten the moment, "Then we must love many times before you leave, thinking only of when we will next be together." I realized too late that I had assumed there would be other times when he would be here in Meuse and we would be together as we were now.

"Yes, Marie, you speak the truth, our truth. For surely we must be together whenever it is possible. I know that it will fall upon me to make that happen. To create the space to be here with you, if you will have me, that is, whenever we can."

He knew my answer even as I took his lovely face between my hands and whispered, "Yes, whenever we can."

Before we came together again, he went to his bag and took out a small packet. He showed me the prophylactics that he had brought to protect me from pregnancy. I had seen them many times, of course, as soldiers often kept them in their pockets or in their kits. Why, I always wondered, would soldiers feel they would have need of them on a battlefield? There was certainly not opportunity to dally with the nurses. And condoms were illegal in France.

I expressed this thought aloud one day as we were preparing for yet another field amputation of a young solder's leg, and I found a prophylactic in his pocket. He looked up at me and asked if we would please spare his "manhood." I told him we would do all we could to keep him as intact as possible. Racked with incredible pain, he still managed to say, "Well then, you can put that right back in my pocket." I thought then that the condoms were perhaps a talisman, helping those frightened boys hold on to their hope for a future beyond the chaos of war. I never removed them from a soldier's uniform again.

I was relieved that Tanvir had thought to bring condoms with him. And we did use them but it bothered me, for I wanted nothing, not even a thin shield, barring his skin from mine. Desired it quite desperately and against all logic. Lust had come to invade me, and I felt completely taken in by this new reality. I knew beyond all else that my life would never be the same.

We both slept till early evening that first day of our being together. I awoke before Tanvir and again lay watching him, pondering how curious it was that I would endure the darkest of life's experiences so early in my years. To live in the midst of war was highly sensual: the sight of bodies blown apart by shells, the stench of the wounded and rotting, and the feel of my fingers as the warm, sticky blood of man after man dried on my hands, to shed off my skin like scales onto my uniform, turning the washing water red and putrid.

And now this sensual experience of ecstasy. I gained an understanding of why men were willing to fight for their country, for their families and their way of life, why we fought desperately to hold onto life even when we saw it ebbing away. For on the other side of possible death was life, and protecting the living of it was worth dying for.

CHAPTER 25

PASSIONS – JUNE 1923

I t was late afternoon on Sunday. We had spent much of the day out of doors, walking through the lavender fields, looking at the beehives, and taking lunch beside the river. Returning to the house after lunch and in need of a nap, I awoke much later to find Tanvir standing in just his trousers, one long arm above his head, leaning against the window frame and looking out across the river. And he began to speak. I do not know if he realized I was awake and if he was talking to me or rather just to himself.

"My mother reminds me I am a man of honor from an esteemed family, a Sikh of Punjab, a citizen of a country with a glorious past. Why would I not want to go home and begin my true life?

"But my country is occupied by foreigners who neither understand nor appreciate our history, our land, or our people. They had no high purpose in declaring India a British colony other than to rape our land and subjugate our people to make the English wealthy. They attempt to import their culture and customs while determining the Indians will be the servants in their homes and the slaves in their fields and fail to see the irony. And I ask, how is this invasion of our land, the forced submission of our people any different than Germany wanting to do the same to England and France?

"Great armies were amassed to prevent Germany from taking by force what they wanted and yet any dissent in India by its people is seen as insurrection. British troops are sent to squelch any signs of protest over the brazen forced occupation of India.

"I have listened to many a philosophical discussion by both military and government men purporting that my country could benefit greatly by Britain's continued influence and example. They determine that if they can successfully form a cadre of Indian men who embody the superior characteristics of being English, then the entire country might come around."

He turned to me, saying, "And here I stand before you, an example of such a man. A traitor to my country. A traitor to myself and my family. I no longer attempt to explain to these righteous men that India is a culture far older than Europe, a country of multiple tribes, religions, and dimensions. A complex country of castes that formed the structure of our people. My English colleagues and friends purport that a caste system is barbaric and fosters superstition and fear. And yet in my work in the English and French hospitals I see a similar hierarchy of social inequity and prejudice. The finest hospital wards are reserved for the wealthy, and those deemed less able to pay are relegated to beds in another part of the hospital where the care can be less than stellar. And the poor? They have no recourse as the social networks that were set up after the war to assist the poor and indigent are underfunded, poorly staffed, and the care often little better than nothing. Physicians like myself are asked to volunteer at free clinics once or twice a month, but nothing is formally orchestrated to allow this to happen. Of course, there are those doctors who feel a sense of obligation and do put much effort into providing their services for free and do so out of a sense of conscience."

I sat up in my bed now, the sheet pulled in a tumble around me. Tanvir walked to the only chair in my room and sat down, saying softly, as though in apology, "I am not one of those physicians, Marie. When I did go with one or two of them, offering my services along with theirs, the patients cringed when I attempted to examine them. My turban was my calling card that broadcast "foreigner"; a bloody Indian. And yet I can teach in the finest hospitals, cut open the bodies of patients high on the European social hierarchy, and am held up as an excellent example of how a lowly Indian provided with a superior English education can, in essence, become English." During this purging of feelings and thoughts, Tanvir frequently ran his hands through his hair, much like I run my hands up and down the front of me when I am perplexed or anxious.

"If you feel so strongly about the future of India, why do you continue to remain in Europe? Why not go home?" I asked.

Pulling a thin, shiny square of paper from his trouser pocket, he began to fold it, saying, "I tell myself it is because of my work, the good I am doing, and when I am lecturing and teaching I am hoping that these young English interns and nurses I am now educating will understand that I am not an Englishman at all but an educated man of India with a different set of values, from an enlightened culture. That I am a rational man of science that has nothing to do with race or culture. That I embrace the study of medicine and purport the advances being made to benefit the health of all people everywhere.

"And the truth is, Marie, my mother is correct. She does not say it in so many words, but she knows I am a coward. What she doesn't understand is I am also afraid. How can I return to my country and accept what is happening there and do nothing? I have seen the world through the eyes of war. The injustice and inequity, the visceral hate between peoples of countries living side by side who are driven by their own egos and pride to subdue other humans. To kill those who are judged to be inferior of mind and body. To kill to acquire lands that are not theirs. Yes, I understand there is nothing new under the sun, and this is the heart of man. But I do not want to be that man who after experiencing such atrocities returns to his homeland nothing better than a servile physician, who quietly steps into his father's shoes in a small village, living a false life knowing that his people are considered little more than chattel by their occupier. That would be the truest cowardly act. My heart longs to see my country free from tyranny. The same tyranny that threatened England and France and was stopped before it was able to take hold and destroy entire cultures."

As he finished folding his crane, a shining red one, he looked up into my eyes, and I saw in his own a man tormented by indecision and passion. "When I return to India it will be as a man hell-bent on educating my people as to their sovereign rights and attempting to build consensus with the English, hopefully with rational dialogue and debate; to make them see, even with what they consider adequate concessions that they have made, that we will never be English any more than they could be German." Standing up from the chair, he pressed the fragile paper bird into my hand and resumed his place at the window, the view toward the river, but I did not know what he truly saw in his mind's eye.

His fervor reminded me of Katy's fiery talk of equality for women and her determination to continue that work back in Boston. I felt my own ambitions pale in comparison. These times of great change in the world led passionate people in a myriad of different directions, their causes and concerns unique yet equally important. My own eyes were seeing beyond my peaceful existence in Meuse, ready to take in a greater view of the world and all that was taking place. Yet my place was here, doing what I could to improve the lives of those I would tend. Although Tanvir offered his services to my clinic, the likelihood that he might soon make the decision to return to India was a reality I would not worry over today. He needed to be free from all encumbrances that would serve as a reason, or an excuse, to hold him here rather than return to his home.

I now sat at the edge of the bed. "Tanvir, while I cannot but listen to your concerns and deeply sympathize, I do encourage you in the way my father has always done with me. He tells me to begin to move toward what I believe is my intention, and that in itself is a step of courage. You are a truly courageous man, and you will know when it is the right time to make changes in your life. These are not small matters, Tanvir, and these decisions require great contemplation. But you also must give yourself some ease of mind or you will not be able to move in any direction. We can sometimes become paralyzed with indecision and guilt and rooted in worry."

He remained at the window, his back to me.

Then I asked, "Have you ever had someone bathe you, Tanvir?"

At that, he turned around, a puzzled look on his face. "Bathe me? Not since I was I child, I am sure. What are you asking, Marie?"

"Because I have a large metal bathing tub, and I would like to bathe away your worries with steaming water and my lovely lavender-scented soap."

He walked the short distance to where I sat and folded to his knees, laying his head upon my lap. The bath, for the moment, was forgotten.

Later, bathed and smelling of lavender, we ate a light supper and took ourselves across the road once more to the river. We walked slowly along its banks, our hands and arms gently brushing against each other as the evening faded to darkness. The air was soft and warm and we lingered long, sitting against the trunks of the poplars.

He was to leave on the morning train this Tuesday to return to Paris and la Pitié-Salpêtrière. I assured him that while I was most grateful that he would act as the initial physician to the clinic, I knew this was only a short-term solution, and one that would resolve itself over time. I was confident another doctor would surely take over the practice in Verdun. He agreed. I sensed he was at peace and was coming to a place where he could make the decision in the not too distant future to return to India. He did not say this, but I saw in his eyes that it was so. And I was here, already at peace, already at home. We did not speak of when we would see one another again.

As we returned to my home in late evening and to my bed, where Tanvir fell soundly into sleep, I lay for some time thinking about what Papa said about passion and courage. Both had found me and I had embraced them wholeheartedly. I realized that passion can take many forms, whether it be for another person, one's work or commitment to a cause, or one's beliefs. As I closed my eyes, I was more than content and forever grateful for this small space in time with Tanvir, confident that whatever lay ahead for each of us we would fulfill our destinies with passion and courage.

CHAPTER 26

PASSAGES – JUNE 1923

Monday morning found us hitching Horse once again to the wagon and discussing the possible medical conditions that I might find coming through the door of the clinic. Tanvir, in asking me what I might expect to see, was attempting to provide me with information regarding diagnosing and treating my patients. In truth, I was more worried about introducing him to the Sisters. I was not sure how to describe our relationship, either to them or to myself.

I would, of course, explain his role as my esteemed physician professor and his kindness in offering to, at least for now, fulfill the role as the clinic's supervisor. A long-distance physician supervisor, but a supervisor nonetheless. And yes, of course they would see that we had become friends. But would they discern that our friendship had extended to something beyond? Would they see in my eyes that I had traveled to a place I did not know existed? Perhaps not, as they, I assumed, had never made that journey themselves. I felt anxious and eager for the introductions to be over and then to proceed quickly to discussing the running of the clinic, a topic more impersonal, which could be made as sterile as the bandages now tucked tightly in my cabinets.

Tanvir seemed more relaxed than at any time since his arrival. He was cheerful and talkative and was looking forward to meeting my friends, visiting their convent and grounds, and, of course, looking at the actual setup of the clinic.

I must, I told myself, remain calm and collected during the visit with the Sisters. I felt once we entered the clinic all would settle, and we could commence with the banal details of documentation, procedures, and inventory.

After stepping up onto the wagon first and offering a hand to help me board, Tanvir asked if he might drive. "I have never done so but would, I think, find it quite invigorating," he said as I handed him the reins. Horse turned his head, giving Tanvir a suspicious eye, but I nodded my assent and told him to head back north.

As we traveled to town, Tanvir focused solely on his driving, and I continued my attempts to compose myself, silently practicing introductions between my friends. I was extremely grateful that Henri was not arriving back home until tomorrow afternoon, hours after Tanvir would have boarded the train to Paris. I did not think I could have emotionally maneuvered my way between the two men.

Tanvir drew the wagon up close to the entrance of the convent. We had barely jumped down from our seats when Félix came barreling out the door, running squarely into the front of me and wrapping his short arms about my legs in his usual greeting.

"Marie! Sisters say there is no more breakfast but to come in for tea," he said eagerly, his mouth buried against my hip.

Taking him by his slim shoulders, I turned him around saying, "Félix, I have brought a visitor. A friend from Paris. This is Dr. Tanvir Singh."

"Bonjour, Docteur. I'm sure we have enough tea for you as well. I do like your hat. How do you wind it around your head so that it stays on?"

Tanvir laughed. "It's a pleasure to meet you, Félix. So you like my turban, do you? It takes much practice to tie a tight turban. And I would like very much to have tea with you."

Félix took Tanvir by the hand and led him into the convent, leaving me with a few moments to take a breath and smooth my dress. Catching myself, I put my hands behind my back and walked none too quickly through the front door. I was the coward this morning, hoping that by now Félix had made the introductions and the Sisters had taken their first appraisal of this new friend of Marie's.

Once inside, I found them all walking into the large refectory and not the familiar kitchen. I understood this to mean that Dr. Singh was to be treated more formally, that as a physician he would be held in high esteem. Following in their wake, I entered silently, mingling into the midst of them as they moved round the table. I sought out Sister Dominique and settled myself beside her. Tanvir was farther down on the same side, and Sister Agnès sat directly across from me.

I knew if I avoided her eyes she would be suspicious of many things but certainly not the truth. I smoothed my dress again upon sitting, looking up at her with what I felt was the most asinine smile I have ever conjured upon my face. She was indeed looking at me and merely tilted her head slightly to the left, raising a single eyebrow, with her mouth forming into something I interpreted as resembling a question mark.

The other Sisters asked Tanvir question after question regarding his work at the hospital in Paris, and he regaled them with stories of his teaching and his surgeries. I was surprised by how easily he engaged with these curious women, but then again, being a teacher he was used to talking with those he hardly knew. I knew also his polite bohemia was meant to explain his professional intentions: that his business here was to inspect La Clinique Meuse, ensuring all was in order, and that both the facility and the nurse were ready to receive patients. I heard him explain as much and more—that he was to be the physician supervisor until such a time as a doctor once again took up practice in Verdun and assumed that role.

I just sat there on the bench, that silly grimace upon my face, looking to all the world—except for Sister Agnès, I was sure—as though I was speechless with appreciation and as surprised and grateful as a nurse could ever be. And it was true, I certainly was surprised and grateful, not only as a nurse, but as a woman could be.

"Dr. Singh leaves tomorrow on the morning train back to Paris," I heard myself say. "We'll spend today going through the clinic inventory of instruments and medicinals, reviewing procedures, setting up the patient documentation and filing system, and the process by which he will supervise from such a distance as Paris or London. His schedule will not allow him to visit frequently but hopefully enough to meet the supervision requirements. And we will talk by telephone twice a month."

Leaning forward in order to see me, he said, "Because you were my gifted student and outstanding surgical assistant during your time at la Pitié-Salpêtrière, Nurse Durant, I need but vouch for your excellent nursing skills. You have proven yourself an enthusiastic and able student. It took you no time at all to learn what I had to teach."

Feeling myself blush and grow feverishly hot, I looked down at the table, muttering, "Merci, Dr. Singh. Your confidence in my abilities is much appreciated." He was toying with me, and I was barely holding myself together. I found it neither amusing nor helpful to have him so lightly traverse between the already muddied waters we stirred up between the personal and professional. Sister Agnès asked not a question nor made any comment throughout tea.

Shortly after our cups were empty, Tanvir placed both hands firmly atop the table and said, "Well, there is much work to be done at the clinic. Nurse Durant? Are you ready to begin?"

I jumped off the bench rather too quickly and stumbled against Sister Dominique. Righting myself, I assured Dr. Singh I was ready for the clinic's inspection. The Sisters all rose as one, and with Félix once again ahold of Tanvir's hand, we walked together to the front door.

Just outside the door, Tanvir stopped and faced the Sisters. "I thank you all for your kindness in making me feel so welcome and for your most gracious hospitality. Nurse Durant has shared with me how much your friendship and comradery mean to her, and I am very happy to have shared this experience."

I appreciated Tanvir's comment and was now able to easily produce a sincere smile and an accompanying head nod as I looked round at my dear friends.

Sister Agnès finally spoke, thanking him for assisting me, that by doing so it was ensured that our community had a much-needed medical clinic. "You are welcome here, Dr. Singh, whenever your clinic responsibilities bring you back. Next time, we will have you as our guest for dinner."

With that, Tanvir released Félix's hand and the good doctor and I jumped atop the wagon and drove the short distance to the clinic. I was nearly faint by the time we got there. I had been holding my breath for what seemed like forever. With slightly shaking hands, I lifted the heavy door key from my pocket and turned the lock, allowing us to escape into the quiet of the empty room. Walking over to the plinth table, I took hold of it as I finally exhaled all that had been held so tightly inside.

"An enthusiastic and able student, you say? A quick learner as well? You nearly had me falling off my seat, Tanvir. That was not kind of you and I really was not amused," I said, watching him still standing by the door with a smug look upon his face.

"Well, it's all true, isn't it? Regarding your nursing as well as your other newly acquired skills." Both of us now smiling, he walked across the room and we but touched hands. Conscious of the fact that there were windows on two of the four walls, we were careful to remain some discreet distance apart. We were both acutely aware we needed to talk seriously of the clinic and set it in order if I was to formally see patients in less than a week's time.

I eagerly and with much pride showed him all of the fine instruments, supplies, and contents of the labeled bottles in the cupboards. He was particularly interested in the microscope, declaring it an excellent choice and that it was made by a very reputable manufacturer in Germany and one of the finest to be purchased.

"I must admit I am rather jealous, Marie. You have put together a first-rate clinic. One I would want for myself when I return one day to India. I am also proud of you; you have made your dream a reality and are passionate about what you have created." He added, sounding forlorn and rather lost, "You will do well, my dear friend. I am sincerely happy for you."

"You know how to make your dream a reality as well, Tanvir. And, dear friend, I am proud of you."

It was curious to me that I no longer felt that initial overwhelming physical need to become absorbed into him, but rather was content to stand side by side, knowing I had experienced with this man a life-changing shift in my perspective of all I thought I knew. We were and would remain good friends.

Tanvir, while strong, was dependent upon many others and circumstances outside of himself and was only beginning to find his own right of way. These few days in Meuse seemed to allow him to step away from all he thought he had to be and look inside himself to find all he wanted to become.

The hours sped away as we worked diligently through the afternoon till early evening. Sister Dominique had brought us lunch earlier in the day and remained in order to become familiar with the filing system and how to record each patient's visit in a folder specific to them. Tanvir and I agreed upon a semimonthly date and time in which he would call me by telephone to discuss the clinic activity. He would provide assistance, answer questions, make recommendations, and provide verbal consent regarding treatment during those future conversations.

I would discuss with Henri having a phone installed in the clinic that, of course, would be my cost alone. This would also allow Sister Dominique and me to schedule patients if they called in to the clinic; however, I knew that most of our patients had no phones. Although the clinic hours, as well as the location and phone number, were to be posted on the flyers I was having made, local patients would simply arrive on my doorstep and wait their turn for care. And that was certainly fine by me.

It was also fine that Tanvir and I could communicate with one another twice each month. At least until he returned home to India, which I was sure he would do in the not too distant future. While that caused me some pain, I also was relieved I could acknowledge that while I would miss my friend, I knew that he and I were not destined to be together but for this brief, illuminating time—a time that proved so enlightening to each of us in different ways.

As the light faded, we headed back to my home. Tanvir again drove the wagon, finding humor in the fact that Horse would take us home without any effort on his part. We were both emotionally and mentally exhausted from the intensity of the past few days and content to merely sit silently beside one another, listening to the strapping of leather against the metal of the harness and bridle as it made music to accompany the setting sun. Once home, I prepared a light meal before we both fell into sleep, our fingers the only part of us entwined.

The next morning, I awoke to the sun streaming through the windows. I had left one partially open, and the birds were chirping madly as they flew over the river, catching the insects from the early hatch. I arose first, bathed and dressed, and then woke Tanvir, allowing enough time for a quick cup of tea and a soft-boiled egg before leaving for Verdun to catch his train.

On the way to the station, we again discussed our twice-a-month plan to connect with one another. He would call from either Paris or London, depending on where he was teaching. Tanvir held onto my hand most of the way into town. I felt a sorrow for him. He seemed at such odds with his place in the world.

"Do you feel good about returning to Paris, Tanvir?" I asked, looking at him.

With a reassuring pat to my hand and a slow smile brightening his solemn face, he responded, "All will be well. I acknowledge that I cannot push into the back of my mind issues that need to be viewed rationally. That there are decisions I will need to make. I now feel better able to do that, and I thank you, Marie, for the time in this beautiful place. Your loving kindness and the solitude of your home was the respite I needed. You are a strong and determined woman. I hope to emulate your example. I will miss you, *ma chérie.*"

It was my turn to pat his hand, which I did in silent reply. We kept our own counsel for the remainder of the journey, each of us thinking our own thoughts as we prepared for what was next in our lives.

The train was sitting on the tracks, her passengers boarding, and we said a quick adieu as he stepped up onto the car and disappeared round the corner. I stood watching the train depart along with a piece of myself, grateful that Tanvir did not appear at a window. Goodbyes were exhausting in the best of circumstances, and our goodbyes today held both the beginnings and endings of our emotional time together.

It was with some relief that I made my way south again. I looked forward to a period of solitude in which to sort my thoughts. But as I approached the clinic and Henri's home I saw his automobile parked outside my office door. He was untying rope and removing oilcloth securing a large piece of what looked like furniture—but not exactly. I could not make out what it was but did know it was intended for my new space.

"Bonjour, Henri, and welcome home," I said, jumping from the wagon. My need to be alone was forgotten as I realized it was indeed good to see him, and I was certainly curious about what was carried on his trailer.

"Your timing is excellent, Marie. You can help move these into the clinic. They are your privacy screens. I was fortunate to find them in Reims and hope they meet your needs."

Henri did not make eye contact or offer any other greeting but continued untying and removing the heavy covering he had placed as protection over the screens.

"I'm sure they will be perfect. You never disappoint, Henri."

"Félix tells me you had a visitor these past few days. A doctor from Paris? How did that come about?" He stopped what he was doing and looked at me intently.

It dawned on me that, of course, Félix had told him of Tanvir's visit both with me and at the convent. I was not sure how to answer, much less explain the past several days. But I realized that I only needed to convey to Henri the doctor's offer of supervision.

"Dr. Singh was one of the professor physicians at la Pitié-Salpêtrière. He taught many of the classes, and I assisted him in surgery several times a week. I told him my plans for the clinic and the concern that I had not found a supervising physician in Verdun nor was it likely I would find one in the near vicinity. He was kind enough to offer to fill this role, at least for a short while." I related this information to Henri all the while feeling duplicitous at my partial omission regarding Tanvir's visit.

"I understand his visit was a surprise. That it was not planned before you left Paris. Were you caught unawares of his intentions?" Henri asked, suddenly straightening his person and looking deliberately into my eyes.

"Yes, Henri. I did not know he was coming to inspect the clinic. When I left we had established a professional comradery, but I was indeed surprised when he appeared at the clinic door. But it was a welcome surprise, as he was able to see where I would be nursing, the setup of the clinic, and to verify for himself that I had everything necessary to run the clinic day to day. He was pleased to know that Sister Dominique would be dealing with the paperwork and filing in addition to scheduling appointments and greeting the patients. He needed to make sure all was in order before he could ever agree to supervise from such a long distance and that could only be done by actually visiting the facility." I felt my defenses rising along with my blood pressure. I did not need to justify Tanvir's intentions or my own.

I expected Henri to ask about Tanvir staying in my home, but thankfully he did not, and I offered no more in the way of explanations but turned abruptly and made for the clinic door. I unlocked it and opened it wide, taking one very needed deep breath as I surveyed the space all arranged and awaiting patients. Turning back to Henri, I walked resolutely to his trailer, ready to assist him in carrying in the needed screens.

Without further conversation, Henri nodded for me to pick up one end of the first screen. I could see it was the smaller of two, and this one we placed in front of my desk from Papa. As we set it upright, Henri unfolded the three sections, and I could only stand amazed. The screens were nothing less than works of extraordinary beauty.

Dark, heavy wood framed the three panels of thick shantung silk the color of emeralds. The sunlight through the window beside my desk caused the fabric to shimmer, and as I stroked the silk, the colors changed from iridescent pales to darker hues. I could not take in the meticulous embroidery; the level of detail was too much for my mind and emotions to make sense of.

Knowing Henri was outside waiting for me to help carry in the larger one, I hurried out the door to find him already attempting to lift it by himself. I took my portion of the heavy load, and we brought it carefully through the door, placing it in front of the plinth table. Unfolding each of the five sections revealed again the breathtaking beauty of the silk and the exquisite designs embroidered in each panel of fabric.

"Henri, from whom did you purchase these beautiful screens? They both seem so delicate, yet the panels are made of such heavy fabric and the wood frames are deceptively sturdy. They most certainly meet my specifications. The clinic will be a place of beauty as well as healing, and I thank you from the bottom of my heart." I approached him, and he acknowledged my appreciation of both the beauty as well as the functionality of these fine pieces and graced me with a smile and kisses to my cheeks.

"You remember, they are my gift to your clinic, Marie. And yes, they are both fragile and deceptively strong. They reminded me of you," he said, still smiling.

I felt the awkwardness of the past hour ebbing away as we stood side by side, caressing the cool feel of the silk and remarking on the fine hand stitching of the needlework. Henri shared that he found the screens at a large estate sale in a centuries-old chateau just outside of Reims proper, but he would not divulge the amount of money he had to part with to acquire such treasures.

He left me, returning to his trailer to fold the oilcloth and coil the ropes. I took a moment alone to stand and look gratefully over every object and all the potential held within this space and to offer my sincere thankfulness to whatever saints and deities might be watching. It was now merely days until the clinic would open. I needed but to hang my sign and all was ready.

My eyes and fingertips lingered on the slightly nubby texture of the rich fabric of the screens, taking in the beauty and feel of the workmanship. I could feel each individual thread of every intricate stitch used in creating these exquisite images, images of stately, graceful birds—cranes with wide wings spread and in flight, looking for all the world like the cranes Tanvir created with his papers. I felt the truth that, like these beautiful birds that had somehow been given to me by both Tanvir and Henri, we were all connected yet each on our own flights, forging passages into a future we could but glimpse.

CHAPTER 27

LA CLINIQUE MEUSE –
2 JULY, 1923

The day dawned pearlescent, dew covering every surface outdoors and lustrous in the sunlight. Leaving the convent at seven, I arrived at the clinic's door shortly thereafter. And whom should I find standing on the wooden stoop but Bernard.

"Bernard, I am more than surprised to find you here. Do you know that today is the opening of *la clinique*? But we do not open for another hour?"

"Oui, *je sais*. And I know that I am early. But I am hoping you would see me before you have others at your door." He leaned in close to my ear, whispering as if to a conspirator. "My business with you is very private."

I reached into the recesses of my bag and produced the key. Once inside, I told him to sit in the waiting area, as I needed a few minutes to prepare.

His face contorted with frustration. "I can't sit. That's why I'm here."

Initially puzzled by his unexpected appearance at my door, I now noticed that his stance and facial expressions indicated he was in pain. Moving behind the partition screen, I donned my nurse's apron and covered the plinth table with a clean linen cloth.

I returned to the reception area, picked up a pen and a new patient folder from the stack on Sister's desk, and took a seat in one of the chairs. "Now, Bernard, tell me why you are here."

Looking right and left, as though there were others in the room with us, he said, "Can we go behind the screen before anyone else comes in and has a listen?"

"Yes, we can. Follow me and then, please, tell me what is going on with you."

He stood beside the cloth-covered table holding onto its edge with a fierce grip. I stood on the other side, watching and waiting for him to share what was so private.

"Arse boils. I have arse boils," he mumbled through tight lips, looking down at the floor.

Straining to hear and repeating in my mind what I thought he said, I asked, "Did you say you have 'arse boils'? If so, tell me why you think that to be true."

"I know it to be true, Marie. There is nothing to think about. My insides are all plugged up, and when I try to sit and . . . and . . . push, nothing comes out but rock-hard coal along with the sores. And then they bleed and hurt like . . . they hurt like fire."

"Sounds as though you have become severely constipated and now have hemorrhoids from pushing so hard."

"That's about it. I can't walk or sit and can hardly sleep. I don't want to eat, thinking it will become worse. You're a nurse, you need to help me," he insisted, relaxing now that he had shared his concerns, which I did understand to be very private and embarrassing.

"First, I need to examine you and assess the problem, meaning I must take a look at your 'arse boils.' You need to take off your trousers and underwear and lie face down on the table. I will leave while you do so. And no arguing. I'll be back in a few minutes." I would complete first the most uncomfortable and embarrassing portion of the exam and then take his vital signs and history, a procedure that would be much less distressing.

I heard the creak of the table as he climbed on. "Are you ready, Bernard?"

"Of course I'm not ready. Who could be ready for this?"

Returning, I scrubbed my hands at the sink and put on rubber gloves to examine my first patient here in my new space, smiling to think that it was Bernard, of all people.

I moved to his side and asked, "How long have you been in this condition?"

"Many months. It's happened before but then would get better. But now, it only seems to get worse."

He had pulled his shirt as low over his buttocks as possible, and as I lifted it to his waist to begin the exam, he said, "Just don't tell anyone I was here. Can I be sure of that?"

"Bernard, I hold the highest degree of nursing to be had in this country, and with that comes an oath of patient confidentiality. What you and I say to each other goes no further than this room. The only other person who will know is Sister Dominique, as she in charge of the patients' files. You can trust both she and myself to never disclose either that you were here or why. Now, please relax your butt muscles so I can look."

He complied, and I saw three external affected veins, swollen and inflamed, and upon further examination three internal veins.

"You indeed have hemorrhoids, Bernard, and they have been there for quite a while. You should have spoken with me weeks ago."

"Your clinic wasn't open weeks ago."

I didn't argue the point but said, "Now, I want you to turn over that I may feel your abdomen. I expect it is hard and probably tender. I'll leave as you rotate yourself and you can put another linen over your privates. I'll return shortly."

After handing him a small cloth to cover himself, I removed my gloves, placing them into the refuse container, and washed my hands. I then went to the front of the clinic to record some notes in his file, allowing him a moment to readjust.

The clinic door opened, and Dominique walked in with a cheerful "bonjour." I motioned to the screened area and quietly told her that our first patient was here, and I was in the middle of an examination.

"Would you please put water on to boil and make an infusion of chamomile— approximately one liter? The patient needs an enema that will hopefully help relieve severe constipation."

"Are you making me tea, Marie? I don't need tea," Bernard hollered from the other side of the screen.

"You need to move your bowels," I said, returning to the table. "The stool is most likely hard-packed inside of you and needs water to loosen it so you can gently push it out. And I mean gently—no hard pushing. It may take two or three enemas, Bernard. Now, let me examine your stomach."

As I suspected, he was bloated, and when I palpated the area he responded with grumbling and low cursing, attesting to tenderness and pain. Sister let me know the infusion was prepared and that she had filled the enema bag and attached the necessary tubing.

"Now, Bernard. I need you to remain on your back. Bend your knees and keep your feet flat on the table. I am going to place a pillow underneath to raise your buttocks and then we will proceed with the enema. Once the liquid has been administered, you are to hold it inside for at least five minutes. Then, when you feel you can no longer hold it, you can sit on the commode and gently expel the liquid. Do not push, Bernard!"

"*Mon Dieu!* I did not expect to be tortured when I walked through your door today. I am already in enough pain. Is this really what needs to be done?"

"Here we go. Lie still, relax your muscles, and do as you are told." This isn't the way I would have spoken to an unfamiliar patient, one who had never come through my door before, but I knew that with Bernard I needed to be firm and confident and give him no chance to jump from the table and bolt out the door.

He did as I instructed and managed to wait the five long minutes before running to the commode. After dressing, he moved slowly back to the table.

"Was any stool expelled with the water?"

"No more than a few hard rabbit turds."

"And that is better than nothing. I want you to come back this afternoon at three, and we will do another enema. I have written a list of what you are to eat and what you are to apply to the hemorrhoids twice a day. Again, if you want to resolve this situation, you must change some habits so you will not find yourself here again for the same reason. And I assume, Bernard, you would not wish to return more than necessary."

"What must I do, Marie? Tell me and I will do so and not complain. I want to get about my life."

"Let's go over the instructions together. I assume you have a bathtub—fill it half full with warm water, adding a tablespoon of witch hazel. You are to sit in the water for ten minutes, twice a day. After drying the affected area completely, you are to apply the ointment I'm giving you." I handed him a small jar of olive oil infused with aloe vera along with a small bottle of witch hazel.

"And you are to have oatmeal every morning for breakfast, eat an apple every afternoon, and drink many glasses of water throughout the day. Your dinner should consist of vegetables and soft meat. If you follow these instructions, Bernard, and your constipation is relieved, your hemorrhoids will begin to diminish and eventually go away. But if you don't eat correctly or if you push too hard when you go to the bathroom, you'll be right back where you are today. Is that understood?"

"I understand, Marie. Will they be gone in a week?"

"It depends on how quickly you can resume normal bowel functions. The better your diet, the better chance you have to quickly resolve the problem. And remember, be back here at three, as I am hoping that with another enema you can experience some relief from the uncomfortable pressure and pain. Drink a lot of water between now and then."

He took the list of instructions along with the jars of medicine and started toward the door. "*Attendez*, I almost forgot! My other concern was about my neighbor. The wife can't seem to get her baby born, and when I looked in on them last evening, the husband, Jacob, told me she was still trying and nothing is happening, that she is now weak. He was worried about his wife and the baby. I told him I would be seeing you and would let you know."

"Bernard, why in the world did you not tell me this when you first arrived? I could have immediately gone to help."

"My arse hurt so much I forgot everything else. Can't you go see them now? I can take you there and bring you back again."

"Yes, of course I need to go now, and yes, please take me," I said, already gathering birthing tools, instruments, ointments, and linens into my leather bag.

I had heard the door to the clinic open and close several times since Sister Dominique arrived, and as I stepped round to her desk, I saw three patients waiting in chairs. With calm efficiency she helped them complete their personal information and history forms.

"Bernard, please wait outside by your truck. I need to triage these patients and then I will be ready to leave."

Sister and I stepped behind the privacy screen about my desk, and she reviewed with me why the new patients were there—two older women who had come together and one elderly gentleman. None of them reported to be suffering from illness or injury that could not wait until the next morning. I explained the situation to them, that I had to leave immediately to assist with a birth, and I would be happy to see them first thing tomorrow. The women were more than understanding and said so, but the man harrumphed out the door. Perhaps he had cranky arse boils as well.

I jumped quickly into Bernard's truck and off we drove.

"Tell me more about the family. Have they lived in this area for long? Do you know them well?"

"There is the father, Jacob Weir, and his wife, Rose, and a little girl. I think her name is Hélène. The father fought in the war, doesn't talk much, and seems to be having a hard time of it all now. Seems a changed man. I hired him a few times to do chores at my place, and I know Henri has often given them food. They have hardly anything. They seem very old, but I know they are as young as you."

We drove thirty minutes west of the clinic, past Bernard's property, to a very small, unkempt house—more hovel than home. There was no sign of life about, and I experienced a feeling of dread at what we might find inside.

Bernard proceeded to the door ahead of me and walked in unannounced. A man I assumed to be Jacob was sitting on a crudely built wooden bench, his head lying on the rough-hewn table in front of him. Other than the table and the two benches either side of it, there was no other furniture in sight. I neither heard sounds nor saw evidence of a baby or impending birth. Complete silence accompanied a terrible raw odor.

"Jacob, I brought Nurse Marie. She can help Rose now," Bernard said as the man raised his head from the table, looking around as though in a daze. He was thin to the point of emaciation, with dry, wrinkled skin lying loose across his bones, his dull hair hanging long and tangled from neglect, his eyes red and runny. It was obvious I needed to get to the wife immediately. I did not wait for an invitation but hurried through the door to the next room. The smell alone would have led me to the woman.

I found her in a soiled bed, breathing so faintly I feared for her life. Her pulse was weak, and as I lifted her arm, it was as lifeless as the blank eyes staring out at me. With hair matted to her head, red, pus-crusted eyes, and her large protruding belly, she looked for all the world a woman in the throes of both agony and despair. A frail young girl sat on a chair some distance from the bed, silently watching the woman. I assumed this was Hélène.

I walked around the bed and knelt down in front of her. "Bonjour, Hélène. I'm here to help your maman. Has she been talking to you at all?"

The child merely shook her head, looking back at me through eyes red and runny, scratching listlessly at her scalp. She presented the same languorous countenance as her parents. They were all obviously in need of care, but I would attend to the mother first.

I turned my attention once again to the woman in bed. "Rose, my name is Marie. I am a nurse. I am here to help you, but first you need to help me understand what is happening to you." I gently moved my hands across her abdomen, searching for her baby's contours.

Rose slowly turned her head and opened her cracked, dry lips. She tried to speak but the sound produced merely a wisp of dry air. I immediately went back to the other room to get her some water. She was severely dehydrated and in a desperate condition. Bernard stood by the table opposite the husband. Neither one spoke. He could at least help me if he had nothing better to occupy himself with.

"Bernard, I need a glass of water and clean bedclothes. You and Jacob need to make yourselves useful. Once I have determined the state of the baby, I will ask you to return to the clinic and request from Sister Dominique everything I might need."

He nodded his head in agreement and hurried to fill a large pitcher. He entered the bedroom with a glass of water but looked as if he wished to be any place other than where he was. "I will look, Marie, but I do not think I will find any clean bedding here," he said, glancing back through the open door. Nothing was clean in this house.

Raising Rose's head and shoulders that she might drink a few swallows, I then applied olive oil to her lips. She was featherlight, with bones protruding at all angles. As I gently laid her down again, she was gripped with a strong contraction, providing me the opportunity to do a more thorough assessment.

The baby was still high up in the birth canal, the bloody discharge now minimal. Her water had yet not broken. After placing several linen cloths between her legs, I removed a sterile hook from my bag and perforated the amniotic sack, allowing the fluid to spill forth and hopefully sending the infant farther down where I might use forceps, if needed. With each contraction, Rose would need to use what little strength she had to push.

I again enlisted Bernard's help and called him into the room. Bernard came in and stood silently beside the bed. "I need you to prop Rose up when I tell you to. You'll need to place your hands behind her shoulders, lifting her back as high as you can."

Rose gave out a weak moan, and as another contraction began, I told Bernard to raise her up.

"Rose, I need you to push as hard as you can. Your baby needs to be born, and you need to help. Open your eyes and look at me, Rose, and push!"

As Bernard provided support, Rose did look at me and attempted to push as strongly as she could manage. The infant descended to where I could feel the head, allowing me to slide the forceps in around each side of the small cranium.

"Now, Rose, at the next contraction, you need to give another long, hard push."

With her eyes on mine and giving a slight nod of her head, she indicated the contraction was upon her. Bernard lifted her back, and as I applied gentle pressure, guiding the baby toward its new world, the head emerged, and I laid the forceps aside. Rose pushed one more time and the still infant slid into my hands. Quickly suctioning the mucus from the baby's nostrils and mouth, I turned her over—yes, it was a girl—and began briskly rubbing her back. She began to squirm and a welcomed sound, the cry for air and life, greeted us all as we looked from one to the other, smiling with relief as I cut the cord.

Bernard gently laid Rose down onto the bed as I laid her new daughter, wrapped in white linen, into her arms.

"Hélène," I said, walking over to the little girl as I wiped my hands, "your maman is fine, and you have a new baby sister. Would you like to see her?"

Nodding her head once, she quietly walked over to her mother as Rose pulled down the cloth to reveal a head of dark fuzz. Hélène reached out to touch her, saying, "I think she will be mine, Maman."

Rose smiled, replying faintly, "Yes, she is yours too, as you are mine."

Returning to the foot of the bed, I had Rose push twice more, expelling the afterbirth, and then massaged her abdomen to help stop any bleeding and aid the uterus in calming. I was grateful that after such an extensive labor both mother and child appeared weak but in no danger. I did not think, though, that Rose would be able to supply her newborn with milk, at least not until she was adequately nourished herself.

Writing quickly, I handed Bernard a piece of paper. "Here is the list of items needed from the clinic and convent. Please give it to Sister Dominique, wait for her to gather everything, and return as quickly as you can. And I thank you for your help today. You made a fine assistant mid-wife," I said, smiling into his face. He just shook his head and hurried out to his truck with my note to Sister.

Jacob followed Bernard out, and as I watched the truck pull away, the father walked off in the other direction. I wondered that he did not want to see his family. He was almost more of a worry than the others.

Bernard was correct, there were no clean linens to be found—no clean clothes or cloths of any sort. I removed the soiled sheet from under Rose and replaced it with one from my bag, the best I could do before Bernard returned. Both mother and baby were sleeping; Hélène stood beside the bed watching as though they might slip away from her.

"Hélène, I have bread and cheese in my bag. Would you like to share some with me?" She nodded, and I took her into the next room and sat on a bench beside her. I surreptitiously examined the child as she took small bites of the food and drank sips of water from the glass I placed in front of her. It was obvious she presented with an infection to both eyes and a scalp full of head lice. The list I gave to Bernard included ointments and tinctures to treat both the conjunctivitis and the lice. And I knew Rose and Jacob required treatment for the same highly contagious conditions. I only hoped the baby would not contract either one.

I would put Bernard and Jacob to work scrubbing the house from top to bottom with lye soap as I bathed and treated Rose and Hélène. Jacob would need to scrub himself as well. I had spied two buckets outside the door and knew they had an adequate supply of water. Jacob could wash outside, using the buckets to rinse. It was curious he had not yet returned.

I needed to remain with this family until I was assured they were fed, clean, and treated and that mother and babe were stable. My note to Sister stated that she should triage all patients arriving at the clinic's door and schedule them for a time to be seen either tomorrow or the next day.

Bernard returned sooner than expected, and I helped unload several boxes from the back of his truck. "The Sisters all helped put together what you requested, Marie. They said if you needed anything else that I could make another trip back. They volunteered me and my truck without even asking if I would be agreeable to that plan."

"They knew that you would help in any way needed, Bernard. That is the kind of man you are, no?" I heard a "humph" as he carried two boxes into the house and set them on the table.

In one of the boxes were the glass baby bottles and rubber nipples I requested and a jug of still-warm goat's milk. Filling one of the clean bottles a quarter full and diluting it with boiled water that had cooled, I stepped again to the mother's bedside and gently woke her.

"Rose, your baby needs to eat. You most likely do not have milk yet to feed her, so we can give her goat's milk until your own comes in."

She nodded her head and struggled to sit upright against the wall. As Rose stroked her infant's head and mouth, the baby woke and was sufficiently able to take the nipple and suckle for a short while before falling once again to sleep. Rose smiled, looking as relieved as I, handed me the bottle, and lay back down upon the bed, her baby cradled in her arms. Before she too fell back asleep, I had her drink a glass of the goat's milk and take some bites of bread. They could both rest now while I set about caring for Hélène and putting Bernard to work on scrubbing the house. Jacob still had not returned.

"Jacob left when you did, Bernard. He needs to be here to wash himself and to help you clean this place. It is infested with lice, and so is each person in this family. But it won't do much good to thoroughly wipe everything down only to leave the mattresses full of vermin to reinfest everyone. We need a clean mattress for both the bed and Hélène's small cot. And a place for the baby to sleep as well. All the linens and clothing must be burned. See if you can find Jacob in the next ten minutes. If you cannot, then go on to the convent and secure two mattresses, clothing for the mother and father, and some of Félix's clothes he keeps there. I know the Sisters have a small collection of used clothing. And more linens and blankets. I am sorry I did not realize these needs when I sent you back the first time."

"I do not mind. It takes my mind off my own pain and keeps your mind off what you might do to me next," he said with what looked almost like a smile.

I walked out with him to his truck. "Merci, Bernard. Your help is invaluable. I haven't forgotten you need to return to the clinic, but I promise to provide you with care as pain-free as possible."

After seeing Bernard off, I returned to the kitchen, adding wood to the fire in the stove and stoking it high, and then placed the heavy metal bucket on top to boil more water. I would first bathe Hélène and treat both her eyes and scalp. Her light brown hair was dull and snarled, the lice so abundant that the many open sores on her scalp were crusted with dried blood from her constant scratching.

"Hélène, I know your head itches you all the time. That is because there are tiny little bugs in your hair that make you want to scratch. Once we get all the bugs out of your hair, you will feel so much better. I'm going to cut your hair, shampoo your head, and then put on some very nice-smelling oils to get all of them out. And then I will do the same for your maman and papa. You will all smell lovely and not itch anymore. Is that alright with you, *mon enfant*?"

This child had acquiesced to everything I had put to her, never uttering a word. She did so again, silently nodding her head and remaining on the bench where she had finished eating. She reminded me of Félix the first time I met him, quietly suffering on many accounts.

"The water is warm, Hélène, and since it is also a warm day, we will give you a bath outside. Our friend Bernard is bringing more food and clean clothes for you, so let's get your bath done and your hair cut and combed before he gets back. Can you open the door for me, please?"

Taking the bucket from the stove, we walked outside. I helped her remove her thin, dirty dress, then cut her hair to just above her ears with the shears from my bag, hoping all the while that she would not protest. She stood perfectly still as I poured water over her head and then lathered her from head to toe with lye soap, scrubbing every inch of her small frame. My heart went out to the poor child. It had obviously been some time since she was properly bathed.

As I poured water over her once again to rinse her thoroughly, she asked, "When the man comes back, can I have more food?"

Back in the kitchen, Hélène sat on the bench wearing my over-blouse and drinking a glass of the goat's milk as I combed and trimmed her hair even shorter, making sure it was straight and even all around. I then massaged her scalp with olive oil and lavender. The olive oil was to smother the lice and the lavender would soothe her irritated scalp. After letting it set on her hair for a time, I combed through the strands, wiping the dead lice into a cloth after each pass. Mixing a pinch of salt with a tablespoon each of honey and cool boiled water, I then applied this soothing ointment to her eyes. Next, I filled a small cup with honey and handed her a spoon, watching as she eagerly licked the sweetness that would both assuage her hunger and help heal her eyes.

Bernard finally returned with Jacob in tow. I did not ask any questions as they helped me move mother and baby into the kitchen, seating them on the bench where Rose and Hélène drank broth and ate pieces of chicken, cheese, and baguette with honey. Bless the Sisters.

I handed Jacob and Bernard some bread and cheese as I instructed them to move the old mattresses and linens outside to burn and to begin scrubbing the bedroom down with lye soap and water. And to do so as quickly as possible that Rose and her baby might return to bed for rest.

While the men cleaned the bedroom, I took the time to explain to Rose that she needed to undergo the same haircutting and bathing routine that Hélène just completed. The mother looked at her daughter, now dressed in some of Félix's clothes, her hair cut short and shiny with oil, and said, "Oui, Mademoiselle, let's do it now."

By the time Rose was sheared, bathed, and dressed in clean clothes, looking a twin to her daughter with their matching lavender-olive-oil-infused hair, it was time again to feed the newborn. Rose put the infant to her breast, where she nursed for several minutes. She then took the bottle of warm goat's milk I handed her and fed the baby until she was full. Rose was quite weak, but she and her infant were both calm and out of any danger.

"There is still water to give your baby her first bath, Rose."

"*Merci infiniment* for all you have helped with. You are such a fine nurse and a good woman. I have no words to express to you my gratitude. Yes, I will wash my baby. Hélène, come help Maman give your baby a bath."

I handed her two heavy towels the Sisters had sent and a bar of gentle olive oil soap, suggesting to Rose that she wash the baby's head thoroughly each day, applying olive oil afterwards to prevent lice. Sisters had sent an adequate supply of clean linens to wrap the infant in after bathing and this would be the child's only covering until clothes could be found. There were also heavier cloths for diapers and a set of large pins. Where in the world had they found these necessities, and so quickly? I wondered if Henri had a hand in it.

The wood of the bedroom's walls and floor was still slightly damp and smelled strongly of lye when the men carried in the fresh mattresses. I made up the beds with clean sheets before Rose and baby returned to their room and then helped them get comfortable. Just before Rose fell to sleep cradling her babe, I again applied the honey ointment to their eyes.

Bernard had taken note of my ministrations to Rose and Hélène and was now outside with a naked Jacob in tow, telling him to "stand still for the water. Soap down and stop your yappin'." The water for Jacob's cleansing was cold, and hearing a loud wail and a curse, I knew Bernard had anointed him.

Jacob being considerably smaller than tall, thickset Bernard had nonetheless donned the pants and shirt his friend gave him from his own wardrobe. I had to quickly cover my mouth when I saw Jacob come into the house. One or the other of them had chopped his hair as short as possible. It stood up in uneven tufts all over his head. And Bernard had had Jacob rub a good amount of oil and lavender onto his scalp, telling him to "rub it in till it hurts."

While the two men scoured the front room, they kept an eye on the flames consuming the infected clothes and linens and the smoldering mattresses. I stayed in the bedroom with the females until Bernard and Jacob completed their tasks. Hélène was tucked in and asleep on her own clean mattress that we pulled close beside her mother's bed. The entire house now smelled of lye and lavender, its occupants clean, clothed, treated, and fed. I would return the next day to check on them, bringing more food and milk.

I planned to speak with Henri concerning Jacob's need for employment. His obvious depression was worrisome, and without him working, his family would remain in this silent despair. His need was greater than the others' in this house and one I remembered well, not only from caring for the traumatized young soldiers in my home after the war but also from my own suffocating depression. He was in a lonely and frightening place. But when you have people relying on you for their very lives you are not free to live in isolation, hoping with time life will once again take on a semblance of meaning.

It was late afternoon when I jumped from Bernard's truck as he stopped in front of my clinic door. Thanking him profusely for his help during this long day, I reminded him to go home and follow my directions to take a sitz bath and apply ointment, that I would see him the next morning at eight. We were both too exhausted to deal with arse boils now.

I walked up the steps and opened the door to find Sister Dominique there, alone, writing in patient files. "Bonjour, Sister. How has the day gone here?"

"There were ten people wanting to see you, but none were bleeding, wounded, or in severe pain. They will all return tomorrow or the day after. I gave them your apologies, explaining you were assisting with a home birth. They were all understanding and bid the family well. And you, Marie? I know from Bernard that your day was more involved than just helping birth a baby."

I gave her a synopsis of the day and thanked her for managing the clinic so well on her own, on this our very first day. "Please relay my sincerest appreciation to the other Sisters for their help in sending all that was needed. Go home now, Sister, and we will begin again tomorrow. I will spend just a short while reading the files you have taken such pains with today." I then sat down to look over all the patient notes Sister Dominique had written, to acquaint myself with what may present itself tomorrow. Over an hour later, with a sense of grateful weariness, I closed the last folder.

Atop the small stove in the clinic, I set water to boil to clean my instruments and scrubbed my hands again before restocking my satchel with fresh supplies. A knock at the door, the door into Henri's home, gave me a start. "Come in," I called.

"Nurse Durant, this first day has been quite a long one, no?" Henri asked, greeting me with warm kindness and concern in his eyes.

"Long, yet fulfilling—like most days of nursing," I replied with a smile.

As I wiped down the instruments, washing them well under the water tap, he took them from me and dropped them slowly into the now-boiling pot. Henri was very familiar with the routine of sterilizing instruments after treatments and many times at the convent had helped me put my tools in order, readying them for the next patient. Falling through the water, the metal pinged softly as it collided with another piece of itself. "Your instruments bring back the music of life to your patients, Marie."

I smiled in response and gave him an abbreviated version of the situation I found upon arriving at the Weirs' and how we worked throughout the day. Pleased to know that Bernard was so helpful and that mother and baby were doing well, he grew thoughtful when I told him my concerns regarding Jacob.

Henri knew the family only slightly, having met Jacob but once when the man worked at Bernard's cleaning the sheep barn and moving hay. "I saw Bernard briefly today on his second trip back to the clinic. He said he was in a great hurry, as you needed his help. He also told me you are a fine nurse, that you are helping him personally, and that he was already in less pain."

"Ah," I said, laughing. "So he told you of his early arrival at my door this morning and my subsequent intervention on his behalf?"

"Oui, he did, and he also said you 'took charge of a bad situation' at the Weirs'. I think you greatly impressed a man who is impressed by little and compliments few."

"Well, if that is so, then the day truly has been a success. I will need to return to the family sometime tomorrow morning, probably late morning, as they will need more food and goat's milk for the baby. The mother is so undernourished that supplementing what she might provide to her baby will ease her worry and increase the infant's strength. Who knew what a blessing the convent's mama goat would become?"

All the implements were now boiled and set on clean linen to dry. I took a long breath and realized how very hungry I was.

As if reading my mind, Henri asked, "When did you last eat, Nurse Durant?"

"This morning before leaving the convent, and oui, I am famished. The Sisters will have something laid out for me to nibble on before I fall into bed."

"There is more than a little something to eat now lying on my table awaiting those who are hungry, along with hot water for tea or perhaps a small glass of brandy. Félix is fidgeting in his bed, hoping you would consent to tell him goodnight. He has been most eager to learn how the first day of La Clinique Meuse went. I promised I would wait for you and, if he was not sleeping, take advantage of your good nature to speak to him, your faithful boy."

"Of course. Seeing Félix will be a wonderful end to an arduous day. And I gratefully accept your offer of a meal."

Walking through the door, we were instantly bathed in candlelight. The *bougies*, as on my earlier visit, were placed on many different surfaces. Immediately I let go of the day's worries, the comfortable ambience familiar and soothing.

Félix, obviously hearing the closing of the door, rushed at me and launched himself into my arms. "How was your first day, Marie? Was it like my first day at school? Did you have worms in your stomach?"

Hugging him tightly, smelling his little boy smell, I told him the day was busy and a great deal was accomplished. "And I met a little girl your age who might become a new friend."

Yawning wide, he whispered into my ear, "I waited up for you, Marie."

"Yes, I know," I whispered in return. "And I thank you, Félix, as seeing you is the best way to end my day."

"Henri said I have to go back to bed after saying goodnight to you," he said, burying his face against my neck. And with a final hug I put him down, and he skipped off to his room.

While I had been speaking to Félix, Henri had busied himself rearranging the table with olives, sliced meats, cheeses, fruit, baguettes, and small glasses of shimmering red brandy. I wanted to gobble it all down in large bites.

"How very kind of you, Henri, to invite me to share your supper. Wherever do you find these delicacies?" I asked, popping another tangy black olive into my mouth.

"The meats and olives were traded in barter to a railroad administrator. He was short on monies for a painting he wished to purchase for his wife, so I accepted both his cash on hand and his good food in exchange."

"Ah, so you are still bartering with customers. I thought your bartering days were done."

"Bartering can be more excellent than money as you exchange what you have to give for what you might not otherwise receive. You will most likely be asked many times to barter in exchange for your medical services. However, some, like the Weirs, have little to barter with and no money to pay for what they need."

"And little do I care, Henri. Restoring them to health is my payment. Although I realize that if I receive no monies, then neither do you."

Without a moment's hesitation, he picked up his glass of brandy and held it forth to me, saying, "Then we can barter, Marie, you and I. Your presence in my home at my table sharing an occasional meal is the payment I will exact." He smiled then, the lines about his softly weathered face appearing as he took my hand from the tabletop and placed it into his own.

Returning his smile, a rush of warmth rising up through my soul, I raised my glass to his, acknowledging the culmination of so much effort and collaboration. So much to be grateful for, especially all of those I had come to love who contributed to the success of my dream.

And so, this first day of La Clinique Meuse was all I had wanted and everything I needed. I was off on my great adventure wondering what more was to come.

HISTORICAL PERSPECTIVES

PEDDLERS OF EUROPE

The history of peddling in Europe dates back to before the Middle Ages, and through time, peddlers have been viewed with an air of mistrust and even mystique. *Mercelots*, wandering traders, as they were known in France, were viewed with great suspicion and disparity by the organized trade guilds, which considered them part huckster and part merchant.

Peddlers were sometimes mountain people, solitary men who wandered into towns to sell merchandise acquired along the way. There were, however, peddlers who were part of a large family, often owning a communal farm, and when not planting or harvesting, more than one man would take to the road selling merchandise to established customers. These peddlers, such as Henri in *The Passage Home to Meuse*, were part of an extended family. They made their living between what they earned from their crops and the selling of goods deemed essential or in high demand by those they sold to along their extended route where most items were not readily available.

There were three designations of peddlers. The destitute peddler was a solitary trader, with few ties or connections to others in the trade. He could be from anywhere going to anywhere and was considered to be on the fringes of merchant society. This is the rogue peddler often depicted in stories.

Regular peddlers, the second category, had trustworthy suppliers, loyal customers, and well-established routes of commerce. They sometimes sold and bought on credit, and bartering was part of their business. Often they were family men from the farms who peddled after the seeds were planted and again following the harvest. Henri was, for most of his career, a regular peddler, who was trusted and depended upon to bring essential goods to those unable to acquire the scarce necessities of daily living on their own, especially in the many months following the decimation of towns and villages during World War I.

The third category, the merchant peddler, might have kept his inventory in a rented building and sometimes owned a storefront out of which he also sold goods and merchandise. When he was out procuring items or on the road selling, he would have someone else conducting business in his shop. Upon her return to Meuse, Marie found that Henri had become a merchant peddler, both owning his shop in Verdun and continuing to travel to acquire goods and sometimes peddling them in addition to selling them in his store. He became an established businessman but remained a *mercelot* at heart, finding for others what they didn't know they needed until he had acquired it for them.

Resources:

Fontaine, Laurence. *History of Pedlars in Europe*. Durham, NC: Duke University Press, 1996.

ART DECO STYLE

Radical! Geometric! Technological! Bold! Contradictory! Decorative! All of these adjectives provide but a partial description of the Art Deco style of design. "Arts Décoratifs" made its first appearance at the Exposition Internationale des Arts Décoratifs et Industriels Modernes, in Paris, in 1925. Combining bold geometric patterns, bright colors, and clashing hues orchestrated into masterpieces using unique and sometimes rare materials, its influence was present in paintings, sculpture, furniture, architecture, textiles, automobiles, ocean liners, and jewelry. All things created in the Art Deco style found a worldwide audience during its heyday in the 1920s and '30s.

Many of the buildings familiar to us all were designed and built in the style of Art Deco. For example, New York City's Chrysler Building, Empire State Building, General Electric Building, and 30 Rockefeller Center, in addition to opera houses, skyscrapers and museums across the world, including the Louvre, represent what was a new and revolutionary school of design. Many believe this new style, free and unconventional, reflected the feelings of hope and revitalization following "the war to end all wars." It was a new day, a new age, requiring a new and novel way to express the relief the world felt with the fall of oppressive monarchies and dictators. A way to celebrate the beginning of a world constructed and governed by its citizens for the good of all. Cities around the globe have moved to preserve and restore the hundreds of buildings and sculptures representing this unique period in art history.

The *SS Paris* was the first ocean liner in the world to embrace the dynamic new mode, and Marie's cabin was furnished in every detail in the Art Deco style, including its unique square portholes. Numerous aspects of the ocean liner, especially its grand staircase and many public first class areas, from the flooring to the lighting fixtures were constructed, designed, and furnished using the bold designs and vivid colors of the reigning style.

Following World War II, the Art Deco period virtually ended. However, it had a revival in the 1960s (of course!) and continues to inspire artists of all ages and genres. I would encourage you to seek out images of Art Deco in all its many forms. Its beauty might inspire you to think and act in bold, new, and creative ways.

Resources:

"Art Deco; Art Movement," Encyclopædia Britannica. https://www.britannica.com/art/Art-Deco

Benton, Charlene, Tim Benton, and Ghislaine Wood. *Art Deco: 1910-1939*. New York: Bulfinch, 2003.

COMING TO AMERICA

Twenty million people from Central, Eastern, and Southern Europe immigrated to America between 1880 and 1920. This included over two million Jews fleeing persecution in Eastern Europe. Their destinations were the cities where jobs in growing industries were available, such as steel, coal, automotive, and textile and garment production. The work of these immigrants propelled America to the forefront as a major economic force in the world's economy.

In 1917, the passage of the Immigration Act limited the number of people deemed as having "low skills" coming into the country. The Emergency Quota Act in 1921 and the Immigration Act of 1924 set even narrower parameters for immigration, consequently restricting the immigration of Jews fleeing Nazi persecution.

Immigration laws continued to be frequently passed and revised, sometimes appearing reactionary when those already on our shores felt threatened by the further influx of more people vying for precious jobs and resources. The National Origins Formula of 1921 and 1924 gave preference to emigrants from Central, Northern, and Western Europe and enacted lower quotas for those from Southern Europe and Russia. Asians were actually declared "unworthy" of entry into the United States.

These laws remained in place until 1965. During the forty-plus years between 1923 and 1965, the U.S. did allow on a case-by-case basis refugees from Nazi Germany before WWII, Holocaust survivors after the war, and non-Jewish peoples from Central Europe and Russia attempting to flee communism.

Jewish immigrants tended to settle in the poorer neighborhoods of major cities such as Philadelphia, Boston, Baltimore, Chicago, and New York City, where Marie's sister, Solange, and their father settled. Over time, these cities all developed large Jewish sections with synagogues, schools, and markets that helped to ensure their religion and culture remained central to their lives while they assimilated to life in a new country. Finding work in factories, especially in the garment industry, cigar manufacturing, food production, and construction, they established strong communities, and many were involved in the struggle for workers' rights, including the need for better working conditions.

Papa, Solange, and Philippe were among the exceptions rather than the rule. They came to New York moneyed, highly educated, and knowing full well they were a small minority among the throngs of immigrants from all across Europe who would strive diligently and succeed in making new lives in a land now adopted as their own.

Resources:

"A History of Immigration in the USA" https://www.sutori.com/story/a-history-of-immigration-in-the-usa

U.S. Department of State. Office of the Historian. *Milestones: 1921-1936 https://history.state.gov/milestones/1921-1936/immigration-act*

WOMEN AND POST-TRAUMATIC STRESS DISORDER (PTSD)

Both women and men suffer from post-traumatic stress disorder; however, the experiences they have that produce this effect can be quite different. The most common event in a woman's life likely to cause PTSD is sexual assault and/or abuse as a child or an adult, or domestic violence. Research comparing male veterans with PTSD following the Vietnam War and early studies on women following a traumatic event found that women's response to trauma is similar to that of men returning from combat, with symptoms including avoidance, hyperarousal, re-experiencing, and numbing.

Men and women may respond to their symptoms of PTSD differently. Females may have anxiety, difficulty expressing feelings and emotions, or may avoid situations and people that remind them of or might trigger memories of the trauma. Men also often have outbursts of anger and difficulty controlling rage. While both men and women may experience depression and anxiety, women are more prone to both and, in addition, may develop health challenges as a result. Men often turn to self-medicating through the use of alcohol or drugs.

With more women now serving in combat zones in the military, there is a high risk for exposure to wartime trauma. Female soldiers are also at greater risk for sexual harassment and sexual assault than men, again increasing a woman's chance of an experience resulting in a PTSD diagnosis.

During the Civil War, PTSD was referred to as "soldier's heart." Following World War I and World War II it was known as "combat fatigue" and "gross stress reaction," respectively. And veterans returning from Vietnam might exhibit symptoms of "post-Vietnam syndrome." Most people are familiar with the common names "battle fatigue" and "shell shock."

There are effective treatments for PTSD including both pharmacological and cognitive behavioral therapies. Some studies indicate women are more likely than men to seek treatment for PTSD, perhaps because women in general may be more willing to express emotions and share feelings.

For Marie, the horrific experiences of living through the shelling of the field hospital coupled with the day-to-day trauma of nursing the severely wounded and dying on an active battlefield contributed to her diagnosis of "*crise de tristesse sombre*," a crisis of black melancholy. As was true for her, many with PTSD suffer periods of depression, anxiety, guilt, and flashbacks for many years, or sometimes just randomly, throughout their lifetime. Marie, along with scores of other brave women, decided to carry on and found the courage to live and love again. The wounds and scars they bore were reminders of what they lived through, knowing all the while we were never meant to kill one another and daring to hope for a peaceful world.

Resources:

"Women, Trauma and PTSD" The website of the U.S. Department of Veterans Affairs, PTSD: National Center for PTSD. http://www.ptsd.va.gov/public/PTSD-overview/women/women-trauma-and-ptsd.asp

German, Lindsey. *How a Century of War Changed the Lives of Women (Counterfire)*. London: Pluto Press, 2013.

ACKNOWLEDGEMENTS

While writing is a "solitary experience" for an author as the words make their way to the page, it is also true that a book only becomes a finely finished piece of work with the assistance of many people.

My editor, Sally Carr, rallied alongside me toward the finish line, going above and beyond and exceeding all my expectations. I am more than thankful for your generosity and expertise. I look forward to working with you on future projects.

Thank you to Ginger Nocera fellow author, for your willingness to read the manuscript and provide feedback.

I sincerely appreciate Orly Ziv-Maxim's reviewing the portions of the book that describe the observance of Shabbat and references to Jewish traditions.

What fun it was to collaborate with Saroj Gill in finding an appropriate name for Dr. Tanvir Singh and discussing with me aspects of the Sikh religion and customs.

My sincere thanks to Kari Hock for your early support and insightful critiquing as the story unfolded. You pushed me to become a better writer and I am very grateful.

Dominique Dailly, your French spirit illuminates this book. How thankful I am for your insight and friendship.

My talented sister, Kathleen Noble, has done the beautiful cover artwork for both books. My heartfelt thanks to you Kathy. Your inspired paintings bring the stories to life.

Terry, my husband and partner in this wondrous life of ours, my forever gratitude for your constant love, support, and good humor.

READER'S GUIDE

1. Many of the characters in *The Passage Home to Meuse* experience profound changes in their lives. What passages have you experienced in your life that have changed the course of your journey?

2. Fearing that her family may attempt to persuade her to leave France and immigrate to the United States, Marie is initially reluctant to travel to New York City. Have you ever been worried that your family or friends might try to coerce you into a change you did not want to make? If so, how did you respond?

3. In what ways do you think Marie's ocean voyage aboard the *SS Paris* helped prepare her for her time in New York City?

4. Katy and Marie, though very different personalities, bonded quickly and became close friends. Is there a person in your life that although very different from you is a close friend and confidant? What do you think bonds the two of you together?

5. Marie's experience at the Bastion of Beauty was indeed transformative. Have you ever had a makeover (mental or physical) and if so, how did it change the way you felt about yourself? Do you think it changed the way others perceived you?

6. Many of the events that occurred during Marie's time in New York City were unexpected—some were welcomed and others not so much. Think of a time when you traveled to visit family and the time together was so different than what you anticipated. Was that time of "surprises" a positive or negative memory for you or some of both? Have your perceptions changed over time?

7. Marie was stunned by Henri's proposal of marriage. Do you think she knew of his feelings before his declarations? Why do you think she felt so strongly that she would never want to marry? Do you think if Marie had not gone through the devastation of the war her attitude toward marriage and having children would have been different?

8. This was Marie's third time at Pitié-Salpêtrière Hospital in Paris: first, as a Red Cross nurse in training at the age of seventeen; next, as a veteran nurse wounded in the Battle of Verdun; and this third time, returning as a student. Has there been a place in your life that you have returned to again and again that served as a touchstone?

9. As the author of the story, I was very surprised by the appearance of Tanvir and the role he played. I was also surprised that he and Marie went their separate ways with seeming ease after they spent such an intimate three days together. How did you feel about Tanvir? What purpose do you think he and Marie played in each other's lives? What did she learn about herself following their time together in Meuse?

10. Have you ever experienced a similar relationship where you thought it would become one thing and it became another? Was this of your own choosing or the other person's?

11. Many of the characters go through post-war metamorphosis. Which characters do you think changed the most? Have you experienced such a "metamorphosis" in your life?

12. What was your reaction to the changes that Henri made? Why do you think the changes were initially difficult for Marie? Have there been people close to you who have undergone unexpected changes? How did you respond?

13. *The Passage Home to Meuse* takes place over a seven-month period, from December 1922 through June 1923. Has there been a time in your own life when profound changes occurred over a short period of time? For the characters in the book, the impetus for change was recovery and moving on after World War I. What was the impetus for the changes in your own life that sent you on a journey of self-discovery?

CPSIA information can be obtained
at www.ICGtesting.com
Printed in the USA
FSHW010059220421
80632FS